MW00612684

DAUNTLESS HEARTS

A Novel

Lincoln Tuvelais

ARBORVALE
BOOKS

Kenosha Wisconsin

Copyright © 2021 Lincoln Tuvelais

All rights reserved. No part of this publication may be reproduced, distributed, or transmitted in any form or by any means, including photocopying, recording, or other electronic or mechanical methods, without the prior written permission of the publisher, except in the case of brief quotations embodied in critical reviews and certain other non-commercial uses permitted by copyright law. For permission requests, write to Arborvale Books at the address below.

ISBN: 978-1-7351043-4-8 (paperback)
ISBN: 978-1-7351043-3-1 (eBook)
Library of Congress Control Number: 2021901370

Any references to historical events, real people, or real places are used fictitiously. Names, characters, and events in real places are products of the author's imagination.

Book interior by Eugene Rijn Saratorio, https://www.fiverr.com/xchatz
Cover design by Nirosha, www.fiverr.com/printok.
First printing edition 2021. Second printing edition 2023.

For special discounts available for bulk purchases, fundraising, and sales promotions, contact Arborvale Books or admin@arborvalebooks.com.

ARBORVALE BOOKS
6332 39th Avenue Kenosha, Wisconsin 53142
www.arborvalebooks.com
admin@arborvalebooks.com

CONTENTS

FOREWORD

This account of my parents' courtship, published in their loving memory, is based on my mother's extensive correspondence and diaries. The story is further enriched by many interviews with my mother, her relations, and my father, embroidered with as little imagination as possible. My parents were such a remarkably happy couple that they seemed destined for one another. Yet their fates were not so assured and certainly did not seem so to them at the time. I hope, Dear Reader, that this account will prove as entertaining and instructive for you as it was for my siblings.

With my most humble thanks,
Mrs. Lane Phillips
London, 1888, Wilcox & Sons, Publishers

MISS OTIS FINDS A NEW HOME

Kitty Otis, handsome, clever, comfortably affluent, with a lively disposition, seemed to unite some of the best blessings of existence. She had lived nearly eighteen years with very little to distress her until, seemingly as penance for a blessed beginning, every woe imaginable was visited upon her and she lost the privilege of living in the rectory.

Kitty spied Uncle Tinsley's coach through the parlour window and impatiently threw open the door for him herself. He was a tall, handsome man and groomed to perfection. His black hair had dimmed to grey, but he still possessed the penetrating dark eyes and black brows of his youth. His parents had named him Pericles, which suited his appearance perfectly. After he put off his hat and gloves, she greeted him warmly with a peck on the cheek.

Once they were seated in the spacious parlour with silk damask walls, Uncle Tinsley began, "I have received an encouraging reply from an agent regarding Dixon Cottage. It is only sixteen miles to the west of here. They offer it complete with furnishings for seven hundred pounds. That is a bit costly for its size, but it gives me hope that it is well fitted up. I have set an appointment for three days hence."

"I have long dreamt of the day when I would manage my own household," Kitty replied. "But now that the necessity is thrust upon me, I find I don't want it at all! I am grateful to be your ward, but I find it impossible to be happy about leaving the rectory."

Uncle Tinsley patted her hand. "Do not be anxious, my dear. You are a remarkably clever young woman, and your Aunt Tinsley and I will guide you."

At the appointed hour, Kitty, Uncle Tinsley, and their servants set out early on a bright, cold late winter morning in Papa's conservative black coach drawn by Castor and Pollux, teamed under Pike's expert driving.

Kitty twisted the ends of her bonnet ribbons. "Well, Uncle, let us hope that Dixon Cottage suits. For if it does not, I do not know what is to become of Father and me. Although it will only be for three days, I am uneasy leaving him."

Uncle Tinsley laced his hands together in his lap. "Your father's valet is excellent and will take good care of Merit. I am more anxious about so great a burden being thrust onto your shoulders. My invitation to live with Aunt Eliza and me still stands. You need not create a new establishment if you don't want to."

Uncle Tinsley's speech only served to remind Kitty of every painful feeling. She avoided thinking about her situation unless she was alone and could give full vent to her emotions.

She attempted a light-hearted response. "As I recall, Uncle, bachelors are thin on the ground near your estate. No, I am better served establishing a new house in a more populous district. Besides, I believe that with thrift, I shall be able to keep Othello and my wheelers, Castor and Pollux, which is the crux of the matter for me."

Her uncle frowned. "My dear girl, even if you keep your horses, I worry for you. I find it difficult to believe that you will achieve a brilliant match without your mother sponsoring you for a London season. Do not give up hope—"

"Give up hope?" Kitty interrupted, "Certainly not! I only turned eighteen last week. I will not be in danger of spinsterhood for another *five* years. Surely, in all that time, we can contrive a respectable come-out."

Their interest was then engaged by the wild beauties of the landscape. As they made their way west, the ground rose from hills of lush pastures to high fells. The carriage rumbled across uncounted ancient stone bridges. The spectacular broad-shouldered peaks were almost level at the top, with cliffs plunging into narrow valleys. Dark swaths of still-bare bushes marched along the valleys and gave way to heather on the wind-swept tops. The sky was the deep blue only achieved at high elevations. Innumerable little streams wound their way through the valleys, most still frozen to glittering immobility.

Kitty exclaimed, "How picturesque!" or "How striking!" as she discovered various local beauties. Soon they arrived at the *Horse and Farrier* in Threlkeld, where they were to lodge for two nights before retracing their steps.

The innkeeper and his wife, Mr. and Mrs. Brown, unused to trade from the Quality at that season, greeted them with enthusiasm. Mrs. Brown ushered Kitty and her abigail, Betsy Taylor, to the room. Kitty endeared herself by announcing, "How lovely. Taylor, you may have luncheon before unpacking my things."

Taylor, a handsome woman in her mid-thirties with fair auburn colouring and an attractively rounded figure, had worked as Kitty's abigail for nearly seven years. She smiled and replied, "Aye, Miss. Only let me shake out yer pink muslin afore I go t' kitchen."

Mrs. Brown then ushered Kitty to the private dining room Uncle Tinsley had reserved.

"Are you familiar with Dixon Cottage, Mrs. Brown? We are come here to determine if it suits."

"Oh, aye, Miss, I know it well. Mr. Dixon built it when—Lord!—I was but a lass. My sister kept house there for years. His heirs have their own estates, and no-one wants the place. Ah, here ye are."

Kitty said eagerly, "I should like to learn of the house from your sister. Is she near? Would you introduce her?"

Mrs. Brown chuckled. "Near? I should say so. She come to help me in kitchen since Mr. Dixon passed and is in this house even now." Kitty's stomach gave an audible growl, much to her chagrin.

Mrs. Brown smiled indulgently. "Tea and bread and butter's out, and the rest'll be along shortly. I'll send my widowed sister up, Mrs. Abernathy she is, when yer done."

As Mrs. Brown curtsied herself out of the room, Uncle Tinsley arrived.

Kitty began, "Uncle, I made several important discoveries."

Uncle Tinsley smiled and shook his head. "You are so like your mother."

A servant entered with ham, pickles, boiled eggs, and dried fruit tarts. Once the girl had departed, they resumed their conversation.

"How so, sir? Everyone says I resemble my father."

"With your brunette curls and dark eyes, you are assuredly your father's daughter. But in mind and spirit, I hold you most resemble your mama. God pity the tradesman who tried to overcharge Mrs. Otis! Your father was a brilliant man, but not at all practical. It was your *mother* who managed the rectory with economy."

Kitty's eyes filled with tears. "Oh! Uncle, you cannot imagine what comfort these simple reminiscences afford me. No one—almost no one—I know wishes to speak of her for fear of giving me pain or because they have no idea what to say. But these little stories of her are what I most particularly wish to hear."

Uncle Tinsley smiled. "Then I shall include her in more of our conversations."

Kitty smiled, blinked away her tears, and they ate a hearty lunch. Mrs. Abernathy arrived shortly thereafter. She was taller than her younger sister, raw-boned, and ruddy, with the first strands of silver showing in her brown hair.

"Mrs. Abernathy, what can you tell me of the house?" Kitty inquired.

"It is solidly built an' Mr. Dixon kept it up quite well when his family was about him. But as he declined, the staff dwindled. It was down to me an' Toby, his man of all work, at the end. We couldn't keep up with the place."

Uncle Tinsley asked, "What, in your view, is the worst thing about the house?"

"The road to it!" Mrs. Abernathy replied. "The lane is narrow an' has a section carved into the north side of a hill. It gets so clogged with snow in winter that it's impassable."

Following her uncle's lead, Kitty asked, "And what did you like best about the house?"

"Mr. Dixon put a modern draw pump right outside the kitchen," she replied. "It's the greatest convenience. And it's deep enough that we got water even during the worst winter freezes."

"Is there anything else you can tell me about Dixon Cottage?" Kitty asked.

"Well, miss, not of the cottage itself... but...Mr. Peale is the agent, an' you should be warned. He's a sharp'un. He's never broken the law, mind, but he's bent it to his own advantage pretty sharply from time to time."

"Thank you, Mrs. Abernathy." Kitty grinned. "I am in luck, then! Mr. Tinsley here is an excellent solicitor."

After the interview, Kitty rented two hacks from the inn to explore the town. Kitty exchanged her dress for a more practical riding habit, Pike was mounted, and off they set. Meanwhile, Mr. Tinsley made pertinent inquiries about Threlkeld. They spent all evening exchanging their respective discoveries.

The next morning, after an early and excellent breakfast, they set out to inspect the property. The agent, Mr. John Peale, was in his mid-twenties, sandy-haired, freckled, and somewhat stout. He was dressed in a vulgar apple green waistcoat.

He kept up a paean of praise for the village of Threlkeld to the east, the beauties of Keswick to the west. He described the house and its home farm in glowing terms. Kitty could barely restrain from laughing at him. Kitty caught Uncle Tinsley's eye, and they shared a private joke at Mr. Peale's expense. But even Mr. Peale was hard-pressed to extol the excellence of the interior after they startled some bats out of the library chimney.

Dixon Cottage, although smothered in weeds, was built of the native buff-coloured stone. At only 4,600 square feet, it was less than half the size of the rectory but was well proportioned with excellent prospects. Uncle Tinsley noticed the gravel approach was more weeds than gravel, the chimneys needed pointing up, three windows were broken, and an enterprising ash had sprung up through a crack in the front flagstones.

The trio returned to the *Horse and Farrier* and entered a private parlour. Uncle Tinsley and Kitty were seated, and Mr. Peale stood in eager attendance. Mr. Peale seemed somewhat flustered when Kitty, instead of Mr. Tinsley, began negotiations. "Mr. Peale, what price has your principal set for the property?"

With his smile now more blinding than ever before, Mr. Peale made a slight bow. "My principal set the price at seven hundred pounds, entire, to include all the furnishings."

"No doubt in ignorance of its true value!" Uncle Tinsley scowled.

"Aye, it has a bonnie prospect, and we've had many inquiries, sir," Mr. Peale replied, deliberately misunderstanding him.

Uncle Tinsley leaned forward and tapped the table with his forefinger. "However, it is between Threlkeld and Keswick, not in Grosvenor Square."

Kitty turned to Mr. Peale with a mischievous smile. "How odd! It is widely known in town that Dixon Cottage has stood vacant for over two years, and no one else has been to see it." Mr. Peale's smile became more fixed.

Uncle Tinsley turned to Kitty. "Dixon Cottage appears to be a property whose owner has set too optimistic a price, does it not?"

Kitty drew a pencil and small notes-book from her reticule and began figuring. "Yes, it certainly does. Upon my word, a reduction is required for the repairs. Mr. Tinsley, what do you think repairs will amount to?"

Eyes sparkling, lips twitching in a poorly suppressed smile, Uncle Tinsley responded, "Remember, Kitty, whatever repairs you can see are accompanied by at least two others you cannot see. I advise you to set aside at least a hundred pounds for repairs."

Mr. Peale interrupted, "Nay! Repairs will not come to anything like a hundred pounds!"

Kitty ignored the interruption and went on pointedly, "Thank you, Uncle, I rely *entirely* upon your judgement in these matters." Simultaneously excited and nervous, Kitty was determined to live up to Mother's example.

She took a deep breath and turned back to Mr. Peale. "I do not wish to wound you, Mr. Peale, but you led me to believe the home farm consisted of twenty-four usable acres. However, with the steep bits and the boggy bottoms, there are less than twenty usable acres." Kitty appealed to Uncle Tinsley, "Surely that discrepancy requires a reduction. Say, fifteen pounds per acre or sixty pounds total. Does my calculation seem correct to you, Uncle?"

Mr. Peale's smile became more wooden.

Uncle Tinsley reminded Kitty, "But you forgot the problem of the furnishings."

Kitty smiled. "Whatever would I do without your advice, Uncle?" Kitty turned to Mr. Peale. "From your description, the house is offered fully furnished. But the best of the furnishings are gone."

Mr. Peale went a little pink in the face. "But nobody expects to find everything to their liking in a furnished house!"

Kitty's voice became sarcastic. "*Everything?* The dining room has no sideboard, the library no desk, the bedrooms only have Dutch presses, not wardrobes. Most of the upholstered furnishings should be burned, and *all* the mouldering linens will be consigned to the fire.

"Whilst I never expected to find everything to my taste, I did expect to find it *fully* furnished. A farther fifty pounds will be necessary to provide furnishings." Kitty's palms began to sweat as she felt she was acting the shrew. But she also felt oppressed by the urgency of saving the settlements she inherited from Mama. So, she consciously held her head high.

Uncle Tinsley shook his head, now openly amused. "No, my dear. I cannot quite agree with you. You should allow at least seventy pounds for furnishings. The kitchen ovens are in such poor repair that you need to install a modern closed stove. Does that not bring the total down to four hundred seventy pounds?"

Kitty checked her numbers. "Yes, sir, it does. Howsoever, we forgot the chicken coop is a menace and must be torn down. Most of the fences and *all* the gates need repair. The well lost its roof, and no doubt the waters are fouled."

Mr. Peale wrung his hands. "Nay, Miss! The water's as clear and as sweet as can be, and there's a pump for drawing off water t' th' beastie troughs."

She smiled sweetly up at Mr. Peale. "Yes? Well, I will only deduct fifty pounds for those repairs. But there is also the matter of the road which I have on good authority is often impassable in winter. That should reduce the value of the property a farther one hundred pounds. That brings the total to three hundred twenty pounds. Do you agree, Uncle?"

Mr. Peale, quite red in the face, was reduced to spluttering. "Impassable! But ... but, Miss, if ye like the cottage so little, are ye even goin' to make an offer?"

Uncle Tinsley intervened. "Oh, yes, my niece cannot resist a bargain. And a bargain this must be if you are to sell it to anyone in its current state."

Mr. Peale went pale about the mouth. "But, sir, I cannot present my principal with such a paltry offer!"

Beneath the bluster, Mr. Peale was very close to panic. Seized by compassion, Kitty said, "Very well, Mr. Peale, I do not wish to be unjust."

Uncle Tinsley smiled proudly at Kitty. "Vicar's daughter."

Kitty returned his smile. "Yes, indeed. We shall add thirty pounds to the offer price. Do you approve of offering three hundred fifty pounds for Dixon Cottage, then, Mr. Tinsley?"

Her uncle considered carefully. "Upon my word, that seems a fair figure to both parties."

Mr. Peale's brows shot up. "To *both* parties? How is that fair to my principal, sir?"

Uncle Tinsley adopted his most authoritative solicitor voice. "Your principal will have sold Dixon Cottage instead of letting it decay until it is impossible to sell. I believe, on good authority, the heirs wish to be shot of it at whatever price. Present this offer. After all, your principal may still choose to reject it or make a counter-offer."

Uncle Tinsley drew out five ten-pound notes and laid them on the table. "Produce a receipt for the fifty pounds and draft an offer for the property for the remaining three hundred pounds, entire. I shall sign it today, so you may post it to your principal straightaway."

Apparently mesmerised by the money, Mr. Peale nodded mute agreement. When he had written out and handed the receipt to Mr. Tinsley, he bowed himself out of the room.

With a chuckle, Uncle Tinsley turned to Kitty. "Just like your mother!" Kitty laughed, alive to the full force of the compliment.

Mr. Peale returned with an offer letter that evening. Uncle Tinsley corrected the document so that the three hundred fifty pounds *included* all agent's fees and transfer stamp taxes. He signed it and bade Mr. Peale a polite *adieu*. The next morning, the entourage arrived back at Crosthwaite and awaited developments.

REMOVAL

Kitty smiled and kissed Uncle Tinsley's cheek. "Uncle, delighted to see you. What occasions this honour?" She ushered him into the parlour. "Do sit down."

"I just received a letter accepting the offer for Dixon Cottage with no change in terms."

Kitty bounced on her seat, just as she had as a child. "In less than a fortnight! They *were* eager to sell. Now I regret adding thirty pounds to the offer."

"Don't fret about that; it was a good bargain. Thirty pounds less, and they might have stalled. I shall make arrangements to transfer funds from your father's accounts so we don't undermine your settlements."

"I shall ring for tea and let Papa know you are here." With a worried frown, she turned back to her uncle. "This is the moment I have been dreading; telling him."

Uncle Tinsley reassured her. "Your father is made of sterner stuff than you know."

Kitty nodded and left to collect her father. When they returned, Papa greeted his first cousin and life-long best friend warmly.

Kitty moved next to him on the settee and tenderly took his hand in her own. "Bishop Rickman is concerned for your health and wishes to engage a new vicar."

Uncle Tinsley leaned forward in his chair, brow furrowed, and clasped his hands between his knees. "I made arrangements to sell your living, Merit."

Papa's voice remained calm. "Sell my living?" But his hands betrayed him. He withdrew from Kitty's clasp. His hands fluttered about his person like agitated birds, touching first his face, then his waistcoat, then the settee arm. Finally, he interlaced his fingers in his lap.

Uncle Tinsley nodded sharply once. "Yes, sell. In fact, I have received several inquiries. As you know, this will preserve your estate for Kitty's benefit."

Merit turned back to his daughter. "But your mother and I always supposed we would sell after you got married."

"Oh, Papa. You need not worry on that. We will live near Keswick, which is quite the watering hole for gentlemen."

Uncle Tinsley explained, "We already bought a new house, Dixon Cottage. There is a bed chamber on the ground floor, so you will not have to manage stairs."

Merit nodded. "But who will care for the congregation?"

"The new vicar will care for them, Papa."

Merit shifted restlessly. "But, Tinsley, how can losing her home benefit Kitty?"

Kitty suppressed a sigh. "We will have a nice snug cottage as our home."

Papa's shoulders hunched forward, and a glum frown appeared on his face. "It grieves me to leave my parish and all our acquaintance. I am a bit beyond gallivanting about the kingdom."

Tinsley nodded. "Dixon Cottage is not so far, only an hour by carriage, less than that on a good horse. Eliza and I shall visit you there regularly."

Merit nodded. "Yes, yes. But why do we have to move instead of just sending Kitty off to London for a proper season?"

Tinsley sighed. "Your health prevents you from furnishing the pulpit, old boy. You must sell your living. I have already placed it for sale."

By practice of repeated explanations, poor Merit was brought to both understand and be reconciled with the change. Once satisfied with his grasp of the situation, Kitty called for Biddle.

Kitty turned toward her father. "Papa, I fear Uncle Tinsley and I have imposed on you too long. You are wearied. Let your man help you to bed so you may rest."

Merit passed his hand over his face. "Hmm? You are no doubt right, dearest daughter."

Once Biddle had ushered his employer from the room, Uncle Tinsley stood and scrubbed his face with his hands. "*That* was the fellow who published in the *Proceedings of the Royal Society*? *He* is the

Merit Otis who wrote the definitive refutation of Deism? His illness has deprived us of a great light."

Kitty blinked back her tears. "Yes, but the bedrock of his character still shone through. He only worried for me and his congregation. That is what I think upon, nowadays."

Uncle Tinsley gave her the startled look parents reserve for precocious children. "Wise beyond your years, Kitty. You would make your mother proud."

Kitty and her groom, Tom Pike, began jaunting back and forth to Dixon Cottage daily, constrained only by poor weather. On one of her many visits to Threlkeld, Kitty called in on Mr. and Mrs. Brown.

"Hello, Mrs. Brown. I have purchased Dixon Cottage and must hire staff. I have no acquaintance nearby. I hope that you can help me."

Mrs. Brown replied, "Me daughter is getting to a useful age and will soon take over for me sister. Would you be interested in talking to Mrs. Abernathy?"

Having tasted Abernathy's excellent cooking, Kitty promptly agreed to hire her. With Abernathy's help, she retained Edward Hart, a widower, as the man of all work, and his daughter, Mary Hart, as a housemaid. After extensive inquiries in Threlkeld, she could find no farm manager. So, Kitty temporarily gave up the search.

Back home, Kitty showed the rectory to several gentlemen interested in buying the living. Mr. Granger seemed especially eager. Slow and pompous in speech, narrow-minded, and gossipy, Kitty did not like him. He inspected every square inch of the house, the glebe with its farming operations, and the park. He scrutinised all the furnishings. He questioned Kitty minutely about the silver plate, china, draperies, and management of the house. He interviewed several of the more important servants. Although disappointed that Kitty's inherited silver did not go with the Rectory, Mr. Granger made an offer. Uncle Tinsley quickly concluded a sale for five thousand pounds.

Kitty thanked God that her guardian was such an astute man of business. Although not yet hers (and she fervently hoped would not be hers for many more years), Kitty could now claim a respectable eight thousand pounds as her fortune. Mr. Granger began imposing his unwanted and uninvited company nearly daily.

Whenever weather or home duties kept her from Dixon Cottage, Kitty avoided conversation with Mr. Granger by surrounding herself with an impenetrable wall of friends at sewing parties. They prepared house linens and slip covers for furnishings too sturdy to burn but too ugly to look upon. Kitty inventoried the rectory furnishings that were hers to take, each piece burdened with meaning both sentimental and practical. She made many sketches and one oil painting of her mother's garden as *aides de mémoire* against her impending loss. Although she looked forward to managing Dixon Cottage, it still wrung her heart to leave the rectory. Her favourite mount, Othello, became the most heavily exercised hunter in the kingdom.

Workmen restored the Cottage and repaired its home farm. She hired two sturdy village girls. Their ongoing application of elbow-grease brought the house into habitable condition. While there was still much to be done, the Cottage was soon liveable.

On her next visit to Dixon Cottage, Kitty and Tom Pike met a rotund, middle-aged, good-humoured man who introduced himself as Robert Smith. Mr. Smith applied for the job of farm manager and presented two letters of reference. Kitty warned him that he would be sleeping rough until repairs could be made to the quarters above the stables. Mr. Smith amiably agreed. Pleased with his references and his cheerful nature, she hired him.

Kitty left him with orders to hire labourers to plough the nearest fields and prune the fruit trees to improve their productivity. Kitty was full of bustle and efficiency until only a week remained until the removal. But the evil task could not be put off any longer. She called for Betsy Taylor.

Kitty sat at her writing desk, stiff as a cat's whisker, hands clenched together in her lap. "Taylor, it is my sad duty to let you go. You are as beloved to me as Nurse McKittrick was before she retired." Tears formed in her eyes, and she continued with some difficulty. "But I cannot take you to Dixon Cottage. Whoever I engage will have to be laundress as well as abigail, which I know you are unused to."

Taylor responded softly with a twinkle in her eye, "Now dun fret, Miss. What do ye think I done afore coming to this house? 'Asides, who's to give ye countenance?"

Kitty peered up into her face. "*Really*, Taylor? Are you quite sure?" Taylor nodded agreement. Kitty relaxed with dawning hope.

"Aye, I knowed how it'd be when yer pap didn't recover. Since my husband passed, I'd as soon take more and harder work as try and find a new situation."

Kitty impulsively hopped up and took Taylor's hands. "Oh, Taylor. You and Pike are the only faces that Papa and I will know once we get there. You shall be such a comfort to me!"

Taylor, slightly red in the face and with tears in her eyes, responded, "Oh, no need fer all that, Miss! Run along with ye, now. You've a job of work gettin' ready fer the carters."

Kitty bestowed gifts on the needy, visited parishioners, and made ready for the move. In their part, parishioners supplied her with a Tamworth sow piglet and a dozen chickens. The vestments committee subscribed to buy a Jersey heifer. Many of the ladies of the parish donated decorative and useful seeds and cuttings. Tom Pike drove the livestock to Dixon Cottage and stayed there to tend to them.

At last, the fateful day arrived. The Tinsleys and some of their servants arrived early to lend Kitty their farm wagon and their coach. With all of the household staff, the Tinsley's servants, and the carters on hand, loading was done in a trice.

The Tinsleys also supplied material aid on the last inspection. Aunt Eliza discovered a miniature of Kitty's mother still hanging on a wall. Uncle Tinsley discovered Kitty's best silver tea set had mysteriously moved out of its shipping box and into a closed corner cupboard in the butler's pantry.

Kitty looked to Heaven. "I take this as authorisation to continue to despise Mr. Granger!" The Tinsleys laughed. She retrieved her silver, and they entered the carriages in good spirits.

Even after many trips carrying smaller articles, the carriages and wagons were over-burdened. Uncle Tinsley and Kitty acted as tour guides for Aunt Eliza and Father. They arrived at one o'clock in the afternoon, and Abernathy had a hearty meal awaiting them.

Energised by an excellent lunch, everyone hauled belongings into the house. Kitty and Aunt Tinsley directed where pieces of furniture and crates were to go. Abernathy and Mary soon put household staples delivered during the day into their rightful places. Kitty, who had been nervous about sleeping under a strange roof, thanked God for a safe journey. Exhausted by the unaccustomed work, she tumbled into bed promptly after tea and did not stir until morning.

The next morning, Kitty bounded out of bed. She shuffled into her dressing gown and admired the dazzling view of Threlkeld's tumbling fells through her window. After many months of grief, worry, and uncertainty, the weight of her worries lifted. She threw open the window and deeply inhaled the fresh cold spring air. Kitty threw her arms out to her sides and twirled around, belling out her night dress, until the chill from the window penetrated. She shut the window and cheerfully thumbed through her *Book of Common Prayer* until she found what she wanted.

> *O, most merciful Father, who of thy gracious goodness hast turned our dearth and scarcity into cheapness and plenty; We give thee humble thanks for this thy special bounty; beseeching thee to continue thy loving-kindness unto us, through Jesus Christ our Lord. Amen.*

Taylor greeted her with a cup of tea. "Good mornin', Miss, I've yer cuppa tea, and a copy of the *London Times* waits ye in the dining parlour!"

"Oh, Taylor, you are a wonder!" At which point, Mary came in with a pitcher of hot water and filled the wash basin. She moved to make up the bed.

Taylor frowned. "Nay, lass. Leave off with that 'til Miss is dressed." Mary, flustered, started to withdraw.

Kitty softened the blow. "Thank you for your diligence, Mary. No doubt, you will learn our ways in a trice."

Downstairs, Kitty marvelled that the *Times* was only four days old due to improvements in the shipping canals. Uncle Tinsley and Aunt Eliza appeared shortly thereafter. Once various sections had been distributed, they looked up from reading when Hart and her father entered the dining room. Kitty was pleasantly surprised to see Papa so early.

Kitty greeted him with a small kiss on the cheek. "Good morning, Papa."

Papa emerged from his fog and sounded so much like his old self that tears sprang to Kitty's eyes. "Kitty, you have decorated very well. This is elegant but isn't ebony too costly?"

"Why, no, Papa. This is merely painted pine. And see, the French rug has a black background and is figured in blues, tan, and ivory, which inspired my scheme."

By the end of breakfast, however, the fog of confusion had once again descended upon him. "This is nice, Kitty, but when are we going home?"

Tinsley sighed. "The rectory is no longer your home, Merit. I sold your living, and you are to live here from now on."

Kitty had thought she was resigned to his condition but found her heart aching all over again. She said a silent prayer, asking that Papa be happy in his new home.

Uncle Tinsley kissed his wife on the cheek. "I shall be off home directly, Eliza. Enjoy your stay. Do not hesitate to send for me should the need arise."

Kitty sought out Hart after breakfast. "However did you manage to get Father to breakfast on time?"

"Well, Miss, I told a bit of a white lie. I claimed you had given him a new shaving kit, an' that was enough of an excuse fer him to let me shave him."

Kitty awarded him a brilliant smile. "Well done, Hart!"

MISS OTIS MAKES SOME ACQUAINTANCE

After a bustling week of unpacking, arranging, cleaning, and saying farewell to Aunt Tinsley, Sunday arrived. The entire household set out for Church. Kitty was especially careful in her dress. She hoped to make a good impression on her new neighbours and establish some local acquaintance. Once they entered the Church, Mr. Otis headed straightaway to the sacristy, only to be restrained by his daughter.

"Papa!" Kitty blushed beet red and clutched his elbow, whispered urgently, "We are *not* at All Saints; we are at Crosthwaite, and the pulpit is furnished by another. You are not giving services today!" Startled and quite confused, Mr. Otis at length allowed himself to be drawn by his daughter and his valet, Hart, to the pews reserved for the Quality.

Once Hart withdrew to the general pews, another family entered. A slight, balding country squire, his wife, three diminutive daughters, and a son made their way to the pew behind Kitty. Their pew overflowing, the eldest daughter of the family curtsied herself in beside Kitty and nodded hello.

Kitty noted that while quite pretty, the young lady was dowdy. She had large brown eyes fringed with long thick lashes, delicate features, and her hair shaded from very light blond at the crown to rich honey tones at the nape. Her hair was constrained to braids more suitable for an ageing governess than a fresh-faced young lady. She wore a straw yellow round-necked gown with a mismatched pelisse, green shoes, and a tiny chip straw hat. Services started immediately thereafter, so Kitty devoted no more thought to her until the middle of the sermon.

Mr. Sumner at the pulpit advised his parishioners to "... avail themselves of those objects which can only be achieved through intercourse ... ah, *the* intercourse of sociality ..." but too late did he correct himself. Many gasps and titters from the pews greeted his gaffe.

Kitty, while nearly choking to stifle her own laughter, felt the pew vibrating beneath her. Kitty glanced over and saw the other young lady in similar circumstance, quaking with such a violent fit of silent giggles that she rocked the pew. This only added to Kitty's difficulties, as when she caught the young lady's eye, they set themselves off into more whoops choked down only with the greatest exertion.

Later in the receiving line, Kitty introduced her father and herself to their new vicar, Mr. Sumner. A wiry man of average height with an unfortunate receding chin, who now without his wig, proved to have thinning mouse-brown wavy hair. After they had shaken hands, Mr. Sumner introduced them to the young lady with whom they had shared a pew, Miss Marianne Warden. During the tea that followed services, Kitty sought out Marianne, and they were soon conversing with the familiarity and ease of youth.

"Do tell me of your family," Marianne said.

"We lost my mother a year ago to pneumonia," Kitty explained. "My father did not take her passing well, and only five months later, he was seized by apoplexy. He has never fully recovered and has retired from his duties as vicar for All Saints. So, we moved here. Now it is your turn."

"My sincerest condolences. My family has not suffered the tragedies that yours has." Marianne took up Kitty's hand and gave it a little sympathetic squeeze. "I am the eldest; there is my brother, Hal, my sister, Jane, and my youngest sister, Elinor, who has just turned twelve."

"It appears we are similar in age. My birthday is March 1, 1795, and you were born?" Kitty asked.

"On October 3, 1795," Marianne responded.

"So, I am to be the old maid in our little duo." Kitty smiled. "Tell me of your handsome brother."

"Hal?" Marianne asked. "Yes, I believe he got the best looks in the family. He just turned sixteen. If you attach him, you will be able to train him up as you like."

"Too much effort." Kitty made shooing motions with her hands. "I would rather get a husband already formed. Are there any interesting men hereabouts?"

"Not in this season." Marianne sipped her punch. "But come autumn, all the hunt boxes fill up, and it is a regular feast of parties."

"I shall look forward, then." Kitty pressed on. "Have you read any good books of late?"

"I just finished *Fordyce's Sermons.* Although somewhat flowery, still solid."

"That prosy old bore?" Kitty's mouth dropped open before she recollected herself and schooled her expression. "There are very few people who make me feel like a feather-brain, but you have managed it. I am accused of being mannish because of my interest in science. But I try to balance that with lighter prose. Do you ever indulge in *Ackerman's Repository* or a novel?"

"Novels, certainly." Marianne nodded. "But I could not care two pins for fashion."

Kitty felt that was obvious at a glance, but refrained from saying so. "I do believe we could play Rose Red and Rose White in a play. My hair being so black, and yours so blond."

"And so unalike in figure, too." They compared each other and discovered Marianne was exactly of a height to Kitty at 5'3", but only a dainty 98 pounds compared to Kitty's robust 125 pounds. Kitty's little finger ring was a perfect fit for Marianne's ring finger.

"Do you hunt?" Kitty asked.

"Good Heavens, no!" Marianne touched the cross she wore on a neck chain. "Hal indulges, but I avoid riding. I was never any good at it, and horses make me sneeze."

"What a shame. My horses are my greatest companions, and I love them like family."

They parted soon afterwards with promises of mutual visits.

Later that afternoon, Kitty called for Othello to be saddled. She put on her warmest riding coat against the unseasonable cool, foggy afternoon. She declined Pike's escort as she was only riding on her own property.

Othello, ears pricked, and tail held high in excitement, moved easily through the steep country. Kitty, also eager to explore her new surroundings, urged Othello to greater speed. A low stone bridge, only wide enough to be a footpath, crossed a tiny stream ahead of her. She attempted to jump it. However, she did not place Othello correctly, and he took an extra, odd stride just as he launched. With his back arched, he dropped his shoulders, dislodging Kitty.

Kitty landed on her left side in the ditch mud. She was winded and suffered the usual stiffness and minor bruises of a fall but sustained no other hurt. Othello landed awkward but safe. The horse scrambled up and cantered away. No amount of calling or whistling prevailed upon him to return.

Kitty was relieved she and Othello had survived without significant injury. Her riding habit, though, was much the worse for wear. Her left side was besmirched by heavy clay mud from head to toe. Kitty sat down on the top of the stone wall to compose herself. After plucking vegetation from her garments, she spread out her drenched skirts to dry the mud. Kitty rubbed her arms and hands to warm herself, and shook clods of drying clay from her habit. She was debating whether to catch Othello on foot or strike out for home when another rider came clopping through the vale.

Turning, she perceived an enormous young gentleman seated on a vast bay horse leading Othello. Kitty smiled as she hopped up from the wall. "Oh, I see you caught Othello. Well done! However did you manage?"

The colossus spoke in a pleasant, well-educated voice, only marred by a slight Irish accent. "Carrots. I always carry a pocketful when riding. Also, I had the advantage of being on another horse. Horses are much less suspicious of a man on a horse than of a man alone. How did you come to grief?"

"Oh, Othello jumps like an angel, but I misjudged the distance. He went right, and I went left. Where did you find him?"

The gentleman leaned over his saddle, resting his arm on the pommel. "He made it up to the road and was nibbling on the verge. It was obvious from the empty lady's saddle that someone had come to grief. Are you all right?"

"Yes, thank you. A few minor bruises, but quite fit otherwise. But I am et up by curiosity. How did you find me?"

He grinned, displaying perfect white teeth. "The ground is so soft from the rains, it was a simple matter of following his tracks back."

Kitty smiled up at him. "My goodness! Your horse looks to be eighteen hands, at least. Is he part draft horse?"

"I suspect so. I purchased Hercules on the Peninsula to save him from the abuse and neglect of the idiot he was assigned to." His face hardened at the memory.

Kitty eyed Hercules with admiration. "It is obvious he can take your weight, but I have never known of a horse this heavy who could jump well."

In reply, he handed Othello's reins to Kitty, wheeled his horse around, and went sailing in perfect form over the low stone footbridge. Once neatly landed, he wheeled on the instant and returned.

Kitty's jaw dropped before she recollected herself and exclaimed, "Good God! You have a magnificent horse, sir."

"Thank you. Your gelding is also a very fine bit of blood and bone."

The gentleman dismounted, and Kitty got her first good look at him. Kitty thought he could be an understudy for Atlas. He was a bit over six feet tall, but his shoulders were well over a yard wide, so he seemed shorter. His tailoring was impeccable. His well-tailored breeches were stretched over heavily muscled thighs. Even his boots seemed out-sized, although quite elegant. He had black curly hair, dark eyes, and a classically handsome countenance. Kitty felt the breathless thrill of meeting a very handsome man.

He swept off his hat and made a very creditable bow. "Please allow me to introduce myself. Lieutenant Joseph McLaughlin, of the Royal Irish Fourth Dragoon Guards."

Kitty curtsied. "Very pleased to meet you, Lieutenant, in spite of the irregular introduction. Would you be so kind as to help me mount?"

He grinned wickedly and stepped back. "Oh, I think I will exact a toll for that service!"

"How crassly mercenary of you. What payment do you demand, sir?"

Lieutenant McLaughlin's eyes sparkled. "Not mercenary at all. I demand your hand in marriage in exchange for returning your horse. Is that not the usual reward for knights who rescue damsels in distress?"

Kitty rolled her eyes in exasperation, gathered her skirts and quirt, and turned toward home, leading Othello. "Not *this* damsel! My hand is worth considerably more than a horse, even one as marvellous as Othello!"

Lieutenant McLaughlin followed on foot, leading Hercules.

"I will settle for knowing your name."

Kitty came to an abrupt halt and with a hot flush stealing across her cheeks, responded, "I am *not* in the habit of bestowing my name upon strange men! Are manners so different in Ireland, or the Peninsula, or wherever you have been, that ladies act so forward?" She resumed marching home.

"My humblest apologies, Miss. Will you please accept my aid in mounting him?"

Kitty took a deep breath. "Apology accepted."

She thoughtfully knocked the mud from her boot with her quirt. Lieutenant McLaughlin cupped his hands, and she stepped up to mount. As soon as Kitty did so, he flung her so high that she almost flew over Othello's back. She caught herself with her leg against Othello's side and startled Othello into bucking. She bruised her knee on the pommel and fell awkwardly into her saddle. Furious, she lashed out with her foot and kicked Lieutenant McLaughlin in the shoulder.

He flinched. "Ow! You kick like a mule!"

Kitty put on an insincere smile. "Oh, so sorry. You tossed me so hard I had to flail about to regain my balance." She threaded her foot through the iron as she spoke, Kitty tapped her quirt to her hat in mock salute. "Good day, Lieutenant." Kitty took off towards home.

Lieutenant McLaughlin leapt into his saddle and followed. Kitty urged Othello to greater speed. It soon became a high-speed chase over the fells of Cumberland.

As she raced towards home, Kitty was suddenly seized by anxiety. It occurred to her she was alone in the middle of nowhere being pursued by an powerful man on a powerful horse. Even as she scolded herself for being missish, Othello sensed her distress with the telepathy of a good horse, flattened his ears back and leapt forward with a powerful burst of speed.

She guided Othello up narrow ravines, and astonishingly for such a heavy horse, Hercules pursued. Kitty and Othello ducked around thickets of gorse, nimbly rounded stands of trees, always with Hercules and the Lieutenant in hot pursuit. Kitty's blood raced. She leaned close to Othello, and they moved as one. Between the exercise and the heat Othello threw off, Kitty grew quite warm. Kitty felt anxiety over her pursuer and admiration for Othello's power and grace by turns.

As they approached the peak of the fell that sloped towards her house, she could neither hear nor see her pursuer, so she eased Othello into a canter. As they drew closer to the house, she slowed to a trot, and finally entering the stable yard, to a walk. Othello, heavily lathered and head down with fatigue, seemed relieved to be in his own stable yard.

Kitty patted Othello's neck. "Oh! You ran a famous race! Good boy, Othello." Othello tossed his head, accepting her praise as his due.

Pike did not appear after calling several times, so she let Othello drink a little and tied him up. Kitty limped as rapidly as the painful bruise behind her knee would allow to the kitchen to rouse some help. Pike was in the kitchen drinking mulled cider with Mary and Abernathy.

Kitty was relieved. "Oh, Pike, there you are! Othello and I had a famous gallop, and the poor fellow needs to be hot walked. I let him drink a little, but I did not unsaddle him, and he shall need more water and some warm mash, too."

Pike rose. "I was nay expectin' ye back so soon, Miss. Looks like ye've had a tumble—yet another reason ye should let me go with ye."

Kitty nodded agreement. "After today's adventure, you can be sure I shall keep you glued to my side even on my own property."

He shrugged on his coat and hurried out to tend to Othello. Once safely indoors, Kitty began shivering violently. Her damp skirts, unnoticed before, chilled her to the bone.

"There, Miss, sit by the fire afore ye shake yerself to pieces," Abernathy said and turned to Mary. "Get a hot bath drawn fer Miss. Make up a good fire in the bed chamber and get Taylor to set out a warm gown and boots."

Mary nodded and set about heating the large kettle on the stove.

Abernathy thrust a cup of hot cider into Kitty's hands and wrapped her knees with a shawl. "What happened to ye, Miss? You look sore troubled?"

When she had first arrived, Kitty had been bursting with news. But now, she was embarrassed and reluctant to speak. "I was annoyed by a huge man on an enormous horse. He introduced himself as Lieutenant McLaughlin and demanded my hand in marriage in exchange for capturing Othello! A terribly rude joke, don't you agree? To this moment, I do not know whether to be flattered, offended, or frightened. Or am I being missish?"

"Well, I've never seen nor heard tell of ye bein' missish, so don't ye fret about it. Ye're home safe and warm now. I'll just get ye some of me arnica liniment for yer bruises."

Abernathy bundled off, and Kitty slowly thawed. After a hot bath, with her bruises anointed, dressed in a warm gown and boots, Kitty felt much restored.

MORE NEW ACQUAINTANCE

Mrs. and Miss Warden paid a morning call the next day. Kitty gave her guests a tour of the work being done in the garden. As she and her guests re-entered the house and were putting off parasols and gloves, Mr. Hart announced Mrs. John Sumner, the vicar's wife.

"How do you do, Mrs. Sumner?" Kitty greeted her. "I presume you are all acquainted?"

Mrs. Sumner approached Mrs. Warden and shook her hand warmly. "Oh, indeed! For Mrs. Warden is one of our most active parishioners."

"Please, do sit down. I would be delighted to eschew etiquette and converse all together," Kitty offered as she ordered tea. The ladies agreed with smiles and nods.

Mrs. Sumner advanced the conversation with, "I must say, Miss Otis, Dixon Cottage has not looked this well in many a long year."

Kitty smiled and bobbed her curls. "Oh, I am so pleased to hear you say so. I am at the stage when all I can see are all the things still left to do."

Mrs. Warden looked surprised. "But you have rescued the house from near-ruin, from what I gathered. What more could you wish to do?"

Kitty launched into a detailed description of the new southern terrace she wished to build, the additions to the park, the new wallpapers to be installed, the plane tree *allée* she would plant on the approach, the enclosed stove in the kitchen, the scientific farming innovations she would introduce.

Kitty ground to an abrupt halt as she realised from her guest's frozen expressions that her soaring aspirations were boring. "How rude of me! I am so new to managing my own establishment that I have run on inexcusably."

"You are certainly ambitious!" Marianne teased. "Other than the fact that you haven't revolutionised local farming practices, installed

Vauxhall Gardens, and transformed Dixon Cottage into Kensington Palace, how do you like it here?"

Kitty, blushing and giggling along with everyone else, replied, "The natural beauties of the place are enchanting, and the company hereabouts *quite* amusing!"

Mrs. Sumner gracefully rescued Kitty. "I still remember how ambitious I was when learning to manage my own first house. It was both nerve-wracking and a delight. Did not you find it so when you first set up housekeeping, Mrs. Warden?"

Mrs. Warden nodded agreement.

Hart returned with the refreshments, Kitty poured out, and the ladies helped themselves.

"Oh! Nothing your mother can teach you prepares you for keeping house," Mrs. Warden said. "I remember my *bête noire* was the household accounts. I was so afraid of getting everything into a muddle. With Mr. Warden being equally raw and checking everything I did, and making me do it over, I was ever so anxious. But I grew to understand my business eventually. He never checks on me now."

Mrs. Sumner and Marianne appeared unruffled, but Kitty was startled by this glimpse of domestic tyranny. Her father had always shown the highest regard for his wife's intelligence. He sought her help editing his scientific papers and asked her opinion on everything from calming petty squabbles between parishioners to national politics. He would never have dreamt of interfering with domestic management.

"Perhaps Miss Otis would like to expand her acquaintance locally?" Mrs. Sumner asked. "If you were to hold an open house, I could introduce you to everyone."

Mrs. Warden leaned forward eagerly. "Upon my word, Mrs. Sumner, that is an excellent notion. I would be happy to help and donate produce from our home farm."

With so much kind support offered to her, Kitty agreed. After an animated discussion, an excellent plan was outlined.

Immediately after her guests departed, Kitty wrote to Uncle Tinsley and Aunt Eliza.

April 27, 1813
Dixon Cottage, Threlkeld

Dearest Uncle Tinsley and Aunt Eliza,

I pen this brief note to invite you to visit and express my hope that you and yours are well. We are all quite well and settling in here. I have made a wonderful new friend, Miss Marianne Warden, whom I am eager to present to you.

I am planning an open-house on the seventh of May. I will sponsor a fair in the pasture closest to the road for townsfolk and offer a cold collation for my more particular acquaintance. I have already invited some of our friends.

Please come and visit me week after next. I hope you will grace my affaire with your excellent conversation, and I also wish to consult with you on a matter of business.

Yr. Most Affectionate Niece, Kitty

That afternoon, during Marianne's visit, the young ladies discussed Kitty's meeting with Lieutenant McLaughlin. Marianne smiled. "So, you have turned down your first proposal of marriage, and the season has not yet begun."

Kitty bounced her curls with a giggle. "No. Actually, I turned down my *first* proposal when I was only fourteen years old. A boy in our congregation, aged twelve, declared his undying love for me and wished to know when I was to make him the happiest of *men*."

Marianne put her hand to her face in mock censure. "Aha! I perceive now that you are naught but a hoyden toying with these poor fellow's tender feelings. But seriously, I would not take alarm. I suspect that he only pursued you to discover your direction and ceased pursuing you when he realised that you were alarmed."

"Yes, but he threw me up onto Othello so hard, I shall be bruised for days."

Marianne shrugged. "That *does* argue against him. But I doubt he intended or even realised he had injured you. Besides, he was wonderful with Othello, which I know weighs heavily with you."

"True. A gentleman whom the horses like cannot be all bad!"

The Farm Manager

Aunt and Uncle Tinsley accepted Kitty's invitation and arrived on the appointed day. After the first raptures of greeting, Uncle Tinsley withdrew to the library to converse privately with his ward. They left Aunt Eliza and Merit Otis to entertain themselves.

"Now, what matter of business did you wish to discuss, Kitty?" Uncle Tinsley began.

Kitty began pacing about the room as she unburdened herself, "Oh, Uncle, I was never so vexed! It is Smith, my farm manager. I bought modern labour-saving farm equipment which he refuses to use. He hires far more men than are required or than I can afford, instead. When I try to get him to adopt new techniques, he bodges the job badly. I think he does it to teach me to leave him alone. He will not mind me. Worse, when he will not mind me, none of the day labourers will, either. I try to be forceful with him, but he just smiles and tells me that 'grey heads know better than green' and other such trite drivel."

"Have you this difficulty with any of the other servants?"

"Not in the least. In fact, Hart is a far better valet to Papa than Biddle was, and I am much indebted to him."

"I suspect that is because Hart is starting from a clean slate, so to speak, and can see clearly what poor Merit needs now. And the rest?"

"Abernathy is a very skilled cook and thrifty housekeeper. Pike, for all of his sour grumbling, is marvelous with the horses and accomplishes the work of two men. Mary is cheerful and cleans my house as though it were a religious duty. I am prodigiously happy with all of them except *him*," Kitty replied.

Mr. Tinsley rubbed his chin. "The solution to your problem with Smith is blindingly obvious; turn him off."

Kitty blanched. "Oh! What a wretch I shall feel to deprive that amiable man of his livelihood."

Hands clasped behind his back. His penetrating dark eyes bored into her from beneath frowning brows. Uncle Tinsley advised her, "That is not your concern, Kitty! If you wish your house to run comfortably, you must dismiss him. If you wish to drain your settlements by turning your household into a charity, then, by all means, keep him. After all, he brought this on himself through his own stubbornness and ignorance."

Uncle Tinsley paced before her fireplace. "Think what harm he is doing with the other staff. His dissatisfaction and lack of respect is bound to influence them and make for an unhappy house. No, my dear, however painful it is to draw the infected tooth, it must be done before it poisons the body."

Kitty sighed. "I know you are right, though I cringe to think on it. I cannot turn him off without a reference, though. What am I to write of him?"

Uncle Tinsley relaxed. "Well, why did you hire him in the first place?"

"He is cheerful and honest."

Uncle Tinsley smiled. "I advise you say so and remain mute as to the reason he was let go."

Kitty suddenly felt daunted and ill-prepared. "Cannot *you* do it, Uncle, on my behalf?"

Uncle Tinsley replied with some force, "Not unless you wish to lose all credibility with the rest of your staff! If you wish to manage your own establishment, you have to accept the responsibilities that go with it."

After a painful hour spent composing and copying out a reference that was truthful without destroying Smith's hopes for employment, Kitty summoned him to the library. In the briefest interview she could manage, she dismissed him from her service.

"Well, Miss, ye must know yer own mind, but ye're green as spring grass, and ye'll ruin this farm quick as a cock's craw!" Smith said before stalking out the door. Kitty's mopes were dispelled, though, when she re-entered the drawing-room.

Kitty turned to her Uncle, seated next to her father, "Oh, Uncle Tinsley, thank you so much! It was awful, but such a relief."

Papa rose from his usual fog to ask, "What is a relief, dear?"

"Oh, Papa, it is the most provoking thing. I have been obliged to dismiss the farm manager. It was quite disagreeable, but I am much more comfortable now it is done."

Uncle Tinsley interjected, "As I advised you, my dear, you should be."

Papa asked, "Does the fellow have another situation?"

Kitty sat on the settee and fretted. "No, Papa, and I own, that is the circumstance that bothers me the most."

Papa suggested, "Since this fellow needs a situation and you need a farm manager, I suggest throwing your troubles at the foot of the Cross."

Uncle Tinsley, eyebrows raised in surprise, approved. "Excellent, Merit."

Papa led the group in a brief prayer.

Oh God, we humbly beseech thee for Robert Smith who has been dismissed from his post and pray that it may please thee to comfort and relieve him, according to his several necessities, giving him a happy issue out of all his afflictions. God, have mercy upon us, increase the fruits of the earth by sending us a new farm manager; through Jesus Christ, our Lord. Amen.

After this simple impromptu address, Kitty asked the Tinsleys, "Would you care for the shilling tour of the improvements so far?"

The Tinsleys assented and were shown the continuing work of the plasterers in the attics.

"I was unpleasantly surprised when I discovered the servant's quarters to be almost without light or ventilation," Kitty said. "I had large dormer windows built. The attic is now divided so that each servant has a reasonable room lit by a dormer window. It only remains to finish the plaster and nail down rush matting."

Uncle Tinsley declared, "Upon my word, this is fine as a five-pence. Your servants shall be better housed than half the town."

Later that afternoon, Uncle Tinsley made his way to the *Horse and Farrier* to post notice of the vacancy. Applicants were to be interviewed at Dixon Cottage, beginning at 10:00 a.m. the following morning. Hart assumed the duty of turning away unsuitable applicants at the kitchen door. He turned away two fellows with liquor on their breath, several who were far too young to be managers, one who was far too old, and passed on three likely candidates to Kitty. One suffered from a complete lack of respect for Kitty. The other two flatly refused the post when they saw their quarters over the stables, in spite of Kitty's protests that repairs were on-going.

All of the labourers, except for Andy, vanished that day. Kitty asked Andy to keep on ploughing and promised that she was interviewing farm managers. While Andy laboured alone in the fields, it was mostly the same story the next morning.

Finally, a ginger-haired young giant met with Hart's approval and was passed on to Kitty. She and the Tinsleys made their way out to the stable yard where the applicant was waiting. When they arrived, they discovered him crawling about the Worlidge seed drill in the stable yard. As they approached, the young man scrambled up from beneath the equipment and snatched his cap from his head.

He grinned. "Sir, Ma'am, Miss, good day to ye."

Uncle Tinsley addressed him, "What are you about, young man?"

His face aglow with enthusiasm, he explained, "Well, sir, that there's a Worlidge Seed Drill, and a rum goer, sir. I seen pictures, but never the real thing. So, I scratched my curiosity, like, and got a good look."

Kitty smiled. "Delighted to meet you, Mr. ...?"

He made a creditable bow. "I be Robert MacDonald, late o' the Scots Dragoons."

Uncle Tinsley responded, "I am Mr. Tinsley, my wife, and my niece, Miss Otis, the mistress of the house. How do you know about the Worlidge Drill?"

"Oh, well, my dad's got a mite over 100 acres north o' Carlisle, and he subscribes to the *Farmer's Almanac*, an' that's where I read about it."

Kitty fiddled with her parasol handle. "I, too, read about it in an article. It is just the innovation we need hereabouts. But I do not understand it. Could you explain it to us?"

The party were then treated to the amiable farmer explaining the Drill. He demonstrated how light it would be for a horse to pull by snatching up the shafts and wheeling it back and forth.

"See, the lads, they don't like 'em, fer they think it'll take away their livelihood. It can furrow, drop the corn, and cover eight rows in a single pass. Why, with a decent horse, a man can plant over an acre a day!"

Kitty eagerly snapped up the information. "And it takes how many men to plant an acre in one day by hand?"

"Oh, at least four, and usually five. But see, the Drill is *better'n* that. With hand casting, some gets et by birds, and some comes up too thick and fails to head, and some of it is so thin that ye waste the corn and the labour of sowing it. But Mr. Worlidge's Drill prevents all that. Why, ye'd need nowt but *half* the seed corn ye would with hand sowing."

"Fascinating. What would you do with the boggy fields?"

MacDonald gestured expansively. "Most people'd put in French drains. But that's quite a load o' brass, and there's no good outlet for drainin' 'em, the way them fields is situated. So, I'd plant beech, alder, and willow at the top of the fields to take up the water. And ye'll need a horse-drawn hoe to put Sir Townshend's crop rotation into practice. And, er, ye main wish for a farm wagon afore ye're croppin'."

With acute and painful insight, Kitty realised a *desire* to practice scientific farming, and some knowledge gleaned from articles, had left her woefully unprepared for *actual* farming.

"Oh, I have made a mull of things!" Kitty pressed her hand to her blushing cheek. "I had clean forgot we shall need a wagon, and a horse-drawn hoe never occurred to me, either."

Uncle Tinsley interrupted, smiling, "Ah, the good Lord has made fast work of your request, my dear. Though I do not recommend you expect such alacrity in future."

"Oh? Oh! Thank you, Uncle." She turned to MacDonald. "I have just dismissed Mr. Smith from this post and offer sixty guineas a year, paid on quarter day, and a ten per cent share of the harvest. Would you be interested in accepting a permanent post as farm manager for Dixon Cottage?"

MacDonald looked uncomfortable and squinted, mangling his cloth cap between his hands, and harrumphed. "Ah, meaning no disrespect, mind. But I'd be more easy if I knowed *why* ye dismissed Mr. Smith?"

"No offence taken. I can show you more easily than I can explain it to you." Kitty then led the whole party to what she thought of as 'the butchered apple tree.' It stood, stiff as a soldier, sheared into an unnatural smooth globe, awkward and graceless, distinct from the other trees in the grove.

"Och!" MacDonald exclaimed.

"I perceive you understand the difficulty. I asked Smith to prune lightly this year and save as many fruiting spurs as he could while opening up the centre to light and air."

McDonald gesticulated broadly, "He's cut off most of the spurs, and the centre'll grow moss, it's so shaded! It'll take *years* to bring that poor thing back to productivity."

Kitty nodded. "Precisely. Mr. Smith was *not* a very scientific farmer, I am afraid. So, are you easier in your mind, Mr. MacDonald?"

"Yes, indeed, Miss! I'll be happy to accept yer post!"

Kitty extended her hand. "Let us strike hands on the bargain, Mr. MacDonald."

He vigorously brushed off his palms on his clothing and gently engulfed her hand. "My apologies, I bin crawling about on't ground. I go by th'name o' Mac, Miss."

AN OPEN HOUSE

K itty invited her own particular acquaintance from Crosthwaite, the Sumners, the Wardens, Mrs. Fletcher, and several other families on the suggestion of her excellent consultants. She let the open-air-fair be known about town by authorising Mr. and Mrs. Brown to circulate the news.

Once Kitty's guests had been greeted, fed, and given a tour of the principal rooms of the house, she invited everyone out into the sunshine to find what amusement they could at the fair. She noticed a flock of gypsy children peering into the field with longing and approached them.

Eyes twinkling, Kitty smiled. "You may enter the fair and play all day long, but you must do one thing first."

The eldest, a boy of about ten or twelve, squinted suspiciously. "Whassat?"

"You must come to the kitchen door and get treats first!"

All of them grinned, and the youngest children squealed and hopped up and down in their excitement. Kitty led them to the door. "Abernathy, please arrange platters of left-overs for the children. Perhaps sit them down in the grass outside?"

Abernathy looked startled, then grinned. "I'd be happy to, Miss."

Once Kitty stepped away, Mary asked, "Why on earth would she encourage *gypsy* children? They're trained as pickpockets as soon as they can walk!"

"Christian charity, fer one. Fer another, she's clever. They love her now and are far less likely to cause trouble," Abernathy replied.

Kitty saw Mr. Peale, the house agent, who had turned up with the other townsfolk, hurl more quoits closer to the hob than anyone else. His victory earned a prize of a hideous orange shawl. Mr. Peale promptly bestowed his prize on Kitty, who bestowed it on a gypsy child with equal alacrity.

Over the course of the next two weeks, Mr. Peale deposited his card, imposed his company without invitation, and bestowed numerous small gifts on Kitty. Although she returned all his gifts, no gentle hint would quell his absurd advances.

Mr. Peale, wearing a florid waist coat and a new jacket, accosted Kitty during one morning visit whilst seated across from her on her best settee.

"My dear Miss Otis, ye can't but help be aware of my increasin' attentions. Ye're universally charming! Ye're everything a man ... ahem"—he clasped his hands between his knees—"that *I* could wish for in a wife, and I'm here to secure yer consent before approachin' yer father."

Kitty choked off a shout of laughter, attempting to disguise it as a cough before replying, "Well, Mr. Peale, I praise your straightforward manner. I realise this proposal is a compliment to me, although one I never sought. I am afraid I must decline your offer." Kitty concluded with as much grace as she could command.

"Now, don't be hasty, Miss Otis; there is much to consider. I've my own house. Though not as well fitted up as Dixon Cottage, it could be sold or let profitably. I'm also due to inherit my maternal grandparents' farm, which is nigh on forty acres. I enjoy a gentleman's income of two hundred pounds per annum, and with shrewd management, expect that to increase. Since ye're semi-orphaned, it would seem ... ah ... *imprudent* to decline the protection of marriage without due consideration." Mr. Peale smiled urbanely.

With lowered brow, Kitty smoothed her dress before replying. "Mr. Peale, you cannot have considered how we would get on. Whilst you are alive to the fact that marriage is an economic partnership, marriage is also a lifetime companionship. I fear we would not contribute to each other's domestic comfort."

"With yer fortune and mine, what domestic comfort could we possibly lack?" he demanded, still smiling.

Kitty frowned and responded with some asperity, "Companionship, Mr. Peale. Can you name my favourite pursuits, or authors, my political views? You know virtually nothing about me! But I know you well enough to know we would not suit."

"Surely, ye know I'd indulge ye in any of yer favourite pursuits. I dare say ye're bookish enough for the both of us, and what does a *woman* need with political opinions?" Mr. Peale countered, looking less urbane. "Come, come, Miss Otis, these arguments are nonsensical."

With great resolution, Kitty restrained from rolling her eyes. "Mr. Peale, I shall not wrap it up in clean linen: I am only eighteen years old ... I can afford to wait."

Mr. Peale sat up very straight, looking disbelieving. "Ye would sport with ye're future on the hope ye can attach a more accomplished gentleman?"

Kitty, growing red in the face, snapped, "It is hardly a slender hope! I am the granddaughter of a Knight of the Realm, daughter of a respected clergyman, the niece of a countess, and have a respectable fortune. Can you conceive my guardian would approve such a connection for me? But more important to *me* is that you have declared *no* tender feelings for me. May I remind you ladies do not view a marriage offer as a business negotiation!"

"A business negotiation?" Mr. Peale cried in astonishment.

Kitty replied in peevish tones, "Yes, Mr. Peale, this conversation savours of a business negotiation, not a declaration of tender feelings! I shall not embarrass either of us any further by prolonging a pointless discussion. Goodbye." She rose and dropped a curtsy.

Finally taking the hint, Mr. Peale rose and made his bow. He said not one word and stalked out of the room, the very picture of offended dignity.

Later, whilst she and Marianne wandered through the gardens at Marianne's home, they discussed this latest event.

"Never once?" Marianne demanded incredulous.

"Not one time did he declare any tender feelings for me." Kitty walked tall, her parasol at rest. "No, for Mr. Peale, marrying me would have furthered his ambitions. He was astonished that I thought it would take more than our combined incomes to make me happy. I declared I sought companionship. He told me my arguments against the match were nonsense. He even advised me not to 'sport with my future.'"

"'Sport with your future'?" Marianne came to an abrupt halt. "*Surely* he did not mean to imply he is your *last chance!*?"

"That, dearest friend, is *precisely* what he meant." Kitty tossed her head, bouncing her curls. "I told him, with no bark on it, he had not attached my affections. Trying to bribe me into marriage with two hundred pounds a year, a house, and the expectation of forty acres! I am not accomplished the way London ladies are, nor do I come with an heiress's fortune, but I do believe I can do better than that presumptuous little social climber!"

"Certainly, you can! Goodness, if musical accomplishment were the only thing gentlemen sought in a wife, I would never marry. But, Kitty, you *are* accomplished. Your drawings and paintings are delightful. 'Sport with your future', indeed!" Marianne concluded loyally. Then, looking stricken, she asked, "Did he seem upset, or ..."

Kitty replied, "He seemed amazed I did not view marriage as an exclusively financial contract. He was angry his ambitions had been thwarted. But I am convinced his heart was untouched."

"Then he really is a mushroom!" Marianne said, "And deserves such a harsh rejection."

"Oh, do you think I was too harsh?" Kitty asked, a tiny furrow between her brows. "I tried so hard not to lose my temper. But after he told me my arguments were nonsensical, I rather fear I did."

Marianne reassured her, "Yes, but you declined his offer gracefully, and he refused to accept, so he brought it on himself."

"Mushroom!" Kitty called out gaily.

Marianne agreed with a twinkle in her eye. "Mushroom!"

DAVEY

As damp spring gave way to golden summer, Kitty adopted the eccentric practice of bathing in the afternoons in the still room behind the kitchen. It was a tiny room with a very small, high window. The scents of the herbs stored in that room were inviting, the flagstone floor cool in the warm summer afternoons.

Mary was overjoyed since she only had to haul hot water from the stove ten feet to the bath basin instead of across the entire length of the house and up the stairs. So, the staff soon accepted her odd choice, and Kitty fell into the habit of bathing once a week.

Kitty had just completed her bath and toilette. She emerged from the still room to discover the entire household grouped around a tiny, angry figure in the kitchen.

"I din't do nothin'! Lemme go!" A filthy little boy was shouting more or less the same message repeatedly. He squirmed whilst attempting to kick Mac, who held him single-handedly at some distance above the floor. Mac seemed more amused than annoyed.

Mary and Abernathy were discussing the urchin's discovery with Hart. Pike came in to investigate and was lending his opinions. The cacophony was deafening. Kitty attempted to interrupt several times until, exasperated, she clapped her hands and shouted, "Enough!"

Instantaneous silence fell. The child recovered first and resumed his complaints.

Kitty rounded on him and said with perfect gravity, "Young man, if you will be quiet and speak only when spoken to for *five* minutes, I shall feed you cider and biscuits. If you continue to shout at me and carry on, I shall have Mr. Mac knock you senseless."

Mac grinned and gently set the child in a chair at the kitchen table. The child mulishly shut his mouth and folded his arms across his chest.

"Now, Mac, please tell me how you came across this child?"

Mac smiled. "Ah. Well, he was courtin' a belly-ache by stealing green apples from the orchard, Miss."

The child glowered at Mac and shouted, "Windfall's fair game!"

Kitty glared at the child. "Speak only when spoken to, if you please."

Mac grinned and folded his arms across his chest. "Well, it ain't windfall when ye find it by climbing up a tree."

Kitty frowned when the child dared to open his mouth again. "I see. Now, then, young man, what is your name?"

He scowled at her, his shoulders hunched. "Davey."

Kitty pulled out a chair and sat down opposite the boy at the kitchen table. "Davey. Well, and what is your other name, your family name? Your mother and father must live near here."

Davey blanched, and a look of terror crossed his face. "Ain't got none."

"No mother? No father?"

Davey squirmed and stared down at the table. "None."

Kitty was appalled at Davey's appearance. Even gypsy children looked better fed and clothed. Davey's hair was thin and lank, his complexion was an unhealthy grey, and he was visibly crawling with vermin. His skin stretched across fragile-seeming, almost meatless bones. Filthy from head to toe, dressed in rags, with two broken front teeth, he was obviously hungry, unloved, and terrified of his parents.

"How old are you, Davey?"

"Eight, I reckon."

Abernathy gasped behind her. The boy appeared to be no more than five years old, and a measly five, at that. "You reckon? You mean, you are not sure?"

Davey shook his head silently in response, still staring at the table.

"Well, Davey, do you like horses?"

Davey squinted at her with obvious suspicion. "Aye."

Kitty nodded with a firm tilt to her chin. "I believe Mr. Pike could use a stable boy to help with our horses and chores, like leading the cow. So, you shall stay here as a stable boy."

Davey blinked at her dumbly, his jaw hanging slack. "Huh? Yer gonna *keep* me?"

"As a stable-boy, yes. You will have to work for your keep. You shall do whatever chores Mr. Mac, or Mr. Pike, or Mrs. Abernathy give you to do," Kitty gestured to each as she named them. She turned back to Davey. "You shall eat Mrs. Abernathy's excellent cooking right along with the rest of us. Provided you mind your manners and do not shout at me."

Turning to Abernathy, Kitty indicated the cider jug, and Abernathy poured out a cup of cider and filled a plate with biscuits.

Kitty extended her clean, soft hand. "What do you say, Davey, shall we strike hands on the bargain?"

Davey eyed the cider and biscuits with longing and nodded mutely, obviously not quite believing his luck, and extended his bony filthy paw.

"There is one other thing you must do, Davey."

Davey, suspicion alight in his face, growled, "Whassat?"

"You must have a bath every month from now on."

Davey blanched and startled everyone by shrieking, "Noooh!" whilst he sprinted for the door. Mac nabbed him in passing, catching him up under his arms. Davey shrieked, sobbing, terrified beyond words.

Kitty was seized by compassion and, with no thought of propriety, raced around the table and snatched him from Mac. She held Davey on her lap as tenderly as his squirming, heel-drumming, fist-flailing fit would allow.

Kitty petted him and murmured as though to a much younger child. "What is wrong, Davey? Why are you so upset?"

After several minutes of struggle, Davey choked out, "Yer gonna drownd me!"

Kitty coloured and declaimed passionately, "No, *no*, **no** Davey! We do not drown little boys in my bath tub! We mean you no harm. Nobody is going to drown you, Davey." Kitty kept on murmuring assurances and sometimes just soothed, "Hush, hush, God loves you, child."

Davey writhed and kicked and sobbed in her lap as she comforted him over and over again. Davey quieted once he exhausted himself. Though still sobbing, Davey began to look Kitty in the face with brief and furtive glances. As his sobs quieted, he looked at her a bit more steadily, as though tracing a wondrous miracle.

At that moment, her cap askew, her face red, her fresh gown soiled beyond use, Kitty did not feel wonderful.

Davey whispered, "Yer not like ... yer a *good* lady, ain't ye?"

Kitty smiled and released him. "Well, I try, Davey-boy." He impulsively threw his grubby arms about her neck, and Kitty withstood this affection as gracefully as she could.

Kitty took him by the shoulders. She looked him straight in the eyes and commanded, "Now, Davey, you must get in the bath and scrub with soap all over. Then, we shall contrive something clean for you to wear and Abernathy will trim your hair, comb out all the fleas. When you are presentable, we shall feed you a good dinner and let you sleep."

Davey fidgeted nervously. "Are *ye* gonna gimme a baf, then?"

"No, Davey, I think not. You are a big boy, so Mr. Mac should help you, not a lady."

Davey darted a fearful glance at Mac. "Ye'll nay let 'im ...?"

Kitty looked around the room and saw it from the perspective of a helpless child. Most of the household had turned up, and the room was thick with terrifying strangers. Kitty was inspired. "Everyone, please listen. Do *not* drown Davey. Do not knock him senseless. I want him hale and hearty, so he can be my stable boy. Understood?"

There were general murmurs of agreement. Mary, tears of sympathy standing in her eyes, struck on a particularly apt promise. "Cross me heart and hope to die, stick a needle in me eye if I tell a lie," then spat in her hand and held it out to him. He spat into his own palm and shook hands with her shyly, and allowed himself to be led off by a bemused Mac towards the still room.

Kitty attempted to smooth out her clothing. "Well, *that* was unexpected!"

Abernathy nodded. "Aye, that it was. Here, ye look like ye could use a cup."

Kitty gratefully accepted the proffered cider. "Thank you, Abernathy. Poor mite, to be so *certain* we meant to drown him. What a horrible life he must have had!"

Taylor, who had come into the kitchen at the height of the fray, offered, "Let's get ye upstairs and into a fresh gown."

Kitty hauled herself up to her room and had Taylor re-do her rag curls. She destroyed several fleas Davey had transferred to her and changed into a fresh gown.

Later, as Kitty set out to meet Marianne for their usual afternoon ramble, Mac reported that Davey's back and legs were covered with bruises, welts, and scars. "I dun think I was soft, but what could a tyke like him 'ave done to get that many beatin's?"

Kitty met Marianne and related the whole story. Kitty practically moaned, "I feel like a complete idiot. I have no idea how to raise a child. By what lunacy did I authorise myself to take on this charge? I have imposed more duties on my already overburdened staff. I should not be at all surprised if this doesn't trigger a general rebellion."

Marianne encouraged her. "I dare say the burden of raising him will be widely shared. Anything you do is bound to be a vast improvement over what he is used to. Besides, generous impulse should not be checked by cold counsel."

The next morning, Kitty crept up to the attic very quietly to check on Davey. He was still dead to the world. She tip-toed over to the back stairs, ready to descend, when she heard the servants at breakfast. Knowing what she did was wrong, but unable to resist the temptation, Kitty hovered near the top of the stairs, noting the servants' conversation below.

Tom Pike's voice rumbled, "Dun know what Miss is about messing with that nasty bit of riff-raff."

Mary replied with some heat, "She's doin' her Christian duty an' savin' that poor laddie from starvation!"

Tom rumbled again, "Be that as it may, ye females is way too soft on him. Even the Good Book says, 'spare the rod and spoil the child.'"

Abernathy's voice floated up, "Pish, he's had more than enough of that! Ye cannae beat a wee laddie into loving ye, nor is the rod a remedy fer ignorance. Why, that boy has never even *heard* o' God nor knowed the simplest prayer! I've nay seen such a bone ignorant bit of humanity afore. He struggles with simple things any normal boy of four years knows."

Mary corroborated, "Ay, it's true. Why, the lad had no idea what to do with a fork, I doubt he'd ever even seen one afore."

Ned Hart's tenor joined in, "Oh, daughter, you've a kind heart. But I confess, I'm keeping a more watchful eye on the silver and the liquor. Sad to think a mite of his age would get into it, but as wild and ignorant as he is, well ..."

Mac, sounding precisely like the sergeant he used to be, contributed next. "Whether tis ill or not, there's no knowin', nor does it matter. Tis what Miss wants, so we'll make the best of it."

Well satisfied with what she had heard, Kitty ended their discussion by descending the stairs.

Kitty was gratified by Davey's rapid progress. At first, Davey had fits of terror almost every day. Also at first, only Kitty could calm him. But after a few days, Mary took up comforting Davey. His fits quieted to only a few times a week, and slowly, they extinguished themselves altogether.

* * *

On one of her many excursions to Threlkeld, Kitty encountered Lieutenant McLaughlin. Again.

Her suspicions aroused, Kitty mentally counted the number of "chance" encounters with Mr. McLaughlin over the past month. She became convinced he intended to flatter her with his attentions. However, since he had already made a heavy-handed play for her, she was also convinced he was only attracted by her looks and had no interest in her character or mind. More annoyed than flattered, she resolved to send Mary to town.

Lieutenant McLaughlin grinned as he approached her, whisking off his hat and half bowing in the saddle. "How d'you do, Miss Otis?"

Kitty reined in Othello. "Very well, thank you, Lieutenant." Pike backed Pollux a short distance away. "It is nice to see Hercules again." The Lieutenant looked a bit nonplussed. Kitty graciously added, "I do hope the two of you are enjoying this fine weather."

The Lieutenant recovered his smile. "Yes, indeed. We have had many a fine gallop."

"So glad. I am so sorry, but time is pressing. If you would be so kind?"

He replied with another half bow. "Of course, Miss Otis, of course. Good day."

Kitty was more unsettled than the brief encounter should have left her. She pondered her feelings whilst absent-mindedly completing her town chores. How could one trivial snub leave her feeling so confused? Perhaps the Lieutenant was not the same as Mr. Peale, and she had been too quick to judge him. If so, her snub was undeserved, and she felt the wrongness.

But many moral extracts and warnings against seducers played in her mind. Kitty rationalised she had not unfairly snubbed the Lieutenant. His intentions could not be honourable, and the encounter was trivial, anyway.

ARTICLES

Davey grew a solid three inches taller and filled out remarkably over the course of the summer. Abernathy and Taylor were hard-pressed to keep up with his wardrobe needs. His lank straggling hair grew into thick light brown curls, and his cheeks went pink and then brown from the summer sun. He was still slender but not painfully so, with sturdy muscle beginning to show.

Mac and Pike, who were most frequently out-of-doors with Davey, struggled to contain his pranks. He terrorized the cow by tying a bell to her tail, used the bee hives as slingshot targets, and made himself sick several times with stolen treats. But slowly, he left off playing pranks. Davey was (understandably) nervous around Pike, but fell in love with Mac and followed him worshipfully whenever possible. He learnt a few simple prayers, to do his chores, and to bathe himself when reminded.

Abernathy was making headway on his letters, sums, and manners when Davey arrived one afternoon, red-faced and bloody, with his clothes torn. Pike brought him into the kitchen, and Kitty was summoned.

Kitty looked him in the eye. "So, why the fisticuffs, Davey?"

Davey defiantly declared, "He pulled my cork, but I darkened his daylights!"

Mystified, Kitty looked to Pike, who translated, "The other boy punched him in the nose, and Davey hit him in the eye."

"I see. But, Davey, why were you brawling, and with whom?"

The whole tale came blurting out at high speed, "I was playin' with Georgie from over Coldbrook Farm, and I won a race, and Georgie, he din't like that, ye see; so he says, 'I won,' and I says, 'Yer lyin,' and he gets wroth and says I'm stupid; and I says, 'nay' an he says, 'yes, ye is, cause yer workin' fer that man inna frock,' and I told him to take it back, and he wouldn't, and I pushed him down, an' he hit me, an' then we was tussling on the ground, an' then *I won*!"

Kitty struggled to maintain a straight face. "Well, Davey, let us see if I have this straight. Georgie insulted me, and you defended my honour?"

"Yers."

Kitty smothered a smile and corrected him. "That's 'yes, Miss' if you please."

"Yers, Miss," Davey replied sullenly.

"Now, you know brawling is not Christian, and I will make you apologise to Georgie."

"Do I *hafta*?" Davey whined.

"Yes, Davey, you must. And as punishment ... I think at least three, no four, biscuits are called for."

Davey blinked in amazement. Mary began bustling about assembling a plate.

Kitty capitalised on the circumstance to teach an important lesson, "I want you to understand, Davey, fisticuffs is a very poor way to resolve disputes. Not at all Christian. You will have to apologise to Georgie and say an extra prayer tonight. On the other hand, you were doing your level best to defend the honour of a lady, which is good. So, no punishment for the brawl other than having to apologise. Do you understand?"

Davey nodded. "Yers, Miss. Ye din't want me to beat nobody, 'cuz God din't like it, but yer not angry at me 'cuz I stuck up fer ye."

"Correct in all essentials, Davey." Kitty smothered a smile. "Now, go wash up."

Whilst Davey noisily attended to washing up outside of the kitchen door, Kitty turned to the others and said, "This is quite a milestone! Proof positive that Davey thinks of this as his home. But I worry his family will snatch him back now that we have got Davey up to the mark, if for no other reason than to sell him as an apprentice."

Mary clasped her hands in front of herself. "Ye could apprentice him yerself."

"An excellent notion, Mary. But how are we to find his family when Davey stubbornly claims he is an orphan?"

Abernathy chimed in, "I'd wager Mac can get him to gab, particularly if we let Davey know we're offerin' apprenticeship Articles fer him."

Kitty slapped her hand down on the table. "I would not take that wager because I think you are absolutely correct, Abernathy. I shall speak to Mac about it directly."

Mac agreed to usher Davey to Coldbrook Farm to make his apology and convinced Davey on the way back to lead him to his family by promising to go with him and protect him from his dad.

Kitty applied to Uncle Tinsley for Articles, and a week later when they arrived, went along with Mac to cajole Davey's mother into giving up her son. The three set off, with the Articles and two pounds in small change.

The hovel was as wretched as any Mac or Kitty had ever seen. There was no sign of industry, no crops in the ground, no pig in the sty, not even any chickens. It took all of Mac's energies to rouse the occupants from their drunken stupor.

Mr. Burton staggered out of the hut, squinting in the grey overcast daylight, "Whassat?"

Kitty put her arm around Davey. "This is your son, Davey, Mr. Burton."

Davey's mother, ashen-faced and with eyes watering, shook her head. "Nay. He run off. 'At's not him. Not that 'un."

Davey fidgeted in his seat. "Aye, it's me, Mum! Don'cha know yer own son?"

"'Course, I do. Ain't seen hide nor hair o' Davey all summer."

Kitty intervened. "Mrs. Burton, that is because Davey has grown so much over the summer. Davey, tell your mother something only you and she know. Prove that you are Davey."

"Pa makes 'is own peat reek, an' hides it in the roof thatch. And Ma, ye keep Mrs. Culver's chickens an' she gives ye food. When I was little, ye would sing me to sleep with the sea song. Don'cha know me now?"

Mrs. Burton's mouth dropped open. She turned to her husband and grabbed his arm. "Dick, it *is* Davey."

Dick Burton swayed and spoke under his breath. "I'll be buggered."

Kitty turned to Mac and gestured to the purse. "We wish to put him under Articles."

Mac jingled the purse. "It's a full pound. All yours, the minute you sign Davey over to us under Articles." Mac counted out the money into his palm, displaying the coins.

Mr. Burton lunged for them, but Mac snatched them back. "Nuh-uh. Not 'til you sign them Articles." Kitty handed down the Articles, a pen, and ink.

Mac laid the paper on the carriage running board, inked the pen, and handed it to Mrs. Burton, who was closer. She signed a wobbling "X" near the spot that Mac indicated, and her husband followed suit. Mac dropped the coins into Mr. Burton's filthy outstretched hand.

Kitty consoled Davey on the ride home. Being the object of drunken rages was bad, but being unrecognised by your own mother was worse. Mrs. Burton hadn't even kissed Davey good-bye, which nearly broke his heart. Upon returning home, Kitty ordered a weekly food basket of bread and left-overs delivered to the Burtons.

HARVEST

It was a golden summer of high spirits as everyone worked long and hard to resuscitate the old family farm. Mac, Pike, and Hart heroically did the work of a dozen men. To preserve the men for essential field work, Mary and Kitty cared for the kitchen gardens, even though it scandalized Taylor. Kitty quite enjoyed quiet moments working in the fresh air and sunshine, and intended to keep it up. Mary even took over her father's chores of dragging water to the kitchen and chopping firewood to free him for field work.

One afternoon, Kitty discovered Mrs. Abernathy snoring softly, her head resting on her arms on the kitchen table. Out in the light of day, Kitty also noticed dark smudges under Mary's eyes. That afternoon she engaged Harriet, the best of the girls-of-all-work who had helped restore the house, as scullery maid.

Kitty and Mac were meeting as usual with Mr. Otis in the library, both for convenience and to maintain the fiction that Mr. Otis managed his own property. At issue was the breeding of the Jersey heifer. Mac suggested a cross breed, and Kitty worried the delicate Jersey could not carry a large breed calf.

Mr. Otis emerged from his fog and contributed, "It is scientific fact that cross-bred animals are frequently stronger, healthier and more productive than either parent breed. I was just reading of it in my *Proceedings of the Royal Society*."

Mac and Kitty both blinked owlishly in surprise. Kitty said, "Well, that is settled, then. You shall cross breed the Jersey, Mac."

As August yielded to September and the days shortened, the pace of harvest quickened. First, it was the berries, reduced to jams or dried for winter. Then Mac hired Andy back to help with the early orchard fruits and the vegetables, which Mrs. Abernathy dried or turned into chutneys, jams, and pickles. They crushed the poorer apples for cider and cooked many down into black butter, packing only the best in straw for the winter.

Davey proved to have an uncanny talent for smoking bees, and soon, all the combs were harvested. Mrs. Abernathy set Harriet to moulding wax candles. When the fruits and vegetables were mostly in, the pace quickened once again. The wheat ripened.

Mac hired a dozen labourers to scythe the fields. Abernathy, Mary and Harriet awoke in the middle of the night to prepare enormous meals in the wee hours for the labourers and their families. The harvesters arrived before dawn, rude and noisy, and gulped down a tremendous meal.

The labourers' wives and children followed the men and gathered the wheat into bundles the farmers called 'stooks'. At mid-day, Castor and Pollux were harnessed to the farm wagon and plodded about the fields almost without pause whilst the stooks were flung from the ground up to catchers on the wagon.

The harvesters ate out in the fields during the day so as to waste no time from the harvest. Davey and the other children ran food and water out to the harvesters. They left when the sun set, tired and silent. Everyone prayed the weather would stay dry.

Their prayers were answered, and at last, the wheat was threshed and stored in the barns. The straw was tucked under the roof for the animals. Abernathy prepared an elaborate dinner, which was set out in the cool early autumn afternoon shade of the orchard.

The Wardens, the Sumners, the Tinsleys, all the labourers and their families graced the tables. Mrs. Abernathy received applause for her excellent catering. Mr. Otis blessed them all with a beautiful convocation, and they celebrated until the stars came out.

Once Mac had sold the harvest that could be spared, he returned with seventy-three pounds. He proudly presented the funds to Kitty and Mr. Otis in the library.

"Mac!" Kitty gasped, ecstatic. "That is almost ... no, that is *more* than twelve pounds per acre under cultivation. That's double what the home farm at the rectory produced!" Kitty turned to her father. "Papa, we have been blessed with a genius!" Kitty carefully counted out ten per cent of the bounty. "Here is your share."

Mac accepted, smiling and somewhat red-faced with pleasure. "Thank ye kindly, Miss. And startin' with about nowt, too! Now, if ye put most of yer brass back into tha' farm next year, ye can lay in more stock, expand from six acres to eighteen, and ye'll triple yer profits."

"Oh! Mac, do not speak nonsense. *You* will triple the profits for me! What shall I do with this fortune?" Kitty asked rhetorically.

"Ask your Uncle Tinsley. He *is* your man of business," Mr. Otis advised.

"Thank you, Father, that is precisely what I shall do after I have distributed presents to the staff." Kitty smiled at Mac. "After all, without you, I should have foundered badly."

Kitty distributed one golden guinea each to Hart, Pike, and Abernathy; and a half-sovereign apiece to Mary, Taylor, and Harriet. Davey was granted a silver shilling, to his round-eyed wonder.

The poor lad was in such a pelter about it, fretting he should lose it and not wanting to give it into anyone else's keeping. Mac took pity on him and crafted a small 'treasure box' with a simple lock mechanism. The two of them contrived a hiding place for it in the little alcove at the top of the backstairs that served as Davey's bed-chamber.

The next day, as Kitty prepared for her visit to the Tinsleys, she stepped into the kitchen to have a word with Abernathy. As they discussed household purchases, Kitty noticed Mac and Mary in the garden. Mac relieved Mary of her heavy basket of wet laundry and escorted her to the drying lines.

Kitty turned to Abernathy. "Am I imagining things…?"

Abernathy smiled and with a twinkle in her eye, she said, "Not if yer imaginin' that Mac's courtin' Mary. And doing a fine job of it, too, from the look o' things."

Kitty smiled in return, and they concluded their business. Shortly thereafter, Kitty presented herself unannounced to her Aunt and Uncle Tinsley. She delivered her earnings and was promptly invited to stay overnight. After the usual civilities, Kitty explained her mission.

"I come bearing the product of our little home farm, a full sixty pounds, twelve shillings! It was over seventy-three pounds, but I paid Mac his agreed-upon ten per cent. Then I made presents to the servants who worked so hard to garner this profit for me," she said as she handed the money to her uncle. "Father suggested I give it to you to invest for me until the money is needed for next season's farming."

"Merit's suggestion?" her uncle inquired, startled.

"Yes. Dear Papa has rare lucid moments before sinking back into the fog. I sense my loss all over again every time he does." All three sighed. "Mac is confident the Dixon Cottage home farm will return another two hundred pounds per year. Prosperity has smiled upon me."

Mr. Tinsley smiled proudly. "Indeed. And should you continue to add a few pounds to your investments each season, you shall soon be counted an heiress!"

Kitty grinned and then continued more soberly, "However, that is not my sole purpose in coming here. I need a new wardrobe as many new families shall arrive for the hunt season. But I have no idea what is a reasonable allowance. Mama always shopped with me, and I am lost without her."

Aunt Eliza patted Kitty's hand sympathetically. "I shall be happy to stand in your mother's stead and go shopping with you." She turned towards her husband. "Dearest, what do you think is a reasonable allowance?"

Uncle Tinsley smiled. "Thirty pounds. You want to make a good first impression on your new acquaintance."

"*Thirty pounds?*" Kitty responded in scandalised tones. "Why, that is almost half of the year's farm production. I should feel extravagant spending so much."

"Oh, tish—tosh." Aunt Eliza leaned forward and patted Kitty's knee. "That is only a fifth of what a wardrobe for a London come-out would cost! You want to be gorgeous for all the eligible bachelors you are bound to meet."

In short order, all was settled and a business meeting melded into a social visit. Kitty returned the next day in raptures about her planned shopping trip to Leeds.

Since Marianne also needed a new wardrobe, Kitty directed a letter to the Tinsleys, and they modified their shopping scheme. Mrs. Warden, Kitty, and Marianne would all travel to Carlisle, escorted by Pike and Mr. Hart. After a night spent there, they were to proceed with Mrs. Tinsley and her man servants to her sister's house in Leeds. Once there, the party would repair for a week's bacchanal of shopping.

Mr. Warden agreed to the scheme after Mrs. Warden pointed out transport and accommodations were provided. Thus, there were no costs except for the purchases. The *same* purchases, whether Marianne laid down his blunt at expensive local shops or at less expensive warehouses in Leeds.

The programme proceeded as planned. Kitty's best bargain was a gorgeous wool velvet in the deepest burgundy red and an enormous black fur muff. Marianne's triumph was an elegant gold-and-peach shot Italian silk taffeta. Kitty calculated with all their purchases, she and Marianne would appear smartly turned out for the whole of the winter. Their voluminous purchases could not be contained within their luggage, and they bought two new travel trunks to contain the lot.

The entire party, with sore feet and weary ankles, light of heart and purse, were enjoying the last luncheon together when Mrs. Tinsley spotted an old acquaintance. They stopped at her table on their way out and were introduced to Mrs. Beckford and her distant cousin, Sir Richard Raleigh.

Sir Richard soon eclipsed Mrs. Beckford in the young ladies' interest. He was tall and slim, with blue eyes and brown hair in a fashionable short layered 'Brutus' style. His address was polished, and his manners relaxed. His tailoring was faultless, fashionable without going over the line to dandified.

"Delighted to make your acquaintance," Sir Richard said, making an impeccable bow. The ladies dropped curtsies, and Mrs. Tinsley took up the conversation.

"What brings you to Leeds, Sir Richard?"

"Aside from the lovely scenery?" He gestured towards Marianne and Kitty. The girls smiled, and Marianne blushed at the compliment. "I keep a hunting box outside of Keswick and am making my way there for this season's sport. In the meantime, I am visiting dear Mrs. Beckford and hope to make my way to the Cramwell Linn Waterfall north of Carlisle."

Mrs. Tinsley responded, "Now, that is a fortunate circumstance, since all of us live near Keswick and shall be able to continue our acquaintance."

Kitty volunteered, "I have long wished to visit Cramwell Linn Waterfall."

"Then I shall delay my visit until after arriving in Keswick, and we shall all assemble to make an expedition," he replied gallantly.

"Oh, dear. I did not intend to beg for an invitation," Kitty replied. "Changing your itinerary would mean doubling back fifty miles at least, as the falls are between here and Keswick."

Sir Richard bowed. "But such an expedition is so much more amusing with others. Besides, it is a trifling distance in a decent carriage."

"And unnecessary," interposed Mrs. Tinsley. "When you mount your expedition, you can rest overnight at my home, west of Carlisle, before continuing to the Gilsland Spa. I understand that is the usual launch for visits to the falls."

The ladies accepted Sir Richard's invitation, and everyone agreed to Mrs. Tinsley's excellent scheme. They exchanged directions, and Kitty's party reversed course, arriving home without incident.

Then the sewing began. The ladies soon fell into a routine, meeting every afternoon for three hours in Kitty's library, which enjoyed even northern light. Kitty, Marianne, Mrs. Warden, Taylor, and Mrs. Warden's abigail, Libby, all sewed industriously. They soon discovered each other's talents and divided up the work accordingly.

Kitty crowed, "I shall never have to appear in the same gown twice! Or, at least, not looking the same way, what with changing sleeves and accessories."

"Oh, yes!" Marianne concurred. "I dare say half of my acquaintance will not recognise me in my new clothes."

"It is certain your father will not," Mrs. Warden agreed. "Thank goodness these are winter gowns, so he cannot take exception to you displaying a quarter-inch more neck than he thinks you should. Even your father can have no objection to them." Sadly, her confidence would prove to be misplaced.

SIR RICHARD'S BALL

The bright colours and crisp, spicy scents of autumn arrived, as did the Quality. They took up their annual residence in various hunting boxes. Mrs. Sumner and Mrs. Warden, in turn, kindly took Kitty on their morning visits.

After leaving her cards, Kitty received a flurry of morning visits in return, including Sir Richard. However, he spent most of the time inquiring after Marianne and her connections. So, Kitty ended the visit, convinced he was much more interested in her friend than herself. Soon thereafter, Kitty and Marianne received their first invitations.

"Did you get one, too?" asked Marianne in breathless accents, showing Kitty her invitation.

Kitty leaned forward. "Yes, indeed. Sir Richard's ball looks to be excellent. I hear almost every officer quartered in Cumberland shall be attending. But has your mama coaxed your papa into letting you go?" Kitty asked.

"Oh, yes, it is the most famous thing. Mama argued if they send me off to my Aunt Beth in London without ever having attended any private balls, I should make a complete prat of myself," Marianne confided.

Kitty arched a brow and tossed her hair back. "Well, I hardly agree with the reasoning. But I must allow your mother has a clever way of bringing your father to heel."

But it appeared Mr. Warden had not shot all his cannon. He insisted, seemingly in penance for attending at all, Marianne must be gowned to his ridiculous ideas of propriety. He demanded an unfashionable style and stark white, which made her look ill. All of Marianne's pleading and Mrs. Warden's argument she had already sewn gowns for just this use were to no avail. If she was to go, Marianne was to go dowdy. When Kitty learnt of this latest disaster, she, Mrs. Warden, and Marianne contrived a plot.

After considerable debate, the ladies decided smuggling one of Marianne's gowns out of the house would result in discovery. Then, Kitty hit upon a useful idea. "I believe Taylor can cut down my ivory dress with the pale primrose bodice; you know the one. It has tiny puft sleeves. I never wear it because I have outgrown it, but it should be quite fetching on you, Marianne. You and your mama will come here, and we will all dress together on the day of the ball. Mr. Warden will be none the wiser!"

Mrs. Warden was obviously relieved. "Yes! I shall make up the gown my odious husband has decreed, and we will bring it over in a bandbox on the day. I know your papa will not let you wear aught but white gloves and slippers. But we can hide the gold Grecian sandals and those lovely ivory kid gloves in the box, as they are small enough to smuggle out of the house safely."

"But Papa will be vexed with me if I cut my hair into a stylish crop. I shall be in braids. As always," fretted Marianne.

They summoned Taylor, and she suggested the mode *a la Grecque.* A style with the hair drawn up in a high-crowned bun and the tail end of the hair set in curls, tumbling down the back. Taylor also advised they cut a delicate fringe to fall in curls around her face.

Mr. Warden was bound to notice this change, but Marianne bravely agreed to weather his wrath in pursuit of a flattering hairstyle. Kitty arranged for delivery of the shoe roses.

On the day, the ladies came together in good time and encountered an unexpected delay. Marianne's hair was so thick and heavy that it could only be coaxed into a curl in the tiniest wisps. There was so much of it that soon Taylor, Libby, Mrs. Warden, and Kitty were all hard at work ironing some curl into her hair.

They rapidly learnt to make haste slowly, since attempts to gather more hair in a single press resulted in unattractive lax curls. Finally, however, Marianne's hair was done.

"Lord! I find I have much more sympathy with your braids!" cried Kitty as she hurried into her own gown.

At last, they arrived. The girls alighted from the carriage, eyes shining and cheeks aglow. Several young officers observed them with admiration. One, howsoever, was more enterprising than the rest and pressed his hostess for an introduction.

"Lady Margaret." The young officer made a bow. "Would you be so kind as to introduce me to the ravishing blonde lady entering?"

Lady Margaret smiled and gestured for the Lieutenant to stand beside her.

Marianne entered. "Marianne Warden, Lady Margaret Raleigh, delighted to meet you."

"So glad you could come." Lady Margaret and Marianne both curtsied. "May I present Lieutenant James Wallace."

He made his bow. "At your service." He offered his arm to Marianne. She glanced at her mother. With a conscious look between Kitty and Mrs. Warden, he was permitted to escort her.

Lieutenant James Wallace wore an immaculate Scottish Greys Dragoons uniform. His red jacket sported blue lapels and cuffs with white frogging across the chest. He looked quite well. Though he was only of average height, he was well-proportioned and broad-shouldered. He had blue eyes and fair, freckled colouring, with thick wavy ginger hair as bright as a new copper penny. The Lieutenant possessed a square jaw, straight nose, and regular features, and was, without doubt, one of the handsomest men at the ball.

When they had traversed the hall, the footman, through some mistake or other, announced them as "Lieutenant and Mrs. Wallace".

Lieutenant Wallace stood pole-axed for an endless moment before rising to the occasion.

"Enter, Sir, enter. There is quite a press!" advised the footman.

Lieutenant Wallace won Mrs. Warden's undying support by replying, "We cannot. For though 'tis tragic, the young lady has not *yet* consented to be my wife and must be announced as 'Miss Warden.'"

Marianne blushed to the roots of her hair and stifled giggles but remained attached to the Lieutenant's arm. Irritated, the footman announced them correctly.

In later years, it would seem to Marianne that she danced with her dear Wallace alone that night. In truth, she danced with many gentlemen but forgot them all. He only possessed her hand for the (perfectly correct) two country dances and escorted her into the ball and out to her carriage. Those few moments in a hot, crowded ballroom with intermittent snatches of conversation were enough to fix the gentleman's interest. Although Marianne was too young to know her own heart as well as the Lieutenant knew his, she too, was well on the way to forming an attachment.

Marianne's new elegance was not wasted on the rest of the gentlemen. Sir Richard also danced with her twice. However, his hands lingered on her too long for her comfort. Completely flustered by his inappropriate attentions, Marianne spent much of her time with him in an agony of shyness.

As soon as they were settled in the carriage to go home, Mrs. Warden began, "I must say I am quite pleased with Lieutenant Wallace; he is a pretty-behaved young gentleman."

"And quite good looking, too," Kitty volunteered with a smile. Privately, she thought the Lieutenant was shy and not as sophisticated as Sir Richard, but she had no intention of throwing a wet blanket on Marianne's happiness.

"Do you think so?" Marianne asked. "I believe so, but first impressions can be so deceiving. Lieutenant Wallace and I spoke with the comfort of long acquaintance. He has a knack for making me brave."

"Sir Richard seemed to give you decided attentions," Kitty observed.

"Yes," Marianne returned with a worried frown. "But he is *so* forward. He had his hands all over me. He makes me very nervous."

"His action rather confirms what I heard of him," Mrs. Warden supplied. "Mrs. Fletcher discovered from the Wright twins that Sir Richard fled London on the heels of scandal. According to their intelligence, for they have just returned from nursing their aunt in London, Sir Richard is reputed to be a libertine."

"Hmm," Kitty disagreed. "Just the sort of rumour I usually attribute to misinformation or jealousy. We shall have to become better acquainted to see."

After taking down Marianne's hair (a second trial like the first), Mrs. Warden and Marianne put on the gown her father had decreed, and they made it home without incident.

The general peace was not to last. Servants will talk, and a juicy titbit like the ladies' plot was too delightful to die an early death. Through a route unknown to any of the ladies, Mr. Warden discovered their plot. Sadly for his dignity, though, he chose to complain of it following church services.

Mr. Warden, hands on hips, lectured Marianne in the chapter house. "What a saucy minx you are, to think a school-room chit can pull the wool over her father's eyes. Whatever made you conceive acting the hussy in a ludicrous gown would improve your consequence or make you appear to advantage? A single party has so overset your judgement, you have taken to folly instead of heeding wiser heads than yours—"

Kitty interrupted with eyes snapping, cheeks flushed, and a glittering smile. "How *fortunate* we have a Tulip of the *ton* to guide us in the latest fashions!"

She raked her eyes over his figure, inspecting his unfashionable buckskins and gaiters. "I dare say, even though my father is a vicar, and my mother nobly born, they misled me in propriety of dress. The dress which you despise as 'ludicrous' was given to me by my aunt, the Countess of Burton Dasset, on the occasion of my sixteenth birthday. I wish to discover in what way my dress, which my noble kin determined was proper for me at age *sixteen*, offends on a woman of *eighteen*?"

Marianne audibly sucked in her breath, and several ladies within earshot tittered.

"I am eager, sir, for your precepts. In particular, I wish to learn how gowning your daughter in the cheapest stuff which could be got, in the least flattering colour available, and in a style appropriate for an ageing relict well beneath Marianne's station, could improve *your* consequence or make either of *you* appear to advantage?" Kitty said to Mr. Warden in a lively tone while a dangerous smile played on her features.

Mr. Warden, now red-faced, attempted to assemble a response that did not make him appear to be either a martinet or a simpleton. Mrs. Fletcher, having suffered from Mr. Warden's pompous dictates herself, could not resist intervening. "Well, Mr. Warden, it seems you are no longer just a better farmer than the rest of us; you are also now an expert in feminine fashion. I marvel at your accomplishments, sir!" General giggling followed this home stroke.

Kitty, her temper much abated after her outburst, decided it would be prudent to retreat. She turned to Mrs. Warden. "Obviously, we need much study on the matter. Would you be agreeable to joining me and Marianne this afternoon for tea and a perusal of fashion plates?"

Mrs. Warden immediately perceived the advantage of allowing Mr. Warden time to regain his temper and hastily accepted. The ladies departed, leaving Mr. Warden highly flustered.

Mr. Sumner approached and said sympathetically, "Never engage in a land war in Asia, hey?"

"Excuse me?" flashed Squire Warden, irritated.

"You know, Asia is foreign territory. Ladies' fashions are foreign territory for a gentleman—"

Seeing the ridiculous in the exchange, the Squire laughed uproariously. "You have a point, Mr. Sumner."

"Yes, and if the ladies take a notion to wear bones in their noses next season, the most us poor fellows can do is hope that they are discreet tasteful bones," finished Mr. Sumner.

SQUIRE WARDEN'S BATTLE

O nce Mrs. Warden, Marianne, and Kitty were settled in Kitty's coach, the ladies had a good laugh at Mr. Warden's expense.

"Oh, Kitty, your comment was excellent!" exulted Marianne. "I never have had the nerve to say those things, though I have thought them often!"

"Yes, dear," Mrs. Warden concurred. "Your father was abandoned by his father when he was but twelve years old, so he received no guidance whatsoever. In his determination to do better by his own children, he attempts to manage every detail of your lives. Poor dear. It does him a world of good to receive a set-down when he oversteps the bounds!"

"Oh, I hope I have not made your lives uncomfortable for you when you go home." Kitty reached over and squeezed Marianne's hand. "He just made me so angry when he started dressing you down in public!"

"Oh, no. Whatever his faults, my husband has an excellent sense of humour. He will have laughed about this and mostly forgotten it by the time we get home. Sadly, this also means he will largely have forgotten his lesson as well. We will fight this battle many more times." Mrs. Warden sighed.

The ladies then began to contrive many strategies to soothe his inevitable sulks so Marianne might have a creditable come-out. Once again, the ladies underestimated Mr. Warden.

October 11, 1813
Warden Grange

My Dearest Kitty,

I write you to cancel our engagement for Monday afternoon. My father has forbidden me to see you ever again! I weep even as I write this. I am also effectively confined to my home, since it is reasonable to assume you will attend any social event that I would normally attend.

I do not know what my father believes he is accomplishing, but all he has done is create a deep and abiding bitterness in my heart!

Oh! How I pray to forgive him. But, as yet, I cannot! He is, in every sense, a tyrant! And, according to my mother (her voice was raised, I could not help but overhear), a fool as well. I can think of nothing either of us or even my mother can do at this point to soften his heart.

Once he makes an idiotic pronouncement, he is apt to dig in his heels and become more stubborn and rigid at any sign of opposition. This is all made worse because, in some part of his autocratic heart, he knows you are right and he is wrong—a situation that will only make him more mulish.

Pity me, Kitty, and pray for me. Perhaps God can amend his hard heart. I know of no way I can.

Yr. Heartbroken Friend, Marianne

Kitty's response to this missive was not unhappiness, but anger. As she sat at the dining table with the note clutched in her hand, her father entered.

"Goodness, Kitty! What has put you in such a state?" her father inquired.

Kitty explained the situation to him as simply as she could. "Marianne is right; her father *is* a tyrant! Oh! I wish I knew how to overthrow him."

"That part is easy. Make being stubborn more difficult for him than being reasonable. Ask the vicar for help. That is what my parishioners did to me all the time," her father advised.

"Papa, you are a genius!" Her face wreathed with smiles; she embraced her father. "I shall apply to the vicar immediately."

Within ten minutes, Kitty was mounted on Othello, as Marianne's missive had arrived just prior to Kitty's daily ride. Within the half-hour, Kitty was in Mrs. Sumner's drawing-room pouring out her troubles.

Mrs. Sumner listened sympathetically when Kitty shared Marianne's letter. "Your father made an excellent suggestion if I had the first notion of how to effect it!" Mrs. Sumner sighed. "I shall have to ponder this thorny problem—how to resist Mr. Warden without putting his back up and making everything worse ..." She trailed off, staring blankly through the window, deep in thought. Kitty wisely left her to it, sipping her tea.

Mrs. Sumner's footman brought in Mrs. Warden's card, who had appeared on much the same mission as had driven Kitty to the rectory.

After the usual civilities, Kitty made ready to leave when Mrs. Warden asked her to stay. After a brief review of Kitty's conversation with Mrs. Sumner, Kitty handed Marianne's letter to Mrs. Warden.

Mrs. Warden read it and was affected, saying with tears in her eyes, "Oh, my poor daughter! I tried to warn Mr. Warden, although Marianne is a loving and obedient child, his restrictions are completely unreasonable. He will only engender bitterness, as she says herself." Mrs. Warden sighed. "Oh! What is to be done?"

"I think ... I believe ... perhaps ..." Mrs. Sumner began, hesitantly, "I may have an idea." The ladies eagerly applied to her to reveal her scheme.

"Well, it appears to me it will be much easier for Mr. Warden to be reasonable if all his acquaintance believe he is *already* being reasonable," Mrs. Sumner began.

Her guests looked puzzled, so she explained. "We shall have to recruit a great number of people to compliment him on how much improved Marianne is under Miss Otis's influence, how much they look forward to seeing her in her best looks ..." The light broke in on both her guests, and they eagerly took up the theme.

"Why, I can ask the Fords and the Browns to speak to him," Mrs. Warden volunteered.

"I think it might be best if you and I"—Kitty motioned to Mrs. Warden—"appear to have no hand in this. Sadly, that leaves most of the work up to Mrs. Sumner."

"Not entirely, Miss Otis. You have an onerous task as well," Mrs. Sumner returned.

"Oh?" Kitty asked.

"Yes, you must issue a very contrite apology," Mrs. Sumner advised. Kitty sighed but nodded her agreement. "And you, Mrs. Warden, will have to make a great show of your concern over insulting all of your acquaintance every time Marianne turns down an invitation. Of course, we shall see she receives a *flood* of invitations!"

The ladies conversed with great spirit as they worked out the details.

The next day, Mr. Warden stopped for an after-business pint at the *Horse and Farrier*. Mr. Brown commented, "Ye're long-headed, ye are, Mr. Warden. The way ye have Miss Warden rigged up, she's bound to attach some top-o'-the-mark gentleman and land ye with a load of brass." Mr. Brown winked. "An' to think she were naught but a school lassie last year!"

Mrs. Brown arrived to deliver the roll and cheese Mr. Warden had ordered. "Aye, me sister tells me t'was Miss Otis what taught her to dress like a London lady. Me sister says Miss Otis has very refined taste, very *haute ton*."

"Well, I know nought of all that." Mr. Brown shifted uneasily. "But I do know Miss Warden has become the prime article this year. I hear the Quality talkin'... she's caught their eye, that's for certain."

Mr. Warden, his mouth busy with beer and cheese, had no reply except for a very surprised expression.

The next day, he met Mr. and Mrs. Ford when he was about his normal business. Mr. Ford approached, smiling. "How do you do, Squire? We had the honour of attending Sir Richard's ball and were very impressed with your daughter's transformation."

In a mode unique to the Fords, Mrs. Ford then echoed him, "Miss Warden was utterly transformed!"

"Transformed!?" cried Mr. Warden.

"She commanded considerable attention from the best of the young officers, did she not, my dear?" Mr. Ford continued.

Mrs. Ford nodded enthusiastically. "Considerable attention. I believe it is due to the good influence of Miss Otis, who has a genius for elegance."

Mr. Ford then took up the role of echo. "Yes, dear. A positive genius for fashion. Miss Warden lost none of her sweetness, though. She was every inch the lady."

Mrs. Ford smiled. "Shan't keep you; please give our regards and compliments to Mrs. Warden."

Mr. Warden, struck dumb by astonishment, hardly knew where to look or what to say, and so bid a hasty farewell to the Fords. Mr. Warden was unable to stir from his house without hearing how well Marianne looked and acted at Lord Raleigh's ball. Several acquaintances bluntly attributed his daughter's improvement to Miss Otis's influence.

Meanwhile, at home, Marianne took to leaving any room he entered unless her mother was there to support her. She never spoke against her father, but she never looked at him, either. She remained silent and grave, and when forced to speak, spoke as little as possible.

One Friday afternoon, she asked to be excused and was heading for the door when her father, completely exasperated, responded, "You are *not* excused! These constant mopes are ridiculous! I have only denied you a single companion. You were perfectly content before Miss Otis moved here and can be so again."

"Please excuse me, Papa, but you are mistaken," Marianne replied sadly. "As long as you deny me Miss Otis, you deny me every acquaintance I have, since it is impossible for me to be invited anywhere where she will not also be invited." She dropped a curtsy and fled the room.

Mrs. Warden judged the time right. "I believe you have been too hasty, Mr. Warden. You only intended to deny her, as you said, a single companion. Howsoever, Miss Otis is everywhere popular, and therefore, bound to be included in any society we would want Marianne to join in."

"Nonsense! How can you say so?" Mr. Warden interrupted.

Taking a deep breath, Mrs. Warden continued. "So, unless you change your mind, everyone will assume you are hiding Marianne because she carries some man's natural child, or worse, has run mad. Once rumours begin, she will be haunted by them even during a Season in London!"

"A Banbury tale if I ever heard one!" cried the beleaguered man. "You cannot possibly believe avoiding Kitty Otis will ruin our daughter in society!"

Seeing her husband's astonishment, Mrs. Warden added in softened tones, "I know you did not intend it, dear, but you have *not* denied her a single companion. You have denied her *all* local society and, because of that, any future at all. You have *ensured* she will dwindle into an old maid." Mrs. Warden then followed her daughter from the room, leaving a bewildered and angry Mr. Warden staring into the fire.

At the church tea after services, Mr. Warden was dealt a double blow. Lady Margaret, Lord Raleigh's mother, who rarely deigned to talk to the Wardens, was terribly amused by Mrs. Sumner's campaign. She approached the Wardens. "Mr. Warden, your liberality in gowning Marianne in the best of taste will permit her to rise to the first ranks of society. I never saw a girl at her first ball so elegant as Miss Warden was on the night of our ball. I must know the London *modiste* you employed."

Mrs. Warden replied with a curtsey, "Why, I shall take that as a great compliment, Lady Margaret. We employed no *modiste*; I made over one of Miss Otis's gowns."

"Otis… that is so familiar … Is she the niece of Lady Vivian, Countess of Burton Dasset?"

"Yes, I believe so. At least, I have heard her refer to her Aunt, the Countess," replied Mrs. Warden.

"Yes, I know her slightly. Lady Vivian was a diamond of the first water in her day. A lady of great delicacy, propriety, and elegance. If her niece is anything like her, your daughter is very lucky in her companion." Lady Margaret nodded majestically and took her leave.

Mr. and Mrs. Tinsley, down for one of their frequent visits, had been apprised by Kitty of the situation. They requested an introduction from Mr. Sumner. Mr. Tinsley said, "We are so delighted Miss Otis has found such respectable neighbours. We are particularly delighted with Miss Warden, who we know from her letters is her dearest companion. With poor Miss Otis's situation, no mother and an ailing father, she needs the support of every friend."

Mrs. Tinsley expanded the theme. "Miss Warden is such an excellent companion for Miss Otis, for her more sober ideas inform Miss Otis's opinions, and Miss Otis is helping Miss Warden conquer her school girl awkwardness. They are so well suited to each other."

Mrs. Warden replied, "Oh! I am so glad to hear it, for that is my opinion exactly."

Mr. Tinsley finished, "Our greatest concern was that Miss Otis would have few opportunities to mingle with society. We are much reassured, now we have had an opportunity to meet Miss Warden. I look forward to making your better acquaintance."

"Likewise, I'm sure," replied Mrs. Warden. The ladies curtsied, and the gentlemen shook hands.

The *coup de grâce* came from Mr. Sumner, who took aside a distinctly ruffled Mr. Warden to counsel him quietly. "Mr. Warden, I wish to urge you to reconsider your probation—I mean—*prohibition* on your daughter. First, I doubt you intended this punishment to be as severe, as far-reaching, and as damaging as it will prove to be.

"Consider the plight of every hostess in the district: what is a hostess to do? Snub Miss Otis or Miss Warden? Either way, the hostess and many of her guests will be unhappy. If you take the approach of simply keeping Marianne at home, people will begin to suspect there is something wrong with her, and the rumours will fly. You will end up doing much greater damage to her reputation than any ball gown ever could ..." Mr. Sumner fidgeted nervously.

Mr. Warden interrupted irritably. "My wife gave me the same Banbury tale..."

"I hate to be the one to disabuse you," Mr. Sumner's fidgeting escalated. "But it is *not* a Banbury tale! Unless your daughter discharges her social hostilities—I mean—*responsibilities*, as usual, rumours will fly. Besides, this punishment is disproportionate to the crime. This was a minor prank, executed with the full permission and approval of your wife. The girls would never have assayed it without Mrs. Warden giving them countenance."

Mr. Warden once again interrupted with, "Was ever there a man so hen-pecked?"

Mr. Sumner replied, embarrassed, "No more than the rest of us! I have actually seen the gown in question on Marianne, which I do not believe you can claim. I assure you, there was nothing improper—"

"It is not the *gown* I object to. I take offence that my wife and daughter deceived me!" Mr. Warden interrupted snappishly.

"Well, as to that, uhm..." The good vicar brushed his hands through his remaining hair in a harried gesture. "You brought that on yourself. Recall in Paul's *Epistle to the Ephesians,* he says, 'And, ye fathers, provoke not your children to wrath.' I am afraid, Sir, you were '*provoking.*'"

Mr. Sumner adopted a lecturing tone. "You left your wife and daughter little choice when you insisted on imposing your masculine ideas in a strictly feminine domain. The punishment you levied will inconvenience every hostess in the district, deprive an orphan girl of necessary society, deprive Marianne of her proper place in society, and subject her to impertinent speculation. Your strictures upon her seem unwarranted, even churlish, as a response to a mild prank authorized by your wife."

"But what else am I to do?" cried Mr. Warden.

Mr. Sumner concluded in mild accents, "I believe you have made your point, Mr. Warden. I merely ask you to reassess the situation and judge that by birth, fortune, education, age, and abilities, Miss Otis is well suited as a companion for your daughter."

As Mr. Sumner departed, he motioned to Kitty, and she approached Mr. Warden. "Good day, Mr. Warden. I have no wish to importune you; I am come to tender an apology. I deeply regret having offended you and promise to never let my fashion sense over-set my common sense again." Kitty blushed furiously from deeply conflicted feelings. Uppermost was embarrassment, mingled with a grudge against the necessity of appeasing so tyrannical a man.

Mr. Warden finally conceded in sarcastic tones. "Humph. Not much of an apology, and tardy, too, but it will have to do. Run along to have your life-sustaining chatter with Marianne."

"Thank you." Kitty curtsied before practically running across the Chapter House to share the good news with Marianne and her mother. The ladies embraced affectionately and spoke with great animation until it was time to go.

HUNT SEASON COMMENCES

Kitty and Marianne were soon caught up in a gay whirl of visits, morning calls, and balls. Local matrons still repeated dark rumours of scandal in London about Sir Richard. Still, he excited the interest of many young ladies. He pursued Marianne at every social function. Marianne, whilst flattered, could not like him. She felt nervous around him and evaded him as much as she could while still being civil.

Mr. Warden was quite pleased with Sir Richard's interest in Marianne. Sir Richard would give his daughter prestige and comfort. He was only dimly aware of Marianne's feelings and did not let his daughter's preference interfere with his delight.

At the next ball, during a break in the dancing, Kitty and Marianne indulged in all the usual chitchat. Marianne complained, "I cannot say 'no' to Sir Richard because I still wish to dance. Oh, I wish he would fix on somebody else!"

"I know, my dear Marianne," Kitty replied. "All we can hope for is some disaster overtakes Sir R, and he bows out."

They were so intent on their whispered conversation that Kitty failed as sentry. Sir Richard appeared with a plate of food for Marianne.

Sir Richard clasped and caressed Marianne's hands as he handed over the plate. Marianne pulled away startled. A cunning gleam entered her eyes. Marianne feigned dropping the plate. Kitty watched, spellbound, as the contents of the plate slid towards the leading edge. Marianne flipped the jam-filled trifle onto Sir Richard's waistcoat as she caught the plate. His waistcoat was ruined, and his jacket and shirt were also besmirched.

"Oh! Sir Richard, I am so sorry! How very clumsy of me. Please do forgive me," Marianne said with perfect propriety but with a devilish gleam in her eye. "Oh, do let me repair the damage." As she spooned the slop on to the plate, she succeeded only in spreading the disaster.

Kitty, proud of Marianne's clever trick, joined in. She snatched up a pitcher of water and a napkin. Kitty began to dab at the stain, thus spreading it even farther. Within seconds, Sir Richard excused himself.

As soon as he left, Kitty turned to Marianne and said, "Well done! How did you learn that trick? It was a very clever way to drive him off?"

Marianne replied with a mischievous look, "Do you think so? Thank you. I devised it as revenge on my brother, Hal, who was fond of pranking me. I was delighted to dodge Sir R while still keeping the privilege of dancing." The girls were still giggling when two gentlemen approached. They asked for the next two and the girls agreed cheerfully.

Lieutenant James Wallace was also paying court to Marianne. She spent the chief part of every afternoon with him. They visited friends together, rambled around Kitty's park, or viewed striking local scenery. Kitty also added to Marianne's happiness by inviting Lieutenant Wallace to many small parties at Dixon Cottage.

Sir Richard was also a frequent visitor to Warden Grange, but saw much less of Marianne than he would have liked. Marianne and her mother believed the dark rumours about Sir Richard and avoided him whenever possible.

The first hunt of the season opened. The field gathered in front of the *Horse and Farrier*. The Browns did a brisk business in hot cider, tea, coffee, rolls, and other such fare. The local hound breeders indulged in good-natured rivalry between their chosen packs. The horses were splendid with braided up manes and ribbon-bound tails. Marianne's brother, Hal Warden, served as one of the Field Masters and was impressive in scarlet.

Kitty was wearing a fetching deep green habit with black velvet facings. A cold foggy morning with heavy ground mist did not dampen the hubbub of the hunt so much as diffuse it. The sounds blended into one babble of cheerful noise. Kitty spied Lady Margaret aboard a beautiful roan mare and made her greeting.

"Oh, how do you do, Miss Otis? Delighted to discover you hunt," said Lady Margaret.

"Oh, yes! I love a hunt as much as anything. What a lovely roan," returned Kitty.

"Gem and I are only hilltoppers now, are we not, old girl?" Lady Margaret replied, genially patting her horse's neck. "She is coming on to 13 years, now. Too old for jumping, as am I. But I cannot resist bringing her out to watch whenever I can."

There followed a genial exchange of hunt lore agreeable to both ladies. Lady Margaret's estimate of Kitty's intelligence and accomplishments rose. Kitty, meanwhile, found herself liking Lady Margaret far more than she ever thought to. They parted amicably with a mutual promise of morning visits.

Soon enough, the hunt masters cried, "Move off!" After drawing blank several coverts, there came the exciting cry of "Tally ho!" and Kitty was off like a shot. She soon realized Lieutenant McLaughlin had joined the hunt. It was impossible to mistake that man or Hercules. Worse, the lieutenant was in the lead, and she was chasing him.

Seized by sudden anxiety, Kitty eased Othello to a canter. She thought furiously as she rode, almost insensible to the countryside around her. Kitty feared any encounter with him at the hunt breakfast. Yet she could not think of any plausible reason to abandon the hunt.

Finally, inspiration struck. She would claim Othello cracked a hoof going over a wall, and she returned home to have him seen to. With one inventive excuse, she could avoid Lieutenant McLaughlin. Ha! Marianne was not the only one who could dodge an inappropriate suitor.

THE EXPEDITION

Sir Richard was good to his word. The girls received invitations to visit Cramwell Linn Waterfall. The ladies learned the Expedition had grown. Mr. and Mrs. Sumner joined them. Some young officers and young ladies of Sir Richard's acquaintance also accepted. With proper chaperones thus assured, the girls agreed to go.

Kitty and Marianne arrived, each with a small trunk, at Sir Richard's hunt box on the day and well in time. Kitty graciously offered her closed carriage to Mr. and Mrs. Sumner. Mrs. Sumner introduced Lieutenant McLaughlin. She paired Kitty with him in a high-perch phaeton.

As she had no wish to be churlish and demand her coach back, Kitty agreed reluctantly, even though the Lieutenant's smug look annoyed her.

"Very clever, Lieutenant, arranging to join the expedition in a two-person *phaeton*. Surely, you are aware I am travelling with you under protest," Kitty snapped.

"I suspected as much, but my design is to overwhelm you with so much charm I undo all your scruples," he replied. Kitty could scarcely not roll her eyes. "Shall I begin with the riveting story of my life?"

Kitty reminded herself she had withstood Squire Warden's pompous remarks and Mr. Peale's vain pretensions. She was well able to withstand the Lieutenant.

"Proceed, sir," she responded through clenched teeth.

As it happened, Lieutenant McLaughlin did have an interesting life story. The Lieutenant was 24 years old. He was the third son of a wealthy Irish baronet of Gleannri, in County Longford, Ireland. His father had amassed a vast fortune building supply vessels for the English Navy.

His father was now retired and had turned the business over to his two eldest sons. Joseph McLaughlin had travelled most of

England, the low countries, Spain, and France. To Kitty's surprise, he studied at Harrow then Cambridge, taking a Fellowship there.

"Why are you not a college don then?" she interrupted.

"Not enough horses!" he replied with feeling, and Kitty laughed.

He had even joined the Royal Society, like her father. With many witty stories, the Lieutenant kept her well amused during the day. She was so charmed by him she forsook her former reluctance to converse with him.

The *tête-à-tête* was not wholly one-sided. He managed to obtain a fair report of her schooling and life story, too. Kitty and Marianne seized the chance to canvas the morning's events when they paused for luncheon. Whilst Kitty's report was lovely, Marianne's was not.

"Sir Richard never did anything wrong, but he makes me *so* nervous. I am very glad to be going with Mr. and Mrs. Sumner, I assure you! There is more lechery than esteem in his glance. I cannot be at ease and will be relieved when I am not shut up with him all day," Marianne confessed.

"I didn't want to rush to judgment about him—all the rumours clouding his reputation. Now that I see how he treats you, I confess I believe the rumours are truth," Kitty replied.

Kitty resumed her seat in the Lieutenant's phaeton with much better grace than she had that morning. They spent the chief part of the rest of the day chatting about the passing landscape. But they also touched on science, literature, art, drama, and politics. They found a great likeness in taste and views. The Lieutenant was proving to be wholly charming, and Kitty hugely enjoyed herself.

Lieutenant McLaughlin gathered some coins from the Tinsley's groom when they arrived at the Tinsley's, which struck her as odd. However, she had little time to think about it. She learned their host had prepared a small private dance for the evening. Kitty wore her cream-and-pink Russian bodice gown, to the obvious delight of the gentlemen and praise of the matrons.

Kitty and Marianne danced every dance. Sir Richard ushered Marianne into and away from dinner. He trapped her into a *tête-à-tête* whenever possible. But he let his hands linger a bit beyond decency every chance he got.

Kitty found that Lieutenant McLaughlin was a superb dancer, never missing his step. She was amazed. Kitty had not expected grace from a man so heavily built. Kitty was convinced she had never been so happy, feeling a lovely blend of heady delight and fascination.

Her delight was short-lived, however. During a brief break in the dancing, she and the Lieutenant queued up in the buffet line. Kitty heard Mrs. Skelling, who was in front of the Lieutenant. She said, "He is Irish. Which is odd, for the only crop the Irish produce is a vast number of useless children."

Lieutenant McLaughlin stiffened. He replied loudly, so as to be heard by the entire party, and in a broad Irish brogue, "Aye, it's true, so 'tis."

Mrs. Skelling whirled around, flustered, discovering the Lieutenant was behind her.

Lieutenant McLaughlin continued, "It's 'cause t'e women of Ireland are so gran', no man can withstan' 'em. But when t'e men of Ireland see somma the English ladies." He raked his gaze up and down her figure. "We're amazed the English perpetuate t'emselves atall!"

After a brief spatter of swiftly suppressed mirth, a deadly silence descended on the room. Mrs. Skelling promptly left the room, very red in the face. Mrs. Tinsley followed. Mrs. Sumner showed her good breeding by starting fresh discourse. Within moments, the room was buzzing with party banter. Although, judging from some parties' hushed voices, many were talking about Lieutenant McLaughlin's joke.

Kitty's tender delight in him dwindled on the spot. The man she had admired as her father's equal, who seemed to agree with her tastes and views, seemed a monster of ill-breeding. She declined to dance with him again and sat out the rest of the ball with very troubled feelings.

The next morning, Marianne and Kitty were helping each other dress, as Mrs. Tinsley's maids were busy with other guests. They discussed the ball in detail, dodging any mention of the Lieutenant's gaffe, as neither wished to pain the other.

Kitty steeled herself and tossed her head. "I shall arrange to switch places with Mrs. Sumner today, so I will not be trapped with the Lieutenant."

Marianne stood behind her at the dressing table and caught Kitty's eye in the mirror. "But I thought you enjoyed his company so much! Did you want the centre part you wore yesterday?"

Kitty considered herself in the mirror. "Yes, to both. I think the centre part will do nicely; and yes, I delighted in his company. That delight died a fairly miserable death last night when I discovered how ill-bred he is."

Marianne pinned up a high bun for Kitty. "Well, Mrs. Skelling did provoke him, you must allow."

Kitty snatched up a ribbon. "Here, use the black ribbon; my gown has black trim. Yes, I heard her, the ill-bred wretch. But her indiscretion is no excuse for the Lieutenant's rude response. Can you imagine Lieutenant Wallace being so vulgar?"

"No, I cannot," Marianne mumbled around a mouth full of pins. "Imagine my Lieutenant doing what your Lieutenant did, I mean. Lieutenant Wallace is a very well-bred gentleman and reserved as well. I would not give up on your Irish giant just yet, Kitty. After all, he may improve around superior company," Marianne advised.

"Yes, well, I am still too provoked to ride with him today! Oh, that is just right." Kitty smiled at her friend in the mirror. "Now, it is your turn."

Kitty waited for Mrs. Sumner in the hallway before breakfast to switch seating arrangements. However, her plan was overset by Mrs. Tinsley, who wished a long converse with her. So, Kitty left Mrs. Sumner to guard Marianne's virtue and rode with the Tinsleys.

Kitty was spared making excuses to Lieutenant McLaughlin, however, since they never met at breakfast. The Lieutenant had breakfasted early and was out seeing to his cattle. Kitty caught herself approving his care of his wheelers. Then she recalled she was determined not to harbour any congenial feelings towards him. Once settled in the Tinsleys' coach, Kitty's thoughts were more agreeably engaged.

"We have engaged you for ourselves because we wish to convey an invitation." Aunt Eliza and Uncle Tinsley were beaming. Aunt Eliza continued, "My widowed sister, Mrs. Emma Williamson, has invited you to London and will sponsor you for the season. You are to have virtually no expense maintaining yourself whilst there."

Kitty's mouth fell open. "I am to have a London season?" she asked breathlessly.

"Yes, dear." Uncle Tinsley smiled roguishly. "And we also conspired via correspondence with your aunt, Vivian Shackford, who has known Lady Palmerston nearly all of her life. So, you have a voucher to Almack's."

"Further," Aunt Eliza exulted, "your Aunt Vivian volunteered to lend you the Dasset rubies for your formal presentation."

Uncle Tinsley chuckled. "The final victory, though, is Aunt Eliza obtained the services of the most esteemed mantua maker in London. We shall pay for the full-hooped court saque for your court presentation."

"Oh! That is far too much! Why, a presentation gown must cost forty pounds at least. I cannot in good conscience accept your gift!" Kitty cried.

Aunt Eliza smiled fondly at her niece. "Do not be silly, my dear. Who else can I ever indulge in this fashion? My *sons* will not want gowns for their come-outs."

Kitty abandoned adult dignity in her excitement. She threw herself across the carriage and embraced her Aunt Eliza and Uncle Tinsley.

"Was ever a woman more blessed than I? Oh! There is no greater felicity! I thought all my dreams of a London season were destroyed when I lost Mama." Mrs. Tinsley and Kitty both had tears in their eyes remembering her.

Aunt Eliza took Kitty's hand. "She would be so pleased with how you have grown up!"

They spent the chief part of the day in excited speculation. Her uncle, poor patient fellow, rarely contributed to the conversation. The ladies had a lovely time. Aunt Eliza urged Kitty to have dresses made after she arrived and could get advice from Aunt Emma. Mrs. Tinsley extracted a promise from Kitty to hire a dance master to learn how to manage hoops.

When they arrived at the spa, Marianne inquired, "What has sent you into raptures, Kitty?"

"My Aunt and Uncle Tinsley have contrived a London season for me!" Kitty replied. "I shall give you all the particulars after dinner." Kitty was so excited she had very little attention to spare for her meal. The girls excused themselves as soon as civil and talked well into the night.

During the evening, Kitty discovered the full measure of her friend's excellence. Marianne offered advice whenever asked and was a willing audience to Kitty's excited monologues. Never once did she display a single symptom of envy. Her delight was entirely genuine and entirely on Kitty's behalf. Eventually, Kitty's first excitement of communication wore off. She finally awoke to her companion's merits.

Kitty, kneeling on the bed, took Marianne's hands in hers. "Oh! Marianne, if only you were to go as well! I have never loved you so much as I love you now! Your obvious delight in my good fortune is untainted by envy or self-interest. You are an angel, and I hardly deserve you as a friend!"

Blushing, Marianne responded, "Kitty, you would be just as happy for me if the situation were reversed. Besides, a London come-out is no longer such an object with me. I believe—at least, I hope—that Lieutenant Wallace will offer for me. He gave me a book of Burns' poetry, which is quite *risqué* ..."

"I know!" interrupted Kitty, "My father forbade me to read him, so I was obliged to steal him from my Uncle Tinsley's library. A bold move for such a shy fellow!"

This prompted a paean from Marianne on the Lieutenant's virtues. She assured Kitty that, once known, his character was as open and unreserved as anyone's.

This turned the conversation from Kitty's come-out to the even more interesting topic of Marianne's marriage prospects. The girls were hard at it until the wee hours, only going to bed because they were expected to make an early start.

The next morning, Kitty dutifully wrote her thanks to her Aunt Vivian Shackford.

November 12, 1813
Gilsland Spa

Dearest Aunt Vivian,

I write today to express my esteem and fondness for you, which is sharpened by gratitude. My Aunt Tinsley has revealed to me your kind Scheme for my benefit, and I accept with great happiness!

Aunt Tinsley advised I order a court gown trimmed in pale blush pink to set off the pink-toned rubies. I shall have a miniature painted of me in all my finery. I shall send it to you by post, so that you may see the effect of your gifts.

Your kindness has made all my dreams come true. You have supplied everything my beloved Mother would have wished for me.

I know not how to thank you! I shall attempt to conduct myself according to Mother's refined standards and be a credit to you both.

I have also promised my Aunt Tinsley I shall employ a dance master to teach me how to move in a corset and hoops. I shall practice every day.

With all my love and gratitude,
Yr. Very Grateful Niece, Kitty

Then, she sent a note to Mrs. Williamson, whom she had not seen since her mother's funeral. Kitty's second letter to Mrs. Williamson was like the first, although more formal. She was content that she had discharged her social duties. Kitty resolved to enjoy a meander through Gilsland's scenic grounds. She brought pencils and a sketchbook to record the views.

The crisp autumn day dawned so bright and clear that parasols were required. There was enough frost, though, that the girls wore practical walking boots rather than stylish slippers. The party set off in good spirits. Kitty still rode with the Tinsleys rather than brave Lieutenant McLaughlin's *phaeton*. They arrived in good order and broke into small groups to wander along the foot path to the Cramwell Linn Waterfall. Kitty and Marianne were escorted by Sir Richard and Lieutenant McLaughlin.

Lieutenant McLaughlin was an expert with widespread knowledge of history and flora. His lectures as they wandered, observed, and discussed were very helpful. Kitty was impressed with his knowledge. She asked many apt questions, giving him even more occasions for display. Sir Richard bore with being outshone as best he could before he made a daring attempt to secure the ladies' regard. He capered on the edge of a precipice near Cramwell Linn waterfall.

Marianne wore a worried frown. "Sir, I believe that stone to be unsound."

Sir Richard, balanced on the edge of ruin, cried out, "These stones have stood for thousands of years, they shall stand for a few moments more!"

Lieutenant McLaughlin approached the edge. "I must say I agree with Miss Warden; it looks to me as though—"

A brief cry from Sir Richard stopped him. The stone crumbled beneath Sir Richard, and he plunged towards the broken rocks twenty-five feet below.

With a blur of speed Kitty would never have believed if she had not seen it with her own eyes, the Lieutenant lunged forward into a deep crouch. He braced himself by grabbing the edge of the precipice with his left hand. With his right hand, he caught the capelet sewn to the shoulders of Sir Richard's coat.

"Seize my arm," the Lieutenant ordered, and Sir Richard complied. Lieutenant McLaughlin lifted him back onto the edge of the stone cliff with ease. Single-handed! Once Sir Richard was safely seated, the Lieutenant rose from his crouch and lifted him to his feet.

Kitty had always despised women who nattered on about a man's muscles as shallow schoolroom misses. At that moment, she learned the thrill of seeing a powerful man's muscles shifting under a coat of superfine. It was a giddy moment for her and embarrassing as well. She had always thought herself to be above such schoolgirl rubbish. Well, she was *not* above school-girl rubbish when watching the burly life-saving valour of a fascinating man.

"As I was saying before we were so rudely interrupted," Lieutenant McLaughlin continued, "it appears to me the stone could crumble at any moment."

"Erh, quite. I owe you my thanks, Lieutenant." Sir Richard shook the Lieutenant's hand.

The Lieutenant smiled. "Good thing you have an excellent tailor, Sir Richard. If it were not for his work, you would have slipped out of your coat and been lost. Although your man will not thank me for the ruin I've made of it."

Sir Richard quickly regained his poise. "The coat will survive, I dare say. *I* have survived, thanks to your excellent reflexes, sir."

"And your breadth of shoulder!" Kitty exclaimed. "I apologise, but I am et up with curiosity. Just how wide are your shoulders?"

The Lieutenant grinned, and his eyes sparkled. "Last I measured, 54 inches outside to outside. I have the devil of a time getting fitted for coats."

Sir Richard returned to the polished gallantry that marked his manners. "It appears your tailoring has suffered far more than my own."

Lieutenant McLaughlin twisted about, probing his coat's shoulder seams with his fingers. He grunted, "Burst a few seams. Nothing my man can't repair. Just a little extra fresh air for the afternoon!"

The entire pic-a-nic lunch was spent discussing Sir Richard's brush with death. Both men behaved well. Sir Richard made jokes and ceded the spotlight to Lieutenant McLaughlin. The Lieutenant humbly protested any special thanks. Kitty found that she had forgiven the Lieutenant and desired his friendship once again.

DINNER PARTY AT DIXON COTTAGE

"**M**arianne, I have decided to entertain with a dinner party," Kitty announced on one of their nearly daily visits.

Marianne smiled. "And what is the occasion?"

Kitty explained, "Why, an opportunity to enjoy the converse of two lieutenants we are acquainted with. Of course, I cannot just invite them. I was thinking of inviting your whole family and the Tinsleys. With your sisters, there will be too many women, which will be an excellent excuse for inviting the lieutenants."

Kitty called for Mrs. Abernathy, and the girls plunged into an exciting round of party planning.

"This shall be an ideal opportunity for my parents to get to know Lieutenant Wallace better," Marianne declared gleefully.

"Best of all," Kitty bragged, "Mrs. Abernathy will prepare a very elegant meal at very little cost. Almost all of the meal comes from the home farm."

Kitty invited the Tinsleys, the Wardens, and the Lieutenants Wallace and McLaughlin. With her numbers balanced, Kitty gave a great deal of thought to seating arrangements, so everyone should appear to best advantage.

"Oh! Mrs. Abernathy, I am so blessed to have you. Upon my word, any triumph I have as a hostess is entirely due to your skills. Do you know anyone who can provide service? Mr. Hart and Mary will be hard-pressed to serve a table of fourteen," Kitty inquired.

Mrs. Abernathy had several suggestions. Some local help from the village was engaged and a new livery for all created. The gentlemen got to keep the clothes and receive a gratuity of a shilling each for their service.

Mrs. Warden was able to supply white carnations from her hot-house. Kitty arranged and tied them with black ribbons in her mother's silver nut bowls to great effect. Kitty realised she was not only trying to impress the Tinsleys with Lieutenant McLaughlin; she was trying to impress the Lieutenant as well. After a brief moment of embarrassment, she laughed at herself, thinking, "Vanity, thy name is Katherine!"

The day arrived, and Kitty wore her trusty Russian-bodice gown. Marianne wore a primrose gown with lovely matching ribbons. Her sisters were also tolerably dressed, and her mother was in her best looks in a tobacco-coloured silk gown with blonde lace. Even Mr. Warden eschewed buckskins and gaiters and wore a proper suit.

The Lieutenants arrived before the Wardens and were seated in the drawing room when the Wardens were announced. Lieutenant Wallace's countenance seemed to glow with happiness when Marianne entered the room. Mr. Warden, who could not help but perceive the Lieutenant's regard, cast several darkling looks on the pair but said nothing.

Proving his good breeding, Lieutenant Wallace conversed with Marianne's sisters seated together on the settee. Lieutenant McLaughlin was speaking with great wit and flow with Mr. and Mrs. Tinsley. Papa contented himself with sipping sherry and laughing at the amusing anecdotes as came his way from the other members of the party. Kitty was pleased everyone seemed to be well entertained. Dinner was announced and everyone seated according to her design.

Everyone had a suitable conversational partner, Mrs. Abernathy's cooking was praised, and the wines pronounced "quite drinkable". Conversation flowed, none of her temporary footmen made any huge gaffes, and she was complimented on their livery. The ladies settled in the drawing room whilst the gentlemen took port. Mr. Hart approached Kitty.

"Miss, I do apologise for disturbin' ye at this time, but Pike is here with some bad news, I'm afraid. Castor is not well. Quite ill, it seems, and ye're needed in the stables."

Kitty turned to her guests. "Well, it appears my horse needs me! I do apologise for the interruption, but I must off to the stables. Please let my dear Aunt Tinsley stand as hostess in my stead. I shall be back directly." Kitty smiled and made her curtsy before leaving the drawing room for the front hall.

A dismally unhappy Tom Pike awaited her. "It's Castor, Miss. He got into the oats. I dosed him with treacle, and that shifted him. But I was too late. He's got founder."

"Is it a bad case?" inquired Kitty, deeply worried.

"Aye. All four hooves. I can feel the heat and a strong pulse in all of 'em, and he looks miserable right enough."

In a moment of inspiration, Kitty turned to Hart. "Fetch Lieutenant McLaughlin. He is an expert at the care of horses. Perhaps he can suggest something. Pike, you give all the details to Lieutenant McLaughlin and escort him to the stables. I shall get my cloak and meet you there." Kitty hurried off as Pike and Mr. Hart turned to obey her.

Soon, they were all gathered in the stables. Poor Castor was as bad a case as Pike had reported. Mac was trying to soothe him by rubbing him down with a twist of straw. But Castor was hunched, breathing rapidly and sweating, obviously in agony.

Lieutenant McLaughlin immediately proved his worth. Whilst murmuring reassurances to the horse, he expertly ran his massive hands over Castor's legs and feet, clicking his tongue when he felt the hooves. Castor, whilst still trembling, did not cringe away from the big man's hands.

"Where is the nearest shallow beck that's not frozen?" he demanded.

Mac answered, "Down the cow pasture, nowt but a hundred yards."

"Have you a lancing kit?" the Lieutenant inquired. "He'll need to be bled."

"Aye, I've that," Mac responded.

"You—Pike—get a couple heavy rugs and double-rug him."

The Lieutenant turned to Mac. "Get your kit and meet us at the beck."

Castor was reluctant to move, but Lieutenant McLaughlin managed to cluck and chuckle him into it and led him to the beck. Once they arrived by the side of the shallow pebbled stream, the Lieutenant bled the poor horse until Kitty thought she would be sick. However, it was soon done, and the Lieutenant led Castor, whose wound was already clotting, into the beck. Once all four hooves were submerged in the icy water, Castor heaved a deep sigh, obviously relieved.

Lieutenant McLaughlin turned back to the group and explained his treatment. "That's all we can do for him tonight. You'll need to bleed him every day for at least the next three days and keep him on a low diet: hay, no oats. Keep everything but his hooves as warm as you can and let him drink whenever he wants. We'll know we're making progress when he walks out of the beck on his own in the next day or two."

"And if he does not walk out on his own?" Kitty inquired anxiously.

"Shoot him." The Lieutenant's face softened in sympathy to her distress. "It's the only kind thing to do. Even if he recovers somewhat, the coffin bones in his feet will have rotted—he will always be lame and in terrible pain. You don't need to fret yet. He's young and strong, and we caught it early; he should recover."

"Thank you, Lieutenant." Kitty turned to Pike and Mac. "Let us all adjourn to the kitchen, where it is warm."

Once they were all assembled in front of the kitchen stove, Pike announced, "I know I throwed the bolt on his loose box, I'm sure of it. And the oats was all rugged up in a sack. Castor ain't one to escape, so I figger I know who done it. When I gets me mitts on Davey, he'll learn a lesson, I tell ya—"

"Thomas Pike!" Kitty lashed out with the full force of agitated feelings. "I expressly forbid you to lay one finger on that poor boy! He does not know the first thing about horses. It would never occur to him that horses are foolish creatures who will eat themselves to death. But Davey knows all about hunger. That child knew nothing *but* hunger until he came here! Castor always begs for treats. You know he does! Davey, poor boy, believed him. I will not have you punish a kind impulse, even though totally misguided. For pity's sake, man, Davey was trying to be *kind*, which is more than I can say for you!"

Her eyes filled with tears, Kitty flounced out of the kitchen and into the central hall. She dabbed at her tears with her gloved hand and tried to breathe deeply in order to calm down. Lieutenant McLaughlin found her and offered his handkerchief.

"Thank you," Kitty said, after wiping her eyes and blowing her nose. "Just give me a moment to compose myself before returning to my guests. I appreciate your help more than I can say. In fact, if I begin to say, I shall dissolve into tears."

"Oh, can't have that!" Lieutenant McLaughlin replied. "Obviously, I shall be forced to annoy you with vulgar jokes until you come out of it."

"Never mind! I think I am ready now," Kitty returned hastily. She granted him a somewhat watery smile, straightened herself, and tilted her chin up defiantly. "Shall we?"

The Lieutenant offered his arm and escorted her back into the drawing room, where the gentlemen had rejoined the ladies. They were immediately greeted with many kind inquiries about the state of her horse. Kitty left it to Lieutenant McLaughlin to explain.

"Poor bugger got into the oats and gave himself a roaring case of founder—all four hooves. Pike responded promptly and correctly, and we bled him. He's young and strong and should come around quickly," said Lieutenant McLaughlin.

Out of kindness to Kitty, the subject was quickly dropped, and the party struggled back to normalcy. It was soon impossible to tell in that room full of talented conversationalists that there had ever been an interruption.

At last, everyone's *adieux* were tendered. Kitty once again slipped into her warmest cloak and hastened out to check on Castor. She hurried around the stables and was greeted with a singular sight.

An odd bothy of saplings, wood scraps, and old canvas had been built over the stream, so Castor stood in a tunnel-shaped hut protected from wind and snow. Pollux was standing at the head of the bothy. A tiny figure stood beside Pollux. The two horses were nuzzling and scratching each other's necks, obviously delighted with each other's company. Kitty approached quietly.

"Davey, giving Castor a visit was a very good and kind idea, but it is very late now. You should put Pollux back in the barn, as he cannot fit in beside Castor in the bothy. Come along now." Davey fell in place behind Kitty.

Kitty tried to comfort Davey. "Horses are the silliest creatures, are they not? Begging for more food than their belly can hold, eating themselves sick ..." Kitty attempted, but Davey did not respond.

Once they had achieved the barn, she noticed Davey was not only silent, but completely stone-faced. They went about the business of putting Pollux in his loose box. Soon, they returned to the kitchen to find Mac sharing a cup of hot cider with Mary.

"That bothy is an excellent idea, Mac," Kitty began. "Davey had another excellent idea. He led Pollux out to visit with Castor. Both horses were delighted. Castor even lifted his front hooves a bit, which I take as an encouraging sign." Kitty led Davey over to Mac, who scooped Davey up to sit in his lap.

"Now, laddie, ye din't know the oats would do so much harm, did ye?" Mac asked gently. Davey convulsed in sobs and shook his head. "Ye were only bein' kind, like. Ye can't blame yerself that the empty-headed bugger ate hisself sick." Davey buried his face in Mac's waistcoat and wailed pitifully.

Mary comforted Davey by rubbing his back. "Ye're a good laddie, Davey, and ye'll be knowin' the ways o' horses soon enough. The next time Castor or any other beastie looks at ye with them great brown eyes, beggin' fer oats, ye'll know to tell the silly bugger 'no', won't ye?" Davey nodded damply.

Early the next morning, Kitty made her way out to check on Castor and discovered Tom Pike, Mac, and Lieutenant McLaughlin were already there. Tom and Mac appeared to be paying off a bet with the Lieutenant. When they spied her, Lieutenant McLaughlin greeted her, "Good morning to you, Miss Otis. I trust you slept well?"

"Well enough, thank you. I was worried about Castor, though. How is he getting on?"

"Much better, I'm pleased to report," said the Lieutenant. "Mac bled him again this morning, though less than last night. He's been fed, and Davey's off to bring Pollux by for a visit. The pulse in his hooves has gone down considerably, and he's moving his hooves a bit this morning. I am confident we caught it in time, and Castor will be good as new in a few days."

The Lieutenant's estimate proved to be conservative. That afternoon, they discovered Castor had left his odd tunnel bothy for the nearest field and was busily exploring under the snow for a nibble. His recovery was swift, and in only one more day, there was no sign of tenderness or heat in his hooves. By the next week, Castor was back on a full diet and doing duty as a carriage horse again. Kitty found herself thinking very tender thoughts about the Lieutenant, her estimate of his virtues soaring along with Castor's health.

CHRISTMAS APPROACHES

Marianne reported her rapidly growing attachment for Lieutenant Wallace to Kitty nearly daily. He called on her as often as he decently could, and frequently "ran into" Kitty and Marianne on their various walks and trips to the village. He monopolised Marianne at every church function, and their romance was rapidly growing into love.

Lieutenant James Wallace was from a respectable lowlands family, serious in his faith, well-educated and well-read, and very interested in taking up architecture. So much so, in fact, that he proposed an improvement to the construction of the Ellesmere Canal. His suggestion was so well thought of that it was immediately adopted and produced an offer of employment with Thomas Telford, the most famous architect in Scotland.

Lieutenant Wallace accepted the position, sold his colours, and applied to Marianne's father.

"He would not hear of it," reported Marianne sadly. "My father, who married my mother when she was but six months older than I am now, told my dear Wallace I am too young. Mama says he puts too much store in his hopes that Sir Richard will offer for me. But I would not be inclined towards Sir Richard, even if he does offer for me."

"Is that not *just* like your father! To reject an amiable man with a respectable fortune and bright professional future based on his fancy for a title in the family," Kitty sympathised.

"I do not believe his error proceeds entirely from ambition," Marianne continued. "I think he also believes in his heart that I am too young. It is of no great moment, though, as James Wallace has promised me faithfully to return every six months and offer for me again. My work is to remain absolutely unmoved by any other offers. Of course, I promised him my faithfulness most readily."

Kitty did not grant Mr. Warden as much merit as his affectionate daughter did. Kitty thought ambition and a greedy desire to keep his most deserving daughter nearby drove his decision. She did not think Mr. Wallace would have a better reception in six months than he did just recently.

"This will not do!" Kitty declared with a furrow of concentration on her brow. "Your father denies your heart's desire, forcing you to miss months, and possibly years, of happiness, and you say, 'it is no great moment?' *Of course*, it is of great moment! How does your mother feel about all this?"

Marianne replied, "Mama is dear Wallace's champion. She says Sir R's reputation makes her uneasy."

"This is ridiculous!" Kitty gestured emphatically, spilling some of her tea. She hopped up from the settee and began pacing the room. "Your father must be made to see reason. Although I am perfectly aware, you and I are not the ones to manage it. Your father will never consider poor Mr. Wallace unless we take the shine out of Sir Richard. All of those rumours! Three intelligent women united in uneasy distrust of one man. Something *must* be wrong. Let us investigate why Sir Richard excites such anxiety in discerning females! I shall consult my Uncle Tinsley for his advice when he comes to visit me this Christmas. Perhaps he can conceive of a scheme for bringing your father to heel."

Marianne eagerly consented, and the ladies concluded their visit amiably.

Christmas was rapidly approaching, and Kitty and Marianne attended the usual festivities. Once again, they found themselves at Sir Richard's hunting box with James Wallace conspicuously absent. Kitty hugely enjoyed dancing with Lieutenant McLaughlin.

When there was a pause in the dancing, the girls headed to the entrance hall for a quiet conference. As they tidied each other's toilettes, Marianne reported, "Sir Richard's attentions are so embarrassing."

"It never ceases to amaze me that he won't take a hint." Kitty responded, "I have had better luck and thoroughly enjoyed dancing with an excellent partner."

As they were about to re-enter the main hall, Lieutenant McLaughlin's voice floated back to them, "As fer the Widow Fletcher; I hear she's given up on men entirely. And on behalf of men everywhere, let me be the first t' say t'anks and hallelujah!"

Kitty was furiously indignant on Mrs. Fletcher's behalf. She grew quite red in the face and started forward, only to be restrained by Marianne laying a hand on her arm.

"Kitty!" Marianne hissed in a frantic whisper, "You must not descend to his level! You must regain your composure or be forever stained in the eyes of this company as shrewd and vulgar. Kitty, please, consider! Let us regain our composure before re-joining the party."

Kitty's back stiffened, every line of her face and posture betraying her outrage. She sighed. "You are right, Marianne. It would not do any good to scold the Lieutenant. What would I do without you?" Kitty embraced her friend, "How could I ever have thought well of such a vulgar man?" The girls re-joined the party and danced the night away.

Several days later, the Tinsleys arrived for their Christmas visit. After the usual civilities, Kitty showed her Uncle Tinsley into the library to consult with him.

"What an extraordinary application, Kitty! You are convinced the man is a scoundrel. Very well then, snub him," her Uncle Tinsley advised.

"Unfortunately, that will not solve the problem." Kitty outlined Marianne's difficulties and her plan to "take the shine" out of Sir Richard.

"But what do you expect me to do?" Mr. Tinsley replied. "I am no Bow Street Runner."

"Well, and I doubt they would be of any use," Kitty responded, massaging her forehead. "I do not accuse Sir Richard of being *criminal*, but of being ... well, less of a shining knight than Mr. Warden believes him to be. If he were offering for me, and you did not like the cut of his jib, what would you do on my behalf?"

"Oh, ah ..." Her uncle looked thoughtful. "I would write my banker under the guise of assembling a syndicate and try to discover whether he is in debt. Perhaps scour old gossip rags to see if he figured in them prominently. A single or even a few mentions could be a matter of luck. But if he figures in them often, I would assume 'where there is smoke, there is fire.' I would also apply for a reference from the vicar of his home parish."

"A famous plan, Uncle!" Kitty exclaimed, delighted. "I shall take your advice. Would you please undertake to inquire amongst your banking acquaintance after him? It could very well save Marianne from what her mother and I believe to be a most ineligible marriage."

Her uncle made the requested promise, and they discussed Kitty's London *début*.

Just before Christmas, Lieutenant McLaughlin presented himself for a morning call. After Kitty sent Hart off to order tea, the Lieutenant paced nervously in front of the fire, then launched into what was obviously a rehearsed speech.

"Miss Otis, you can hardly be insensible to my increasing admiration of you. I believe my feelings are reciprocated. I wish to know, in fact, if you would be interested in having me address your father."

"Are you offering for me?" Kitty exclaimed in astonishment, "You, who flouts every social convention?" she continued archly with a teasing smile. "Surely you are not offering me a *carte blanche*, so you must intend marriage, but that seems so *bourgeois*, I can hardly credit your offer."

Joseph seemed surprised and replied with mounting colour and obvious agitation, "You doubt my intent? Marriage is an honourable estate, the object of most intelligent men, and I believe virtually all females. How could you doubt me? You, who are renowned as clever?"

"Ah. My apologies, Lieutenant, I see we are to converse seriously," Kitty replied, agitated. Now that she realised Lieutenant McLaughlin was genuine, her feelings were fully aroused, and she had a great deal of difficulty maintaining decent composure. First, she was excited and flattered, but mostly, she felt dreadful anxiety.

Her stomach was in knots; she felt the first tiny whispers of trembling or perhaps a headache, perhaps dizziness. Kitty could not be entirely sure what these symptoms betokened, but she was certain of two facts: First, Lieutenant McLaughlin was the most fascinating man she had ever met; and second, the very thought of being married to him prompted anxiety so intense it threatened to overwhelm her.

With the speed of thought, her conflicted feelings drove her to her feet, and she paced the room as she attempted to marshal her jumbled thoughts. Surprised both by her sudden activity and the unexpected course of the conversation, the Lieutenant promptly sat down.

Kitty stared anxiously into his face and wrung her hands. "I am highly flattered, even gratified, by your proposal, sir. But I am afraid I must decline."

"Have you no feelings for me, then?" he exclaimed in turn.

"Of course, I do," she replied in softened tones. "You are, without doubt, the most fascinating man of my acquaintance *in private*. But your public behaviour is such ... I am convinced, while you are a delightful companion, you are entirely unsuitable as a husband."

"So, your Missish dependence on propriety will deprive us both of a lifetime of happiness?" he asked, disgusted.

"Missish?!" Kitty exclaimed, incredulous and deeply offended. "It is hardly missish to be sensitive to the feelings of others! I think perhaps ..." Torn between sudden compassion and deeply felt offence at his slur, she continued, "I am afraid the war has wounded your sensibilities. You seem not to appreciate true delicacy of mind and elevated principles."

Leaping to his feet in answering agitation, he replied hotly, "It's not *elevated* to timorously consult your neighbour's opinions before your own! Perhaps you are right. I want a bit more spirit in a wife!"

Now fully goaded, all compassion forgotten, Kitty blazed, "It is *not* lack of spirit! Your tasteless jokes put all of my friends to the blush, even the gentlemen! At a dance, instead of enjoying myself, I spend the entire time anxious because I know—*I know*—you will wound someone's feelings; usually, someone who is dear to me, before the evening is out!"

"I never—" he interrupted, his face betraying growing astonishment and confusion.

"Yes, you do! At every opportunity," she insisted, furiously stamping her foot. "If only you would treat people as well as you treat your horses! You are not just careless with other people's feelings, though; you are even careless of my person! When you tossed me up onto Othello as hard as you could, *as a joke*, I caught my leg on the pommel and was lame for a week. And this when you were acting to impress me."

"You never said—" he interrupted again, looking hang-dog guilty.

"As if I would give you the satisfaction!" she cried, exasperated. "What kind of Turkish treatment will I be subjected to once we are married, and the bloom is off the rose?" Contrition was writ large on his face and she continued in much softened tones, "I am very sorry.

I now understand you think civility is spiritless. But I assure you, sir, it is quite the opposite."

His face a frozen mask, his movements wooden, Lieutenant McLaughlin said, "I understand you perfectly." He made his bow.

Kitty felt horribly guilty for having lost her temper. Fully alive to his distress and unable to meet his eye, Kitty said, "I do apologise. I had no wish to wound you, sir. I wish you every happiness." She curtsied him out of the room.

As soon as he had left, the full force of her agitated feelings overwhelmed Kitty, and she fled to her bed-chamber to cry. Turning down the pretensions of a mushroom like Mr. Peale had not touched her in the slightest, but she agonised over every syllable and look of her conversation. Or, with the bark off it, the shrewish scold she had delivered to Lieutenant McLaughlin.

She *knew* herself to be right, but her heart disagreed. She repented losing her temper and deeply regretted wounding him. For she was certain she had wounded him. Mr. Peale had merely been ambitious; the Lieutenant obviously harboured more honourable feelings. Surely, he must have learnt civilised conduct at Cambridge. Why, oh, *why* could he not act the gentleman in public as he did in private? Kitty cried for a full hour before finally falling asleep.

LONDON

January finally arrived, and Kitty convened a staff meeting in the kitchen. "I shall endeavour to distribute the care of my father as equitably as possible. Abernathy, you shall take charge of seeing that Mr. Otis gives Bible lessons to little Davey every day."

Abernathy nodded, and Kitty continued, "Papa grows depressed when he has no visitors, so I have arranged for Mr. Sumner, Mrs. Fletcher and Mrs. Warden to call on him regularly. The Tinsleys will come for a weekend visit every fortnight, weather permitting. So, in addition to your usual household duties, Hart, you are now Papa's social secretary. You must also make sure he walks after every meal."

"No problem, Miss," Hart replied.

"Mac, when you return from delivering Aunt Vivian's presentation jewels to me in London, you must invent questions regarding the management of the home farm to occupy Papa. And you'll need to find excuses to drive him into town for various tasks. Even though he is very deep in his fog, Papa is still a brilliant judge of horseflesh and would be delighted to join you in your search for draft horses, for instance."

"Understood, Miss." Mac grinned. "I'll need quite a bit of consultation to finish the stable quarters. and them horses will need exercise."

Kitty smiled at him fondly. "You too, Pike. You must invent excuses to report to him about the horses at least weekly. And, of course, do whatever you can to rake the road clear of snow."

"Aye, Miss," Pike replied.

"Mary, Papa's vision is growing weaker, and he struggles to read the newspaper. Please read out the headlines and any articles he is interested in after his morning walk."

"Certainly, Miss."

"Does anybody here play backgammon?"

"I do, Miss," Hart answered.

"Do you mind challenging Papa to games on the daily? I have learnt that he is happiest and healthiest when I can arrange to occupy his mind. Even in retirement, he needs occupation."

"It would be my honour, Miss."

"I am so pleased with our little conspiracy. Now, with your help, I can leave for London with a clear conscience."

Kitty gave Mrs. Abernathy ten pounds to settle household expenses and the key to the tea cupboard. Mac went on Othello to her Aunt Vivian's home as he was charged with bringing the loaned jewels to her in London. Kitty travelled in easy stages with Taylor in the carriage whilst Tom Pike managed the hired horses.

Full of anticipation, Kitty hardly noticed the dreary January landscape they rolled through. She amused Taylor with chatter and cries of delight as they passed land-marks. Kitty was as jolted as any traveller but felt very little of it. She and Taylor arrived after a fortnight's travel at the spacious, modern dwelling of Mrs. Williamson in fashionable Bedford Square.

Kitty curtsied when she arrived. "Good day, Mrs. Williamson. Thank you so much for your kind invitation."

"Call me Aunt Emma, dear." She shook hands with Kitty warmly. "I am delighted to meet with you again. It has been nearly two years since your mother's funeral; may God rest her soul. I am so glad to become acquainted under happier circumstances."

Kitty soon discovered Aunt Emma was an endless font of information and an unfailing guide in matters of good *ton*. Aunt Emma decided it was best to have a ball in Kitty's honour after she was presented at Court and had excited some curiosity.

Kitty learnt scheduling a ball was of major strategic importance. The timing of an event could make or break the hostess. A date that did not conflict with any major theatrical opening or another more famous hostess's event was finally decided on.

Aunt Emma advised, "It is important to develop a theme or special quality to the ball in order to make it memorable, or you shall scarcely merit mention in the papers."

In this, Kitty proved her youthful inventiveness. "My absolutely best ball gown is cream-and-pink with a Russian bodice, and your ballroom is decorated in rose and silver ... What do you think of a Russian theme? All the decorations in a Russian style. Russian costumes on the wait staff, in honour of Napoleon's defeat there. Or is that perhaps a bit late, since it's been over a year?"

"Not too late at all, my dear," replied her Aunt Emma with dawning respect. "I have never heard of anything like, and it could be accomplished quite elegantly. All the girls are mad for Gothic or Italian themes, so yours shall be quite memorable and especially impressive for the military set. Shall we adjourn to the ballroom to farther our scheme?"

Aunt Emma ordered gilt-edged cards by the score. Immediately thereafter, the mantua maker arrived, and Kitty submitted to the tedium of her first fitting. With practice corset and hoops provided by Mme. Gaudet, Kitty undertook the study of proper deportment with Mr. Foulis while Aunt Emma served as her coach.

January 25, 1814
Westy House, Bedford Square

My Dearest Marianne,

I am now happily settled in Bedford Square. Mrs. Williamson is a famous hostess, and I am so honoured to be known as her protégé! So much has happened in the two weeks since I sent you a note of my safe arrival. I hope to make amends for my tardiness by writing this long letter to you.

First, the mantua maker, Mme. Gaudet, did a <u>superb</u> job on my presentation gown. It was executed in ivory brocade with delicate pale pink trims. Mme. Gaudet managed to contrive a miserably uncomfortable corset. With today's raised waistlines, it was only a half-corset designed to support the weight of my skirt and hoops. It astonishes me to think our mothers and grandmothers routinely wore full-length versions of those contraptions and even <u>danced</u> in them!

I hired a wonderful abigail recommended by Mme. Gaudet to do my hair. It was a two-and-a-half-hour ordeal. My hair was a towering 12" at the crown, heavily padded, waxed and pomaded, with ringlets down the back, and decorated with a large ivory ostrich plume, two delicate strands of pearls (you know the ones, I have worn them often) and glittering glass 'diamond' pins sprinkled about. The effect against my dark hair was quite dramatic, even if I do say so myself.

I think the artist captured a good likeness for my miniatures. They should be ready in two weeks. You shall be one recipient, my

Aunt Eliza another, Aunt Vivian another. The fourth I shall keep for myself.

I waited hours in the carriage. Pike threw rugs over the horses so they would not take a chill. Once admitted inside, I waited another hour in the frigid St. James Gallery. With all of us wearing hoops, it was rather like navigating a flotilla of colourful earth-bound silk balloons!

My heart went out to Queen Charlotte. Can you imagine a more tedious duty than to watch a parade of young ladies, entirely unknown to you, who kiss your hand, say, "Your Highness," curtsy, and retreat? Yet such was her evening, and she is by reputation quite gay when not "on duty."

I entered past the middle of the line since I am merely the niece of a Countess and a common vicar's daughter. I was announced and curtsied without wobbling. Mme. Gaudet included a cord prettily disguised as a bow that gathered up my train for me. I was able to gracefully retrieve my train and back out of the room without mishap. Several ladies bounced their hoops and managed to flip up their skirts, to everyone's embarrassment.

After that, it was home again to undergo at least an hour and a half ordeal to get undressed and let my hair down. My scalp will be tender for days. But in the end, I think it was worth it.

Almack's was bang up to the mark. I was attended by several elegant young tulips, none of whom had a thing to say above the most commonplace civilities. I had much better luck with Mr. Blanchard, an older widower, who told very amusing anecdotes. Half an hour in his company was no punishment, and we ended up together at table, as he escorted me in to the dinner. Elegant but bland—give me Mrs. Abernathy's cooking any day!

My come-out ball was a triumph, due almost entirely to Mrs. Williamson's formidable skills as a hostess. I invented a Russian theme, and we decorated accordingly. I, of course, wore my trusty cream-and-pink Russian-bodice gown to general acclaim. Mrs. Williamson's skill in hostessing such an enormous fête is awe-inspiring. The come-out received excellent notices in the papers (clippings enclosed). So, I am now well and truly launched!

I have not forgot your predicament and have ordered back copies of all the gossip sheets I can find. So far as I can tell, Uncle Tinsley has not yet received any replies to his inquiries. Please write to me soonest, my dear, about all our acquaintance and your doings at home. Have you had any word about Mr. Wallace?

Yr. Loving Friend, Kitty

In the shortest time post-delivery would allow, Kitty received a very satisfactory reply from Marianne.

January 29, 1814
Warden Grange

Dearest Kitty,

I am delighted to hear about your triumphant début. *Mr. Wallace writes to my brother, Hal, who promptly shares the letter with Mama and me. He has relayed his news by this method ever since. He is currently assisting Mr. Telford with the construction of the Caledonian Canal, which has been fascinating and highly instructional for him.*

My dear Wallace is living on only a small part of his salary. He put all his profit from selling his colours and most of his salary into investments managed by your Uncle Tinsley. He still hopes to marry me and purchase a home for us. He has increased his fortune by almost a thousand pounds, which I hope will lessen my father's objections to him.

I confided your scheme to investigate Sir R to Mrs. Sumner. I thought she would be horrified at our spying. She surprised me by complimenting your "common sense," and urged me to continue our investigations. She will not, however, breathe a word against Sir R.

However, Mrs. Sumner suggested whatever you and your Uncle Tinsley discover should be forwarded to her <u>husband</u>. Papa is much more likely to listen to his vicar than to any of us poor females, no matter how good our information. I think she made a brilliant suggestion.

Mama and I continue to avoid Sir R, but with Papa's eager promotion of a match, it has been very difficult. Sir R persists in courting me even though I have hinted to him my heart belongs to another. My only hope for immediate relief is that he must take himself off to London for the season. Although he promises to return here rather than to his own estate.

Weather brought a temporary halt to work on the Caledonian Canal. My dear Wallace rode down all the way from Scotland to

attend church at All Saints, since Papa can hardly forbid us to talk to
one another at the Chapter House after services!

The conversation turned to favoured foods, and it transpired
Mrs. Fletcher loathes raisins. Mr. Wallace responded with, "Oh, they are
not your raison d'etre? *A long silence followed before everyone began*
to abuse him for his terrible pun. So, now we know the worst of him.
My beloved Wallace is an unrepentant punster!

In other local news, Lady finally had her litter, and there is one
pup I think will be perfect for you. Howsoever, we shall save two from
this litter so you may have your choice when you return at the end
of May.

I am delighted you are enjoying your Season but must confess
how much I miss you. Mr. Otis also complains of your absence, even
though he is truly glad you are having a Season. I wish you the best
success, my dearest friend.

Yr. Loving, Marianne

The season of morning visits arrived, and Aunt Emma introduced Kitty to the most respectable ladies of the ton. Kitty and Taylor began keeping a list of the gowns Kitty had worn in order to avoid appearing in the same outfit twice at the same household.

Aunt Emma took genuine delight in her young *protégé*. She ventured once to give Kitty a hint that politics, war, and science were considered masculine subjects. Kitty took the hint and limited herself to fashion, art, current romances, horses, and gardening. She refused to compromise her principals by gossiping; although she was not so principled, she did not enjoy *listening* to gossip.

THE TRUTH IS REVEALED

A unt Emma also proved to be an invaluable guide to shopping in London. Taylor, relieved of laundry duty by Aunt Emma's upstairs maid, was busy running up new gowns and accessories for old gowns. Eventually, the gossip sheets arrived. Kitty and Taylor combed them for any mention of Sir Richard. They found twenty-seven articles to justify their effort. Uncle Tinsley was also successful and forwarded his information to her. Aunt Emma's footman's cousin, who was in service at Sir Richard's town-house, provided further information. Kitty hastened to assemble her discoveries for Marianne.

February 12, 1814
Westy House, Bedford Square

Beloved Marianne,

> *I have obtained extraordinary intelligence about Sir R. It will diminish his suit in your father's eyes but is so shocking I hardly know where to begin.*
> *First, you have my permission to share this letter and all of its enclosures with Mr. Sumner.*
> *Please ask him to advise Mr. Warden about Sir R's character and the inadvisability of admitting him to your family. I scarcely know how to convey my findings. I would much rather Sir R made a radical reform and save himself financially, socially, and before God, but that seems highly unlikely. So, even with some qualms, I shall share my discoveries with you.*
> *I mentioned I had met Sir R. in Leeds whilst on a morning visit to Mrs. Inchcombe, with Mrs. Palmer and Mrs. Williamson in attendance. The ladies were noticeably cool about him, and Mrs. Inchcombe stated she would not welcome his address to any of her daughters [!].*
> *After exclaiming I thought him quite dashing, the ladies united in their warnings to me. It seems Sir R seeks a bride in a district far from London in the hopes his reputation will not hinder him. His*

address is discouraged by all of the matchmaking mamas of the ton.
Even respectable Cits and the wealthy nabobs of London avoid him,
despite his title!

Mrs. Williamson's footman's cousin is in service at Sir R's
town-house. He reports that Sir R destroys all tradesman's dunning
notices, except for those that arrive the week before quarter day. This,
it seems to me, indicates Sir R. is not a reliable man. Howsoever, there
is more.

We were perfectly right to be uneasy about him. I found
twenty-seven mentions of him in the gossip sheets (clippings enclosed).
It seems Sir R has quite *a reputation as a libertine. He is frequently*
seen escorting notorious Cyprians about town.

Although his lustful tendencies are disgusting to any principled
female, there is still more bad news. Sir R. is never seen attending
church. Although it pains me to say so, his attendance at All Saints is
merely a ruse to secure your family's good opinion. I am afraid his own
vicar at his estate reports he does not keep his tithes (Mr. Poundstone's
reference also enclosed).

Uncle Tinsley has discovered Sir R has mortgaged every brick of
his estate and lives entirely quarter-day to quarter-day, which explains
why he does not keep his tithes and destroys dunning notices. (Uncle's
letter is also enclosed.)

His reputation must be very bad indeed for him to seek an
alliance with a woman who only has £4,500 from her grandmother
and an even smaller settlement when her parents pass. This, I have
no doubt, indicates his desperation. This is no insult to your charms,
Marianne! Having spent some time in London, I can assure you with
absolute sincerity; you are a diamond of the first water.

Sir R is licentious, irreligious, and unreliable. You have no love
for him, and I'm afraid his appreciation of you can only be prompted
by lust and self-interest. Oh! How I pray you will be saved from this
mésalliance!

You will, I know, put all of this information at Mr. Sumner's
disposal. Please write to me as soon as you can to let me know
what becomes of your father's opinions once Mr. Sumner lays this
information before him.

Yr. Most Anxious Friend, Kitty

Kitty was delighted with the opera, the stage, the ballet, and her visits
to famous London sites. She enjoyed the British Museum and the
famed Round Reading Room. Now that the first flush of excitement

was dying down, though, Kitty was becoming bored with *ton* social events. Kitty was astonished to discover that most of the fashionable people she met were insipid. Aside from several clever women who were her Aunt Emma's particular friends, the *haute ton* were dull! Mr. Blanchard, the older widower, always had something interesting to say. Otherwise, the conversational landscape was uninspired.

* * *

Her Aunt Emma hosted an intimate dinner and cards party in honour of Kitty's nineteenth birthday, and invited Mr. Blanchard. His tailoring, while expensive, was quite old-fashioned and not particularly flattering to him. His handsome face was rather weathered from age. In Kitty's view, the only real mar to his masculine beauty, aside from his age, was his teeth. The top row was only slightly disordered, but the bottom row was decidedly crooked. He also displayed some nervous tics—popping his knuckles and fidgeting with his clothes or twisting his signet ring. He escorted her to dinner.

"Your estate in Oxfordshire is well away from any sea, so you could not have had any experience of it. What drew you to the Navy?" Kitty asked.

"I blame Jonathan Swift. I loved *Gulliver's Travels* as a boy. I re-enacted the battle of Lilliput at the island in our little lake, created tiny ships out of fallen twigs and bits of rubbish. I played Gulliver, of course, and dragged them all to the other side of the island. Came home reeking of pond scum; totally ruined my clothes. I remember *that* lecture to this very day."

"Well, I have to confess, Jonathan Swift and complete ignorance of life aboard a ship of the line. In my innocence, the sea seemed so exotic and alluring, with many thrilling adventures awaiting. Then, I discovered it's mostly overcrowded, inconvenient, cold, largely monotonous, and with *terrible* food. I still miss it."

Kitty laughed. "I am now curious to hear your summary of your current career as a landowner."

"Much more varied. Why, we are only now beginning to unlock the potential of scientific agriculture. Not only do I enjoy the privileges of privacy and comfort, I also find the puzzles of improving production endlessly fascinating."

"I agree whole-heartedly," Kitty enthused. "My farm manager has applied scientific principles to the home farm at Dixon Cottage. According to the memories of the locals, it is now more productive and profitable than it has ever been. I just cross-bred my Jersey cow to an Ayrshire bull in the hopes of maintaining milk production while improving size and ease of calving in the get."

"You amaze me, Miss Otis. You are the only woman of my acquaintance who converses intelligently about farming. So, it is my turn to be curious. What excited your interest in scientific agriculture?"

"Well, all four of my siblings were carried off by smallpox before I was born. So, my father gave me a boy's education, although I managed to dodge Latin instruction. Mother rescued me there. My mother gave me lessons on drawing, needlework, managing household accounts, and she insisted on French. So, much to my annoyance in today's political climate, all I can claim now is school-girl French."

"Very balanced, it seems to me. Admirable, in fact." Blanchard smiled.

* * *

Her greatest relief, though, was her daily ride in Hyde Park. Three weeks passed away quietly in this manner with no word from Marianne. After several days of very wet weather, there came a hard frost with weak but clear morning sunshine, and it was dry enough that Kitty risked her favourite crimson riding habit. It was a striking outfit and appeared to best advantage on Othello's glossy black hide.

After a sedate tour of the park, Kitty was growing cold and picked up the pace in order to warm herself. She very nearly lost her seat when she perceived Hercules with Lieutenant McLaughlin astride approaching her.

Her stomach did several flip-flops and settled on a strange, tickling sensation. Her heart leapt in her chest, and she felt light-headed. She commanded herself quite sternly not to be a silly goose. But when the Lieutenant turned to escort her down the park lane, her eyes shone, her colour heightened, and her face was wreathed with smiles.

"Good day, Lieutenant! It is delightful to meet you here. What brings you to London?" Kitty asked while her heart whispered, 'He came for you.'

"Obviously, I yearned for another glimpse of Othello, the handsomest horse in all of London!"

"Oho, so it is my *horse* whom you think handsome? *Touché*," Kitty returned, bubbling over with laughter.

"Well, I have it on good authority that I sadly lack manly civility. So, I am come to get some town bronze." He grinned back at her. "I attended to your reproofs."

"How very flattering! Where have you been in the meantime?" she replied, blushing to the roots of her hair and eager to change the conversation.

"Travelling across the Irish Sea—"

"Madness at this time of year!" Kitty interrupted.

"Yes, there is that, but I needed to consult my father about business and sell my colours. I am properly Mr. McLaughlin now," he continued.

"Sold your colours! What do you plan to do with yourself now?" Kitty asked, genuinely intrigued.

"I would wager you can guess." He smiled.

"Obviously, something to do with horses." She smiled back.

"Indeed, you are correct! I have arranged to return to Ireland this spring to acquire bloodstock"

They spent a very agreeable half-hour in a knowledgeable discussion of the business of horse breeding and training. Kitty issued an invitation for a morning visit and provided Mrs. Williamson's direction, and they parted amicably.

March 10, 1814
Westy House, Bedford Square

Dearest Marianne,

> *I have very exciting news to convey and could no longer
> wait for your reply, however much I long for it. My news is this:
> Mr. McLaughlin is in London and has taken up courting me again!
> He, in his own words, "attended to your reproofs," and sailed home to
> Ireland to sell his colours. So, here he is!*

I knew when I rejected his proposal, I was right, but it nearly broke my heart, as you no doubt recall. Oh, Marianne, I knew I was fond of him, but I did not realise my feelings had sharpened to even more interesting affection until I saw him again.

He is now studying to improve his civility and attends me every time I ride in Hyde Park. And he has escorted me to several different entertainments. Mrs. Williamson thinks he is very witty. Now the first flush of triumph died away. I am bored with the ton *in London. I have never been so well entertained as I am now that he is come.*

But I am concerned about you, Marianne, and long to know what is happening at home. Has Mr. Sumner spoken to your parents? If not, why not? Has Sir R come down to London? Is Mr. Wallace still there, or has he returned to his post? Please reply.

Yrs. Most Affectionately, Kitty

Only days later, Mrs. Inchcombe and Mrs. Palmer paid a morning visit. The gossip turned to Mr. Blanchard, and Mrs. Inchcombe said, "I am so glad to see him mending from grief at last. It has been over two years, I believe, since his wife died, and he is only now regaining the lively wit he was known for."

"I quite agree. Although he appeared in society last Season, he was as wooden as a marionette. This year, he is coming back to life and issuing invitations again. It's a case of 'Time heals all wounds.' I believe the match-making mammas of the *ton* may have better luck this year," Mrs. Palmer replied.

"Let us hope so," Aunt Emma returned. "It would be such a pity for him to throw himself away at such a young age. Have you any news of Hal Linden? I haven't heard of him for ages." Thus, did her Aunt Emma turn the conversation. Kitty was briefly pleased, as Mr. Blanchard seemed like such a nice man.

A few days later, Marianne's long-awaited letter arrived, and Kitty promptly excused herself from the breakfast table and hurried upstairs to read it.

March 18, 1814
Warden Grange

Dear Kitty,

I did not mean to sport with you. Please accept my apologies for the delay. The reason is thus: Mr. Sumner refused to discuss Sir R until he also had similar evidence for my dear Wallace! We have already received letters of reference from his former commanding officer, from Mr. Telford, and from his vicar. Mr. Sumner only awaited confirmation of his financial prudence from your Uncle Tinsley to proceed.

Last night, he spoke to both my parents. Naturally, I was not there, but my dear Mama related the whole to me. The contrast between these two men could not be more profound. Whilst Sir R had all of the advantages of property and title, he has virtually nothing invested. He derives his income almost exclusively from his rents.

James Wallace, by comparison, is the son of an architect with no inherited land and only £3,500 settled on him by his maternal grandmother. Yet he has managed through wise investment and the exercise of thrift to swell that investment to over £4,000. He will receive a farther £2,000 when his paternal grandparents pass on, and some small amount (he is the second son) when he loses his own parents. So, his prudence bids fair to provide us with over half as much income as Sir R, and without any of it being encumbered.

The information about Sir R's irreligious habits shocked my father a great deal, I think; particularly when contrasted with Mr. Wallace's enthusiastic endorsement from his vicar. Evidently, my dear Wallace was led to convert to the Church of England because of what he viewed as weakness in Sacrament and Liturgy in the Church of Scotland. He studied and prayed for over a year and received his father's blessing before making the change and has been steadfast ever since.

Finally, we are to know what Mrs. Sumner refused to reveal. It seems Sir R does not limit his liaisons to London Cyprians. Mrs. S interrupted Sir R while he was attempting to seduce Lizzy Stanhope, Mrs. Sumner's young upstairs maid. Lizzy was crying and begging him to leave off when Mrs. S walked in on them. He extracted a promise from Mrs. S not to reveal his crime in exchange for future good behaviour.

You can imagine Mrs. Sumner's feelings. She was horrified when she realised he was courting me, and still burdened by her promise, did *not know how to warn me or my parents. It is no wonder she endorsed our investigations!*

You are, of course, the <u>second</u> person I have written. I wrote a note to my dearest Wallace to apprise him of the situation, and I expect to hear from him quite soon (no need to go through Hal again, since our engagement is openly acknowledged).

I hope I have satisfied your curiosity, vindicated your investigation, and soothed your concerns. I would continue, but it is the middle of the night here, and I am nodding off over my own writing.

I am so pleased you are once again speaking to your Irish giant.

With love and gratitude,
Marianne

Mr. Blanchard presented himself for a morning visit. After the usual civilities, Mr. Blanchard, twisting his signet ring, issued an invitation. "I hope you will consent to join me and my other guests for the *première* of Hannah Cowley's comedy, "The Belle's Stratagem," which is being revived at the Theatre Royal Friday next."

Mrs. Williamson, wreathed with smiles, countered. "Your invitation is timely, Mr. Blanchard, for we have just had to cancel our cards party for that evening due to Mrs. Whittaker's illness. I would love to go."

Taking the hint, Kitty, who was genuinely interested in seeing the work of a lady dramatist, agreed. "I would be delighted, Mr. Blanchard."

He replied, "I can only hope that you do not take *instruction* from Mrs. Cowley's play. The plot centres on the young lady's stratagem for tricking a happy bachelor into matrimony." The ladies laughed, and the conversation turned to more general subjects. The Brighton Palace came up, and Kitty declared that she was not an admirer.

"Really? Why not?" Blanchard inquired.

"I find it vulgar. It is an ostentatious display of wealth, a masterpiece of bad taste, and an irresponsible waste of the treasury," Kitty said decisively.

"I heartily concur. Can you imagine the effect that spending £700,000 would have had on the war effort?" Mr. Blanchard smiled. "You are the only young lady of my acquaintance who offers political opinion—and a well-reasoned opinion, at that."

"Oh, dear! I have been warned not to discuss politics. Although I am flattered that you consider my opinion to be well-reasoned."

Blanchard laughed. "Excellent advice, no doubt. But you are perfectly safe ignoring that warning with me."

Soon, the discussion evolved into a complex debate about the management of public funds. Mrs. Williamson observed them closely, smiling into her teacup. She remained largely silent until Mr. Blanchard departed.

"Well, my dear, I must congratulate you," her Aunt Emma said, turning toward Kitty as soon as he had departed.

"On what?" Kitty asked, surprised.

"On finding a man who not only *tolerates* your masculine interests, but actually *encourages* them." Her Aunt Emma smiled. "I believe Mr. Blanchard is interested in you. It would be a brilliant match. He is the most eligible bachelor in London."

"Good grief!" Kitty cried, surprised beyond any more fitting response. "He must be twice my age!"

Her Aunt Emma chuckled. "Not quite, my dear. He is not yet thirty, although he is a bit weathered from his service in the Navy. What appears to youth as an insurmountable gulf of time becomes trivial later in life."

Wide-eyed with surprise, Kitty answered, "His suits are so out of fashion that I estimated his age as nearer forty. I must admit to being impressed with his education. Particularly since he went into the Navy rather than attend University, so it comes entirely from his own cleverness. Do you really think he is interested in me?"

"Quite," Aunt Emma replied. "Mr. Blanchard has over five thousand a year and a lovely estate near Oxford. He is widely reputed to be a very reliable man of moderate habits and excellent character. Every match-making mama of the *ton* has set her cap for him. But you have made a splendid conquest, apparently without effort!"

"Believe me, it was unconsciously done!" Kitty responded, embarrassed.

"I believe that is the characteristic of yours that is most appealing to Mr. Blanchard. He has been subjected to so much calculated matrimonial scheming. Now, when you appear at the Theatre Royal, you must be exceptionally well-dressed. You will be minutely examined by everyone of importance. You cannot appear in your favourite pink-and-cream gown, as it has been too widely seen. May I suggest you have Taylor run up an identical gown, but in the stunning blue-grey velvet we found at Grafton's last week?"

Thus did Kitty and Aunt Emma plunge into details of dress and hairstyles, fans and shoe-roses, and abandon thinking about Mr. Blanchard.

MÉSALLIANCE

After composing a light-hearted, rambling reply to Marianne, Kitty changed into her riding habit. She was on her way out to her daily appointment with Mr. McLaughlin when she was detained by Aunt Emma in the front sitting room. Kitty hastened to her side.

"Aunt Emma, you seem so grave! Whatever is the matter?" Kitty blurted out before they were even seated.

Aunt Emma assured her, "Nothing too grave, I hope, my dear. I have no dreadful news to impart. But I must talk to you of serious matters."

Kitty inclined her head, signalling her hostess to proceed.

"You have been seen quite often in the company of Lieutenant McLaughlin of late. So often, in fact, you are in danger of frightening off other, more suitable, *beaux*. I should see much less of him if I were you. You should be encouraging men who would be acceptable to your family."

"Unsuitable? You think Mr. McLaughlin—he has sold his colours—is unacceptable to the family?"

"Yes, of course," Aunt Emma replied, apparently surprised. "He is not of your station and represents a *mésalliance*."

Kitty replied, confused, and becoming upset. "*Mésalliance*? But I thought you liked him. As for his station, he is the son of a baron."

Her aunt replied whilst clasping her hand to offer comfort, "Yes, but my dear, that is *Irish* gentry. Not the same thing at all. And I *do* like him. He is a very handsome and entertaining young man. But that does not mean I think him a suitable husband.

"A handsome countenance, wit, and charm are not all a husband should offer," she explained. "He shows every symptom of being an unreliable gamester, for one thing. But more importantly, you must also think upon your family's position and the status he will convey to his offspring. Should you wed beneath your station, your children's lives will be forever diminished. It is unlikely you would find happiness in Ireland, dear, as you would not be accepted by the

Irish. Mr. McLaughlin will certainly never be accepted by the best of society here, for he is not only Irish, but quite prone to impropriety as well.

"It is not only your own heart you must think upon in these cases, my dearest Kitty. You would be well advised to make a better choice. Not just to please your family, but to secure the best possible future for your children," Aunt Emma explained gently. "Now, I have no wish to pain you, although it was inevitable in this case." She sighed, and patting Kitty's hand, said, "A good ride in the park will clear your head. You are a very clever girl and will make a sensible decision, I am sure."

Heart pounding, her mind in a whirl of confusion, Kitty said something civil to take her leave but could not recollect her own words later. She prepared for her ride and mounted without knowing what she did, numb to all around her.

Head bowed, she rode to her morning ride in uncharacteristic silence, leading the groom to suspect her distress. Othello obviously knew her mood as well and misbehaved in uncharacteristic fashion. When she failed to school him, the groom's suspicions were confirmed. He was used to scrutinizing passing streams of horseflesh with her, gaily mocking or admiring their owners. This day, they rode in silence.

Mr. McLaughlin immediately observed her distress and, after a very civil greeting, asked, "What's troubling you, Miss Otis? It must be terrible to silence you."

"I hardly know how to ... that is, I have been told ..." Stuttering to a stop, she suddenly burst out, irritated, "I am so confused I have been deprived of the power of speech!"

Taking a deep breath and working strenuously to control her voice, she looked straight ahead—she could *not* look him in the face—and finally assayed, "I have been reliably informed that my family will never approve a connection to your family. Further, my aunt informs me that I will never be accepted in your country. She believes that any children arising from our union would have a greatly diminished future. I have been sent ... I mean, Mrs. Williamson expects me to ..."

"Break it off?" Mr. McLaughlin spoke through clenched teeth. With the full force of wounded hopes, he cried, "Why must you always consult the opinions of others over those of your own heart?"

"I cannot break my family and abandon my fortune and my heritage! I cannot, and I will not. While I greatly admire and esteem you, Mr. McLaughlin, I cannot abandon *everything* and *everybody* else I hold dear.

"You know the state of my father's health. Would you have me hasten him to his grave? The Capulets and Montagues make for a wonderful play but a terrible marriage. I can think of nothing to be done to amend the situation. It is not as though there were some way to drain the Irish out of you or make my family suddenly reverse their opinion." Kitty gripped her reins tightly, barely controlling the urge to gallop and upset Othello. She reached forward to reassure her gelding, hanging her head in misery.

"Well, you're right, and you're wrong, darlin." Kitty noticed that Mr. McLaughlin became more Irish when angry. "I can't be less Irish, so our only hope is to reverse your family's opinion. What t'ink you of an invitation to my home, Gleannri Manor?"

"I would never be allowed to go," Kitty replied.

"Nay, you misunderstand me. What if I inveigle my parents to extend an invitation to your uncle's entire family? Then, you may all descend upon us *en masse* early this summer. Gleannri is at its best early in the summer. The passage is fair and quick that time of year. Also, 'twould be an education for your cousins, since Napoleon's ambitions have denied them the opportunity to travel the Continent. I need to go to pick up breeding stock anyway."

As he spoke, he became more animated and less Irish. He continued, "My mother has entertained the Archbishop of Canterbury; your family cannot help but be impressed."

"I dare not hope for success, but I cannot help myself! Oh, my dear McLaughlin, if there is any hope for us, I believe you have hit upon the only tactic for securing it. Now we must induce the Tinsleys to accept," Kitty replied, straightening her back.

With her head held high, much to Mr. McLaughlin's relief, they plotted together for nigh on to half an hour. With regular correspondence forbidden them, they borrowed Mr. Wallace's tactic. Kitty supplied him with Hal Warden's direction as well as her Uncle Tinsley's. They parted with the promise of meeting in two weeks to talk again after Mr. McLaughlin had made arrangements.

When Kitty returned, she had a very pleasant lunch with her hostess and retired in good spirits to prepare for a dinner party.

Unbeknownst to Kitty, her hostess used that time to correspond with her Aunt Eliza Tinsley.

March 18, 1814
Westy House, Bedford Square

My Dear Eli,

I advised Kitty of our objections to this mésalliance *and enumerated the difficulties of the match. When I was done, Kitty looked like marble. The last time I saw that look on her face was at her poor mother's funeral. I knew she was developing a preference for him but did not understand it had grown to attachment until our talk. We are too late, dear sister; she has already given away her heart.*

Kitty then went on her usual morning ride to Hyde Park and encountered Mr. McLaughlin there. He has sold his colours, no doubt, in hopes of matrimony. When she returned, she was bright-eyed and cheerful. I greatly fear she and her Irish giant plan to elope.

May I suggest we invent an excuse to send her back home as soon as might be convenient? Far better that she recover her good sense away from London and return for a second season than to ruin her chances of a good match by pining away for Mr. McLaughlin during this season. Or worse, make a run for Gretna Green.

My apologies for this curt note on such a delicate matter, but I feel great anxiety. Please reply by return post as I believe it is urgent that we resolve this matter to protect Kitty.

With deepest concern, Emmy

Mrs. Williamson's correspondence had its intended effect. The Tinsleys were prompted into immediate action. After a hasty conference, Mrs. Tinsley replied by return post as requested.

March 22, 1814
Elmsreach House, Carlisle

My Dearest Emmy,

Thank you for your concern. We feel that any subterfuge to draw Kitty from London would be immediately obvious to her and create an irreparable breach. Likewise, we cannot believe she plans an elopement. She is too fond of her father and her home and not prone to extravagant romanticism. Under the blandishments of a handsome man though, even very clever young women have been known to do remarkably foolish things. Thus, we rely entirely on your judgement. So, we are forced to believe it at least possible.

Equally, we fear coming to London to retrieve her will simply force her into early flight. Therefore, we have hit on the scheme of pressing her father to write and insist on her return.

Dear Tinsley is making his way to Mr. Otis even as I write this. Merit's letter to Kitty should arrive shortly after this one. I regret thrusting you into the centre of this thorny problem; please accept my apologies.

Tinsley and I are eternally in your debt, my dearest sister. Please accept this brief and unsatisfactory note in gratitude.

In haste, Yr. Sister, Eli

Mr. Tinsley managed by dint of patient explanations to make Mr. Otis both understand and be concerned about Kitty's situation. Mr. Otis dispatched a letter under Mr. Tinsley's coaching.

March 22, 1814
Dixon Cottage

Dearest Daughter,

I take up my pen to felicitate you on your conquest of London. Your accomplishments continue to delight, and I can only believe your mother is equally pleased looking down upon you from heaven.

Your horses are all well, but I am suffering from a cold winter. My very bones ache from the cold. Cook has tempted me with the best of her art, but still, my clothes hang loose on me. The snow is so deep that we are all locked into the house with no visitors. Your excellent conversation is sorely missed.

Do not forego any of the pleasures of London on my account! You are only young once, but I shall be old from now on.

Delighted by your triumphant début,

Your Loving Father

This combination of complaint and sentiment was sure to alarm his daughter and make her consider a quick return. Mr. Otis's letter had the desired result. On the day she received it, Kitty spoke to her Aunt Emma at tea.

"Aunt Emma, I am afraid I am in a bit of a predicament," Kitty said.

"Oh? And what is the nature of this predicament?" Mrs. Williamson inquired.

"Well, I have had a letter from my father." Kitty sighed. "He makes no direct complaint, but I am deeply concerned for his health and happiness."

"I am not surprised. My sister, Eliza, hinted as much to me in a letter, for she too is concerned." Emma said a silent prayer; her slightly vague syntax would disguise the fact Eliza Tinsley was concerned for *Kitty*, not Kitty's father. She continued, "As you are already bereft of one parent, you must fly to his side. With the aid of your excellent abigail, we can arrange for you to leave three days hence. You should keep your engagement this evening, and we shall write out all your apologies and departure notes tomorrow. Would that do?"

"Do? Why, I am so relieved! The only blot on my happiness is that I must leave London." Kitty suddenly realised her highly acute Aunt Emma would interpret this as a complaint for having to leave Mr. McLaughlin. So she hastened to add, "I have learnt so much from you, I shall miss your companionship and unfailing advice every day. I will miss your whist parties terribly. All my acquaintance in the North are indifferent card players. Please forgive me for cutting short this delightful visit."

"I understand perfectly, my dear," her Aunt Emma replied kindly. "Do not fret; this will not be your last season in London, if I have my way. I sincerely hope you may wait on an invitation to return here next season."

"Oh! You are the most generous creature!" Kitty cried, catching her aunt's hand and kissing her cheek like a much younger child. "I shall be delighted to accept. Please excuse me; I must tell Taylor to prepare."

"Of course, dear, I shall make arrangements for post cattle at once. You run along now," said Mrs. Williamson, quietly satisfied.

That evening, she was engaged for a dinner dance hosted by Mrs. Inchcombe and encountered Mr. Blanchard again. They were seated side by side at the dinner.

"Have you heard," Mr. Blanchard began over soup, "of Mr. Smith's excellent Geologic Map of England and Wales with Part of Scotland? While the original map was six by eight feet, I can claim the distinction of having seen a smaller, simplified folio print."

"How interesting," Kitty responded. "That seems like a monumental undertaking on Mr. Smith's part."

"It must have taken him years," Mr. Blanchard agreed. "Worth every minute of it, in my opinion. Think of how useful it will be for the planning of public works or the search for mining opportunities."

"Or even the layout of transportation canals," Kitty volunteered.

They discussed Mr. Smith's work and its many applications through most of dinner.

"Well, Mr. Blanchard," Kitty confided over dessert, "This is a lovely farewell to London. I am off home on the morrow."

"Farewell? How sadly disappointing. May I inquire as to why we are to be deprived of your company so abruptly, Miss Otis?"

"My father is unwell. And although he did not command my return, I feel I must fly to his side."

"I hope your father's condition is not serious," Mr. Blanchard replied.

"No, rest assured it is not terribly serious. I just cannot bear to think of leaving him in the care of servants when he is even the slightest bit unwell. He was seized by apoplexy shortly after my mother's death and has been in delicate health ever since."

"You are willing to abandon the diversions of London for nursing duties in Cumberland?" Mr. Blanchard smiled. "I do hope for his speedy recovery."

Kitty, though, had the distinct impression he was genuinely—as opposed to merely politely—disappointed. As she could scarcely credit her Aunt Emma's opinion, Kitty dismissed her impression as fanciful and forced it from her mind while she danced.

Much later that evening, Blanchard commented to his man, Ambercrombie, "I find myself completely exasperated with a man I have never met. He is ill. So, his daughter, the *only* young lady in London who offers interesting conversation, has abandoned her Season in favour of nursing duty in the frozen North."

"Speaks well of her heart, though," Ambercrombie replied.

"That it does. I shall have some of the Spanish brandy tonight."

His order prompted much speculation in Ambercrombie regarding this particular young lady. Mr. Blanchard always reserved the Spanish brandy for episodes of deep thought.

The next morning, with her notes of regret and apology all written and delivered, Kitty and Taylor once again set forth on the trunk road, with Aunt Emma's loaned coachman driving. Kitty sincerely looked forward to Dixon Cottage and seeing her father. However, every mile took her further from her McLaughlin and the diversions of London.

Torn between anxiety and genuine regret at leaving Mr. McLaughlin and Aunt Emma, Kitty was restless, fidgety, and frequently bored. The return journey was much more tedious than her travels *to* London had been.

HOME AGAIN

It was only early April and still very wintry in the high country. Kitty was forcibly reminded of her first visit to view Dixon Cottage. The timeless hills, the ancient cobbles, and enduring cottages that had seemed so novel and quaint, now betokened "home." Kitty had believed the rectory was her home and was gratified to discover Dixon Cottage now assumed that honour in her heart. Finally, Kitty arrived in the afternoon, too late for supper and too early for tea. She felt much more bruised and battered than she remembered arriving in London.

"Oh! Papa! I am ever so glad to be with you again," Kitty cried as she embraced her father. "You do look thin and tired and a bit pale. Are you taking your daily constitutional?"

"No, no. It has been too cold. But let me rest my eyes upon you. I am glad you are come, daughter."

They plunged into conversation. With Kitty's expert probing, she extracted many details of her father's doings in her absence. She also retold all that she had written with additional details. He repeated, "I am glad you are come," many times. Thus, Kitty was reassured her abrupt journey had been worthwhile. Then she took up a game of backgammon with him, and after an excellent tea, she read him to sleep. Once he nodded off, Mr. Hart had no difficulty guiding his befuddled and half-asleep charge into bed.

After her first anxious reunion with her father, Kitty's next order of business was a visit to Marianne. So, dressed in a smart new gown, she presented herself for a morning visit the very next day.

After the first luxuries of an embrace and exclamations of gladness, Kitty said, "Marianne! I do not believe I have ever seen you in such good looks. Why, you take the shine out of all my London finery."

Marianne clasped Kitty's hands in hers. "Papa has relented, and dear Wallace and I are to be married on the twenty-fifth of April at All Saints. My note to you must have just missed you in London."

Kitty squealed like a school-girl and embraced Marianne heartily. "Oh! Marianne, I wish you much joy!"

"Will you serve as maid of honour?" Marianne asked.

"If you are sure you do not want one of your sisters to serve that office, I would be honoured," Kitty accepted.

"I have also asked Jane to serve, so at least one of my sisters will stand up with me," Marianne explained.

Soon, the young ladies were deep into plans for Marianne's wedding, and were shortly joined by Mrs. Warden. Mr. Tinsley had consented to draw up the settlements for her, and those were expected to arrive in a few days.

Marianne chose a pale primrose gown overlaid with blonde lace and declined the latest fashion of an all-white wedding gown. However, she chose to wear a lace wedding cap *d'Angleterre*, which she had seen in Ackerman's Repository. Ackerman's excellent engraving showed the cap secured with a diamond tiara. Aside from being ridiculously expensive, it would not suit Marianne at all. They secured the cap with one of her mother's pearl ornaments instead. Kitty volunteered to lend her pearl necklaces and earbobs for "Something borrowed."

Once Kitty announced Marianne's engagement to her own household, she was able to solicit promises of assistance from the staff. She was unable to convince Mrs. Abernathy to share her receipt for *blanc mange*, but convinced her to contribute one.

After supper, Mr. Otis descended deep into his fog, and turning to his daughter, inquired, "Where is your mother, Kitty? I haven't seen her all day."

With tears in her eyes, Kitty clasped his hands. "Oh! Papa, I am sorrier than I can say. But you miss Mama so much, your mind is playing tricks on you. Mama has been buried at Crosthwaite these past two years."

His face collapsed in newly discovered grief. Kitty embraced her father and did her best to comfort him. Exhausted by her efforts, she called for Hart to put him to bed.

The next morning brought Mrs. McLaughlin's long-awaited invitation and a boost to Kitty's spirits. She agonized over leaving her father again. But, after much prayer and many long walks, she soothed her conscience by recalling he could not be expected to make the voyage. After reading the invitation several times, she forwarded it to the Tinsleys with an enclosure note:

April 15, 1814
Dixon Cottage, Threlkeld

My Dearest Aunt and Uncle,

I write today to enclose Mrs. McLaughlin's invitation to visit Gleannri Manor. Your dear sister advised me you are not inclined to approve Mr. McLaughlin's suit. I beg you to accept this invitation to become acquainted with his family and his character before you make any final decision.

I hope this visit will be an adventure for your boys since Bonaparte has denied them travel to the Continent. The voyage to Ireland will be swift and the waters calm in the early days of summer. We need only stay a few weeks. I know Uncle's legal practice cannot be suspended for long.

On a completely different note, I need to withdraw fifty pounds from my accounts to purchase new farm equipment and hire farm labourers. Mac is confident we can put eighteen acres under cultivation this spring. It seems so early in the year to start farming with snow and hard frosts every morning. But Mac is already preparing for spring.

Please visit Dixon Cottage as soon as is convenient so we can discuss these matters.

With lively hopes, your niece, Kitty

This letter aroused considerable exertion at the Tinsley household. After the initial rush of relief ("Kitty was *not* thinking of Gretna Green!"), the Tinsleys determined to accept the invitation. They feared if they did not, they might spark rash action on Kitty's part. Mr. Tinsley issued voluminous orders to his clerk and ordered his carriage for the next day, and Mrs. Tinsley wrote to her sister in London:

April 16, 1814
Elmsreach House, Carlisle

My Dearest Sister Emmy,

I have discovered you were absolutely right—Kitty and her dashing Irishman were concocting a plot! Tinsley and I have just accepted an invitation from Mrs. McLaughlin to visit Gleannri Manor, his family's home in Ireland. You only erred slightly in guessing what they were plotting. I sincerely hope this intelligence will vindicate both your (well-founded) suspicions and our faith in Kitty's character.

Kitty, no doubt, hopes we will abandon our scruples and approve the match. Now, dear sister, we must pray this visit reveals flaws in the McLaughlins sufficient to convince Kitty to abandon Mr. McLaughlin. I sincerely doubt Tinsley or I will change our opinion.

We hope it will be a splendid holiday for Phillip and Alexander. Gleannri Manor is famous for its stables, which should please the boys. We shall be gone from the beginning of June until mid-July. Tinsley's clerk is overjoyed at the opportunity, and Tinsley views this as an excellent trial prior to offering him a partnership.

Tinsley and I intend to round out the boys' education by bringing them with us to London next season. I have already secured the house we rented three years ago. A London season should give Phillip some town bronze to balance our excursion to the wilds of Ireland.

Please keep Kitty in your prayers, dear sister, and let us hope that our prayers are answered.

With high hopes, your sister, Eli

As Mrs. Tinsley's missive was making its way to London, Mr. Tinsley was making his way to Dixon Cottage with fifty pounds in hand. After Kitty had invited him to have a seat in the drawing room, Mr. Tinsley declared, "We shall accept Mrs. McLaughlin's invitation, Kitty. Mrs. Tinsley is posting our acceptance, even as we speak."

"Oh! I am so glad, Uncle!" Kitty exclaimed.

"I knew you would be pleased," Mr. Tinsley assured Kitty. "After a brief respite here, I am travelling on to Whitehaven to book passage to Douglas on the Isle of Man, and from thence to Dublin. From Mrs. McLaughlin's directions, it appears to be a full day's travel from Dublin to Gleannri. So, pack your trunks accordingly. Mrs. Tinsley is also writing to Phillip at Oxford and Alexander at Harrow. They will be over the moon about this holiday. It would seem your suggestion has met with success already." He smiled whilst keeping his hopes and motivations for the journey decently hidden.

They passed a very pleasant evening together, although Mr. Tinsley was saddened by how much his oldest friend had declined since his last visit. Mr. Tinsley set off in good order the next morning. He planned to make the nearly thirty-mile journey in two stages to rest his horses and promised to return in five days. Kitty was thrilled at his prompt, vigorous, and unselfish actions. She immediately reported all to Marianne whilst they worked together on the wedding.

At first, it seemed as though the wedding day would never come. Then, when there were dozens of small chores still to be done, it seemed as though the day would come too soon. Finally, James Wallace and his family arrived.

Marianne's brother, Hal, greeted the groom with, "Hallo from the Northern Postal Express. Letters from courting couples whiz back and forth like bullets in a heated battle!"

Mr. Wallace laughed and shook his hand warmly. "You survived the battle without injury, I hope?"

"Indeed, as you can see." Hal continued with a smile. "I found your correspondence most educational. Now successful courtship has been illuminated for me; I hope to profit from that knowledge."

The young gentlemen rode and fished some and had a "bachelor's party" at the *Horse and Farrier*. The chief entertainment was downing Mr. Brown's finest stout and betting on the outcome of darts games.

The last few days before the ceremony melted away in a flurry of preparations. Lowering skies threatened rain first thing in the morning. But, in the event, the skies cleared, and the couple were wed with sunshine streaming through the Church's stained glass.

Kitty and Mrs. Warden were very nearly late, as they conspired to decorate the bridal chamber with flowers, fresh linens, rout cakes, fruit, and champagne. All of Marianne's family and a representative dozen of Mr. Wallace's family attended, together with the usual village gawkers.

Kitty, along with Marianne's oldest sister, Jane, stood up with her as the bridesmaids. Mr. Wallace's brother, Alistair, and Marianne's brother, Hal, performed the same office for the groom. The entire company then repaired to the Wardens' for a lovely wedding breakfast. The happy young couple retired soon afterwards amongst the usual ribaldry from all attending.

Early the next morning, the Wallace family, who had stayed with the Wardens, met Kitty after breakfast to make their final farewells. After many tearful embraces, the young couple set off for Ballanchulish on Loch Leven. They piled their carriage high with

Marianne's trousseau and wedding gifts, including the wedding portrait that Kitty had painted for them. The rest of the Wallace family following closely behind, they made their way north.

IRELAND

M rs. Tinsley dispatched another letter to Gleannri, advising Mrs. McLaughlin of their travel plans. She soon received a reply; Kitty's suitor would meet them in Dublin and accompany the party to Gleannri. When this intelligence was conveyed to Kitty, she was gratified to discover Mr. McLaughlin was improved in civility. She completed her arrangements for the trip gaily.

Unbeknownst to Kitty at the time, Mr. Blanchard was also preparing for travel. He had called on Lady Margaret during the Season and begged for an invitation to her hunting box near Dixon Cottage for the hunt season. Intrigued, Lady Margaret issued the requested invitation.

Amidst the bustle of preparations, Mac promised to bring Kitty vast profits. She purchased two draft horses and appropriate kit and left all of the rest of farm management in Mac's keeping. Kitty once again turned her attention to her father.

Kitty's father had improved under her care and now filled out his clothes, so she was less concerned for his health and more for his mind. During the last whirlwind round of morning calls, Kitty spent most of every evening explaining to her father why she was leaving and where she was going. She instructed Hart to keep at it, so poor Papa would not be too confused in her absence. At last, the Tinsleys arrived, her trunks were loaded, and they left in good time to catch the ferry the next morning for Whitehaven.

May 27, 1814
Douglas Inn, Dublin

My Dear Mrs. Wallace,

I thought I should begin this note properly so that you may luxuriate in your new name. I write to you now from our inn in Dublin; we shall next be able to communicate from Gleannri.

Dublin is a beautiful town, with many modern buildings sited cheek-and-jowl with quaint antiquities. It seems the whole town is

*grey, the colour of the local stone. Rather than making it drab, the
colour seems to grant it an extra measure of dignity.*

*The inn is comfortable, but I am so glad to have Taylor and the
Tinsley's servants with us! The service here is indifferent, at best. I have
not yet seen my Irish giant but expect to before we leave tomorrow. I
shall have sweet dreams tonight!*

*I shall never forgive you, however, if you do not write to me
and give me all of the details of your new home. Give my best to
Mr. Wallace and write soon.*

Your loving friend, Kitty

When Mr. McLaughlin met them the next morning, he had the
foresight to bring two coaches and hacks for the boys who rode
beside the carriages. The Tinsleys rode with Mr. McLaughlin and
Kitty, with the servants in the coach following.

They made their progress through a countryside so green; Kitty
would not have credited it if she had not seen the verdure for herself.
They all chatted and played guessing games. Between sightseeing
and their own amusements, time passed quickly, and they were soon
entering the gates of Gleannri.

It was a vast estate, and they passed through many lush horse
pastures on the drive to the house. Gleannri Manor was easily four
times the size of the All Saints rectory, built in the very latest fashion.
The broad steps to the front door welcomed them in. The butler,
in full livery but with a virtually unintelligible accent, showed
them into an enormous drawing room. The room was elaborately
decorated with many ebony pieces and gilded furnishings.

Mrs. McLaughlin was a stately woman of extraordinary beauty
only just beginning to fade. Her red hair showed the first touches of
grey, and her skin was starting to show signs of wear. But her face was
an ideal oval of beauty, and she was dressed in a very expensive gown.

Kitty was seized by self-consciousness. Mrs. McLaughlin greeted
them civilly, but Kitty's mind was occupied with worries. Her gown
was travel-weary, her hair was not showing to best advantage, her
bonnet was not secured properly, and mostly she was concerned by
the suspicion that Mrs. McLaughlin did not like her.

Tea was brought in, and Mrs. McLaughlin, with perfect
correctness, invited Mrs. Tinsley to pour out. Several minutes were

absorbed with pouring and arranging the tea, serving the delicate cakes and tiny decorated toasts, and exclaiming over their elegance.

Mrs. Tinsley began the conversation. "Mrs. McLaughlin, you have an excellent cook. French, I would guess?"

Mrs. McLaughlin replied with a look of boredom on her face. "Thank you. We have retained M. DuBois, from Paris."

Kitty attempted to participate after finishing a lovely piece of toast. "I understand that Mr. McLaughlin recently built this house for you?"

"Five years ago," Mrs. McLaughlin replied.

Joseph McLaughlin remained uncharacteristically silent. He alternated between fiddling with his teacup and shifting uncomfortably in his chair.

There was a slight hesitation in the conversation, and Mrs. Tinsley stepped in to rescue the situation. "I remember leaving Leeds for Carlisle as a young bride. It was difficult leaving behind family and friends. But I soon became comfortable in my new parish and made new friends. I expect leaving Belfast was a wrench for you, was it not?"

"No. I had long desired a country house," Mrs. McLaughlin replied. The conversation once more lurched to a halt.

"Do you visit your friends and family in Belfast often?" Mrs. Tinsley assayed.

"Annually," Mrs. McLaughlin replied as briefly as possible.

Messers. McLaughlin and Tinsley affected not to notice anything amiss but never once participated in the conversation. Phillip and Alexander Tinsley took the cue from their father and watched, apparently fascinated but silent. Kitty, already ill at ease and now confused and intimidated, fell silent. Thus, they all witnessed an extraordinary, very polite battle of wills between Mrs. Tinsley and Mrs. McLaughlin.

Mrs. Tinsley used every art to maintain conversation, whilst Mrs. McLaughlin did everything in her power to suppress it. After a perfectly correct but excruciating ten minutes, Mrs. Tinsley capitulated. "No doubt, you have many duties pressing, and we must repair before dinner. If you will excuse us?"

Mr. McLaughlin bowed and excused himself. All three ladies stood and curtsied, and Mrs. McLaughlin rang for her butler. "Joyce, show our guests to their rooms." Joyce bowed and mutely gestured the ladies out of the room. They proceeded up a grand double-back stairway to the upper storey and down a long corridor, to rooms at the far reach of the house in total silence. Once the butler had opened the door for her, Kitty turned to him and said, "Send for my abigail at once, please."

Kitty had taken off her bonnet and removed what pins she could reach in her hair, washed her face and hands, and undone her shoes to change into her dinner dress. Still, Taylor did not appear. Finally, she applied to Aunt Eliza's abigail to go in search of Taylor. After a tedious wait, Taylor, somewhat flushed and breathless, arrived.

Kitty opened the door for her. "My goodness, Taylor, you need not have run. But, I have been waiting well on to half an hour. What happened?"

Taylor answered in somewhat breathless accents. "The butler never passed on yer message. Then, when Mrs. Tinsley's abigail came lookin' fer me, all the house servants misdirected her. She finally opened every door in the basement 'til she found me. I'm in a room in the basement clear, on the other side of the house."

"How ridiculous!" Kitty exclaimed, irritated.

"Oh, 'tis the Irish nature. I'm told the whole lot of 'em's got Pooka blood, and they cannae keep from playing tricks," Taylor joked.

"Oh, dear. I am so looking forward to a bath to get rid of all my road dirt. Can you arrange that for me? And a cot for yourself in this room?" Kitty inquired.

"O'course. Now, let's see to yer hair." Taylor released her hair, and the women exited the room together, Taylor to see to the bath and Kitty to see her Aunt Eliza.

Kitty knocked timidly on the door to her aunt's quarters and asked for advice. "Aunt Eliza, I declare I am quite uneasy. I expected the McLaughlins to take some time to warm up to me. After all, I am completely unknown to them. But ..." Kitty trailed off.

Aunt Eliza finished for her. "That was the coldest, most intimidating greeting possible, within the bounds of civility."

"I would not want to think ill of anybody, much less my potential mama-in-law," Kitty countered.

Her aunt took her by the shoulders and, studying her face, replied. "Kitty, you will meet women like her from time to time. Women who use their husband's money as a weapon and etiquette for ammunition. There is but one response: refuse to be intimidated.

You are a true lady of impeccable breeding, delicacy of mind, and strength of character. Just carry on being yourself. If you are every inch a Christian lady, then no 'slings and arrows' will ever touch you. Besides, it is your only hope of winning over the McLaughlins."

Kitty embraced her aunt. "Oh! You are so right, so very right! What would I do without you? Shall we go for a brief walk in the pleasure gardens before dinner? I believe your sons would be eager to escort us."

"Of course, they would. Go and bathe, and we will meet you at the landing in an hour," Mrs. Tinsley promised.

When Kitty returned to her room, she discovered a very breathless, red-faced Taylor and a very shallow bath. Kitty quickly diagnosed the problem. "Would none of the house servants help you with this?"

"Nae. I'll be all right. Jest give me a moment," Taylor declared stoutly.

Instead, Kitty immediately applied to Phillip and Alexander for the loan of their valet, and to Mr. Tinsley for help from his valet. Between the two men, Mrs. Tinsley's abigail, and one last round trip for Taylor, her bath was ready.

Completely refreshed, wearing a lovely blue dinner gown, Kitty met with her aunt and Phillip and Alexander at the stairwell as planned. Kitty was determined to heed Mrs. Tinsley's advice and left it to the servants to concoct a bed for Taylor.

The four of them wandered the house for some time before discovering the garden entry. Once outside, the garden was refreshingly cool after the sultry heat of the day. They talked animatedly about the beauties of the garden, and Kitty's mood improved markedly.

Once they made their way back inside, they discovered a small parlour facing the cool north-eastern side of the house. Phillip rang vigorously for help, and eventually, one of the house servants arrived.

"You rang?" he asked once he finally appeared.

"Just to inquire after supper-time," Phillip Tinsley replied, somewhat crossly.

"Supper's begun already," the footman declared with relish.

At that moment, Joseph McLaughlin burst into the room. "There you are! We're all terribly late. Mr. Tinsley, with your permission." Mr. McLaughlin escorted Mrs. Tinsley. Mr. Tinsley took Kitty on his arm, and they all hustled down an enormously long hallway to the dining room.

Mrs. McLaughlin was wreathed with smiles at the foot of the table. She called out gaily, "Oh, there you are! The servants couldn't find you. Please do sit down."

Kitty was seated next to Mrs. McLaughlin at the foot of the table, Joseph took what was evidently his usual station just below his two oldest brothers. Phillip and Alexander were isolated in a clump of elderly relatives. Mr. and Mrs. Tinsley were seated mid-table, separated only by the McLaughlin's youngest son.

It was not an arrangement calculated to show anyone to advantage. The soup tureen had already been removed, and several platters were empty. The overall effect was to make Kitty and the Tinsleys feel like poor relations come begging rather than honoured guests. Joseph appeared to be completely oblivious of the subtleties and applied himself vigorously to his food.

Kitty's only relief was a few short bursts of conversation with Joseph's youngest sister, Mary, seated next to her. Even that was spoiled by Mary's furtive glances at her mother.

When the second course was served, Kitty looked the footman full in the face. "Please convey my compliments to the chef. M. DuBois is a culinary genius."

The man looked startled and glanced at Mrs. McLaughlin, who nodded consent. Kitty realised immediately that not being called to dinner, or even being informed of the hour, was no accident. All the servants danced to Mrs. McLaughlin's tune.

Bewildered and hurt, Kitty worked hard to keep her head high. The ladies were ushered into the vast drawing room, which was set up for a card party. After tea, the gentlemen joined them. Joseph McLaughlin, his younger sister Mary, and Mr. and Mrs. Tinsley formed a natural conversational group and conversed on a variety of topics. By the end of the evening, Kitty had dismissed most of her earlier discomfiture as insignificant.

As the party was breaking up, the butler brought her a letter from Mrs. Wallace, and with that missive, her day was complete. When she arrived at her room, she discovered Taylor was comfortably perusing the Bible.

"What of the plan to bunk in together, Taylor?" Kitty inquired.

Taylor carefully marked her place and explained with a smile. "Well, it seems Mrs. Tinsley's abigail is already in a bed chamber above this 'un, and there's an extra bed in that room. So, I had the boy's valet move all me things in, and I'll bunk in with her. I felt too fresh bunkin' with you, if ye'll pardon me sayin' so, Miss. We would nay want to harm yer consequence with yer mama-in-law to be, now, would we?"

"I knew I could count on you to work things out to our best advantage, Taylor!" Kitty eagerly read her letter whilst Taylor brushed her hair and braided it up for the night.

May 29, 1814
Loch Leven Cottage, Ballanchulish

Dearest Kitty,

I hope this letter finds you well and happy. I could not wait upon a letter from you, but must spill all my happiness onto paper at once. Our bridal chamber was lovely. Thank you for helping Mama with it. Our drive to Ballachulish was fair and easy, and the countryside picturesque to the highest degree.

We stopped over at my in-laws' house for a few days before making the final journey to our new home. My mama-in-law was very sweet to me. There was nothing she would not do to make me feel welcome. I love them already.

I also met Miss Lucy Miller, fiancée to Wallace's older brother, Alastair, whom I like very much. May I suggest having amiable in-laws is one of the greatest felicities bestowed by marriage?

My new home reminds me of Dixon Cottage. A deliberate resemblance, as Wallace worked diligently to find a comfortable home for me. It is only leased, as my darling husband feels that work on the "locks for the lochs" will be over soon, and we shall soon move. He looks forward to becoming less of a waterworks specialist and more of a general architect.

Within the limited scope offered at a leased property, I am adding homey touches. I just finished netting a fringe curtain for the smaller of our parlours. We have engaged an excellent staff. Although Mrs. MacComber cannot meet Mrs. Abernathy's standards, we eat quite well. She is also thrifty with the household accounts.

I have already had our vicar and his wife over for a small dinner party. I plan a larger entertainment once I have amassed more acquaintance to swell the guest list. My darling husband's older brother will be visiting us soon and plans to stay a fortnight, so I am arranging for his keep and entertainment.

This house has a much smaller home farm than Dixon Cottage. But still, we can support our carriage horse, Grandee, and two milk cows, together with a flock of 28 chickens. The village is quieter than Threlkeld. Nonetheless, I am quite content. I enjoyed reading Sir Scott's "Waverly," and can highly recommend it.

I eagerly await your description of Gleannri.

Yr. Loving, Marianne

As it was so late, Kitty replied briefly.

June 1, 1814
Gleannri Manor, Ireland

My Dearest Mrs. Wallace,

I feel positively churlish for my demands at the end of my last letter. Please disregard me entirely. I shall not repeat my first letter, which has no doubt reached you, but shall plunge into new particulars.

First, I have never stayed at a home quite so large as this one. Gleannri encompasses over 30,000 square feet, not counting terraces, follies, guest houses, stables, workers' cottages &c. Every room is ornamented with elaborate marble or gilded mouldings and panelling. The furniture is heavily carved, inlaid, frequently of rare species, or embellished with gilding. Almack's ballroom is not as large as the vast drawing room here, and they maintain an enormous staff. I must confess, as luxurious as such appointments are, I am more comfortable with a simpler style of housekeeping.

We are being very well entertained. Their cook, M. DuBois, is a genius. I have never eaten so well. The weather has been very fine. Mrs. McLaughlin has planned many events for our amusement, and I shall write to you about all of it soon. I shall seek out a copy of Sir Scott's book.

I have opened the windows, and a balmy breeze, scented with grass, is wafting through the room. I can barely keep my eyes open and must bid you adieu.

Yr. Exhausted Dévotee, *Kitty*

The next day, Joseph McLaughlin invited Kitty to ride. She accepted, as did the Tinsley boys. They all met in front of the magnificent stone stables. A lovely chestnut filly was led forth. As soon as the horse spied Kitty, she began bucking and shying, rolling her eyes, obviously nervous.

Kitty resorted to the old trick of removing her hat, and the filly settled. She mounted without difficulty and saw both of Joseph's older brothers hand him money as she settled her straw chip bonnet back on her head. Kitty felt quite cross that his brothers had been betting against her, and quite smug that they had lost their bet.

They had an enjoyable ride exploring a quarter of the vast Gleannri estate. It was lovely and did much to repair Kitty's mood before returning for lunch. During lunch, it was announced a horse race had been arranged, and thus was their afternoon spent. Soon, the days established a pattern. There was a morning ride, luncheon, various afternoon entertainments, quiet supper followed by tea, card games, or a private dance or music party.

A week after their arrival, Joseph's oldest brother, Patrick, challenged him to a horse race. It was quickly arranged. Only three days later, they were treated to the brothers competing in a match race referred to at the local pub as "a battle of the gods." Joseph had brought Hercules with him, and Patrick was mounted on his favourite, Mercury.

When the tape dropped, the horses were off to a flying start. Hercules grabbed the rail and opened a two-length lead. Mercury cut away a length. He cut away another length as they came to the half-mile post—and now, they were running head and head. For almost a half-mile, they ran as one horse painted against the lush green foliage of the Irish countryside. They were neck and neck—head and head—nose and nose.

They came flying past the mile. Hercules had lost his two-length margin. His velvet had been shot away. Mercury had shown his reserve speed. From two lengths away, he was now on even terms. As they passed the milepost with three-sixteenths left—the stretch that always tells the story--Hercules was keeping up. With barely more than a final furlong left, Hercules surged ahead.

Down the final furlong, the great-hearted Hercules opened a small gap. Nearly every spectator expected Mercury to close the gap again. Yard by yard, they thundered ahead.

Patrick gave Mercury the whip. Mercury battled to the bitter end. Mercury lost by a head—run off the track by a battered five-year-old draft horse, who had more speed and more heart, and Joseph in the saddle.

Hercules' victory was awarded a brief smattering of applause, but no roar from the flabbergasted crowd. As they stood to leave, Kitty overheard his brothers, Michael and Liam discussing the race.

"Well, he's an idiot in most things, but ye have to admit, he's a way wit' horses," his younger brother began.

"Aye, Liam. I only wish he extended t'at intelligence to any other area of his life."

"I t'ink Cambridge ruint him," Liam continued. "He lost whatever sense he had, an' now does little more t'an ape t'e English."

"Disgustin'," Patrick agreed. "'An' him t'inking to make his fortune on the streng't of it. Complete lunacy."

Kitty was shocked to discover how little his brothers thought of Joseph. Now knowing that his family expected nothing of him, she was even more impressed by his education and ambition.

That Sunday, Kitty and the Tinsleys attended church in the modern chapel on the estate. Kitty and Aunt Eliza could understand very little of the Latin service, although her uncle and the boys had enough Latin to follow. But their boredom was not relieved by the homily, as the priest had a brogue so thick as to be unintelligible!

Kitty was paired with Mr. McLaughlin in a two-seat *curricle* on the way back. Once he had handed her in, he said, "Don't know what that was about—Father O'Hare's Irish is so thick, even *I* lost the thread on occasion. Father Miller is our usual priest and has diction as clear as cut glass."

"What a relief; I felt incredibly stupid. I don't have enough Latin to follow the service, nor enough Irish to follow the homily!" It finally occurred to Kitty to ask, "Are you willing to convert to the Church of England?"

Mr. McLaughlin grinned. "For you, certainly. I don't think it matters nearly as much as the priests and vicars would have us believe."

While flattered, Kitty wondered how anyone could hold religious conviction in so little esteem. She was a bit unsettled by his glib reply.

One memorable evening, Mr. McLaughlin senior regaled them with anecdotes of his youth, his business, and of Ireland. His tales were so well told and so funny that Kitty fairly shrieked with laughter most of the evening. She staggered out of the room with her sides aching. Never had she been so well entertained by such a talented *raconteur*. That evening did much to explain Joseph McLaughlin's sense of humour!

The next day whilst riding with Mr. McLaughlin, Kitty complained, "My stamina for such a leisured existence is flagging. I am used to managing my house, looking after my father, and making visits to the poor and the sick of the parish. Here, I am useless. I don't even paint or draw or do needlework. I am discovering that idle luxury does not suit me. I believe that is why I grew tired of London so quickly when I was last there."

"I find that easy to credit. I am impressed by your drive to be useful. Most young ladies would leap at the chance for idle luxury," Mr. McLaughlin replied with a smile.

"Sadly, however, you are the *only* member of your family who is impressed. Your mother never speaks to me unless she must. Your older brothers avoid me entirely. Even your younger sister, Mary, avoids me. I am never invited to participate in morning calls from your acquaintance, nor am I invited to accompany your family in making calls. You and the Tinsleys are my only companions."

Mr. McLaughlin's brow furrowed. "I am aware. I'll ponder on ways to ease them into this. You, on the other hand, could charm the birds out of a tree. Give them time; they'll come around."

"I am reassured. If anyone is clever enough to puzzle this out, it's you." She smiled.

A few days later, however, when walking the park with her Aunt Eliza, Kitty said, "I am becoming more uncomfortable around Mrs. McLaughlin, not less, with time."

"Yes, dear. I had noticed."

"It seems she always has a ready excuse for avoiding all conversation with me," Kitty confided. "I thought Mrs. McLaughlin would want to question me about my upbringing, connections, religious habits, etc. But she appears to be avoiding getting to know me at all. I cannot disabuse myself of the notion that she disapproves of me. Yet, if that were so, then why invite us all?"

Aunt Eliza fiddled with her parasol and answered carefully. "I suspect in order to discourage you. I believe the McLaughlins are as disinclined to this match as we are. Mrs. McLaughlin is but a small taste of the treatment you would receive as an English woman living in Ireland. As much as I admire your dashing Irishman, I doubt the two of you can turn the tide of public opinion by yourselves. You must consider what your life will be like in daily society, Kitty."

Kitty hung her head and replied quietly, "Oh, I know you are right, but I cannot help myself. I cannot bring myself to call it off, though I am sorely troubled by doubt."

"Perfectly understandable, my dear. I suggest consulting your Bible. Not the Song of Solomon," her aunt advised with a conscious smile. "Perhaps Philippians."

That night, Kitty obediently read Philippians and discovered in 4:8, "Finally, brethren, whatsoever things are true, whatsoever things are honest, whatsoever things are just, whatsoever things are pure, whatsoever things are lovely, whatsoever things are of good report; if there be any virtue, and if there be any praise, think on these things." And so, Kitty set out to count her blessings, and finding many to be thankful for, slept peacefully.

A GARDEN WALK

Two days later, Mr. and Mrs. Tinsley were on a sightseeing trip and had not yet returned at the hour of Kitty's usual garden ramble. So, she undertook her walk alone. She was standing in an *allée* of yew when she overheard Joseph McLaughlin's eldest brother, Patrick, and next eldest brother, Michael. They were talking on the other side of the yews.

Kitty was about to retreat rather than eaves-drop but became rooted in place when she realised they were discussing *her*. The young men abused her so viciously and in terms so vulgar that Kitty was frozen in shock. The petty dislikes of her sheltered existence had little prepared Kitty to be the object of true hatred.

Kitty was bereft of movement; her head was spinning; all her limbs grew cold. The blood drained from her face, and her ears buzzed. Kitty felt as though she would faint, but she did not. She soon perceived by the crunch of gravel and movement of the men's voices that they were about to turn the corner and discover her.

In a mad, unthinking panic, she took up her skirts and made for the house, running on the grassy verge to remain undetected. Her flight bolstered by intense distress, she ran like a falling star streaking across the night sky and reached the house before the McLaughlin brothers rounded the bend.

Kitty fervently hoped they had not perceived her and she could maintain her composure as she bolted up the stairs. But the tears flowed even as she attained the landing. Kitty was sobbing lustily when she entered her bed-chamber. She threw herself upon the bed, crushing her finery.

Taylor, having heard her mistress's door slam, knocked and entered shortly thereafter. She was shocked to see Kitty in such a state. Rushing to her lady's side, she rescued the hat, took away the parasol, and attempted to soothe her tears.

At first, Kitty could not even speak, but she finally gulped out, "Please ask for my Aunt Tinsley to come as soon as ..." and could not go on.

"I'll keep a lookout fer Mrs. Tinsley," Taylor offered. She added nervously, "Ye'll be all right, then?"

Still unable to speak, Kitty nodded vigorously, searching for a handkerchief, and waved Taylor out the door. As she sobbed, she reviewed every moment with her beloved Irish giant.

All the combined warnings of her family came to mind. Both Aunt Emma and Aunt Eliza were convinced she would not be accepted in Irish society, and McLaughlin would suffer the same fate in England. With his brothers' crushing opinion fresh in her ears, the truth of their arguments impressed her with particular force.

Mr. McLaughlin had expressed the opinion that importing horses to Australia would be highly profitable. Europe was war-torn, and America already had plenty of horses, in his opinion. Therefore, he wished to venture to Australia.

Perhaps, she thought, they could flee to Australia, and her heart trembled with hope. But then, she thought about her father wasting away a betrayed, broken, and bereaved man; about little Davey out on the streets with inadequate clothing, food, or shelter; of the scandal she would inflict on her beloved Aunt and Uncle Tinsley. Could she live with herself if she inflicted all of that on those nearest and dearest to her in pursuit of her own selfish desires?

Kitty's conscience would not allow. Once she was certain in her heart that she could not and would not run away, Kitty's mind turned to all of the more practical justifications for her decision. She thought of the reality of living in a penal colony. No books, only a makeshift church, none of the comforts of home. She knew herself to be woefully ill-equipped to tame a raw wilderness. She would be worried for her own safety and the safety of their children. Her children ... no sons they had together would have any opportunities for education or professions, her daughters scant choice of marriageable bachelors.

If they did run away together, her entire staff would be in a precarious position—suddenly without employment and with no references. Uncle Tinsley would certainly not approve of an elopement, and she would have to abandon her fortune. They would not have enough to establish a new household and a new business in the wilds of Australia. Furthermore, it occurred to her she would have to abandon Dixon Cottage and everything she had managed to achieve. With so many of her plans unfinished, the very idea of leaving her home wrung her heart.

No, she decided, her heart breaking. Whilst running away together held strong appeal, she knew in her heart it would be impossible. In twenty minutes, her mind was made up, and her tears had abated. Mrs. Tinsley, still in her travel dress and hat, entered. Taylor followed with some tea.

"This is very unlike you, Kitty; whatever is the matter?" Mrs. Tinsley sat on the bed next to Kitty and laid Kitty's head on her shoulder. Supported by her aunt, tears flowing freely once again, Kitty was finally able to make herself understood, and the whole story came out.

"Ah, my dear girl." Aunt Tinsley sighed. "You have loved not too well, but unwisely. I would give anything to have spared you this."

Mrs. Tinsley turned to Taylor. "She is too exhausted for dinner. Arrange for a little soup and some buttered bread. I shall tender her apologies. Please ask Mr. Tinsley to come in."

Once Mr. Tinsley arrived, he immediately perceived his ward's distress. When informed of its source, he was offended, although not surprised. He said with elaborate sarcasm, "Obviously, we must not impose on the McLaughlins any farther. I shall make arrangements to leave immediately."

Mr. Tinsley dispatched Phillip Tinsley on horseback to the village carters to procure coaches and hacks for the following morning. Mrs. Tinsley hurried into her dinner dress. Taylor organised the servants, who took great offence to the slur on their young Miss Otis. By the time Mr. and Mrs. Tinsley returned from dinner, their travel clothes were laid out, trunks all packed, and arrangements for the coaches complete.

At dinner, Mrs. Tinsley insisted on a seat next to her hostess. "Mrs. McLaughlin, it is my sad duty to convey to you that we must cut short our visit. My poor, dear ward, Miss Otis, is greatly indisposed, and we can no longer trespass upon your hospitality. We have made arrangements to leave in the morning."

This announcement soon filtered to the centre of the table, and Joseph McLaughlin excused himself and made his way upstairs.

Taylor reluctantly admitted him to the bed-chamber but remained by Kitty's side for the entire conversation.

"You've been crying!" Mr. McLaughlin exclaimed, his anxiety obvious. "What happened?"

Although Kitty had been preparing herself for this interview and was determined not to embarrass herself, she could not help the tears still rolling down her face.

"I overheard your brothers Patrick and Michael in the garden. They did not perceive me; I was on the other side of the yew hedge. They ..." Kitty's voice faltered, and she continued in a whisper, "Your brothers hate and despise me. And your mother does not approve, either. She never speaks to me if she can avoid it and has played all kinds of mean tricks. I thought ..."

Kitty could barely continue, and taking a deep breath, forced out, "That is, I had *hoped* these were mistakes; that your family would come to know and accept me. But I now perceive that is not—and will never be—the case. There is no hope for us, my dearest McLaughlin. Not when both families so strongly disapprove the match."

"What did they say?" Mr. McLaughlin demanded, his brow darkening.

Kitty gasped. "I cannot ... I *shall* not repeat it! Let us just say it was perfectly clear that if we married, our children would always be despised by your family. I also now plainly see what you would have to endure should we settle in England. No, McLaughlin, should we wed, there would be no future for us."

"England and Ireland are not the only countries on earth! America is not profitable for me, but Australia is opening up for free settlement, and they need horses. We could build a life there, Kitty, and to Hell with all of them!"

Kitty considered for a long moment before answering, "I am sorry to seem paltry, but to betray my father and hasten him to his grave, a bereaved man? To cruelly abandon the staff that has been so loyal to me and leave little Davey to die of starvation and exposure? Run away and inflict scandal on my family, blighting my cousin's standing with the *ton*? Marry against the wishes of my guardian and lose my fortune? Abandon my home? Not to mention the dangers and difficulties of the passage. What kind of a life will we have without my fortune to help establish a business and a household?

Our children will not have the education and opportunities I would want for them in a penal colony.

"As appealing as such daring may be; and I can testify it holds *great* appeal; I cannot do it. I will not succumb to the temptation to pursue my own desires when it will inflict so much harm on so many people I hold dear. No, my dear McLaughlin, there is no hope for us. My heart is breaking in two, but we will not suit, you and I. My conscience will not allow. Our families will not let us. Nay, the whole of society is against us." As she spoke, McLaughlin's face underwent a radical change from distress to rage.

"When I have myself sorted, I shall write to you. Against all your beloved convention, I shall write!" he declared bravely as he stormed out of the door.

"And I shall reply!" Kitty promised to his departing back.

Taylor, herself in tears, comforted Kitty as best she could, whilst the rest of the servants hovered outside the door. Over the course of the evening, the servants and the Tinsleys put together the story of ensuing events.

The McLaughlin brothers were all tall, athletic men, but only Joseph was a giant. He stormed into the dining hall just after the ladies withdrew from the room. He seized his brother Michael from behind as he sat at the table and lifted him—chair and all—in front of himself, using Michael as a club to knock his eldest brother, Patrick, from his chair.

Mr. Tinsley, appalled at this sordid scene, immediately quit the room. He retrieved Mrs. Tinsley from the drawing room and escorted her to their quarters. At this point, all descriptions became confused. But it is certain from Patrick's broken ribs and Michael's broken nose, Joseph landed telling blows before his father and the footmen intervened.

Once released by the footmen, Joseph stalked into the drawing room, followed by his father. He tersely demanded his sisters leave him to converse with his parents. All reports of the conversation between Joseph and his parents are largely conjectured. Howsoever, the English servants, huddled on the staircase landing, heard several shouted exchanges.

Joseph shouted, "Ye're mad! Utterly mad! Her fortune's greater than my own!" And later, "Ye've got that and to spare, 'tis nuttin' to ye!" And still later, "If nay, t'en, I'll make it a matter o' courts and scandal, o' back-stabbin' and lies, and ye'll ne'er lift yer head in society again!" And finally, "I'm shot of t'e whole lot o' ye! And may yer black hearts land ye in Hell!"

The servants deduced the McLaughlins senior accused Miss Otis of being a fortune-hunter. From the next remarks, they surmised Mr. McLaughlin was demanding his inheritance and threatened legal action with all its attendant scandal should his parents not consent. Hence, his remark, "You have that and to spare." Joseph's final shouted remark needed no explanation. All this was reported by the servants to Taylor, and by Taylor to Kitty. It convinced Kitty that Joseph was the noblest of his brothers, whilst reassuring her she was wise not to marry into such a family.

A DAMP BRINE CROSSING

The next morning, Kitty awoke heavy-eyed and tired from all the tears she had shed during a restless night. She dressed and had her trunks transferred to the waiting hired carriages well before the McLaughlins rose for breakfast. Mrs. Tinsley wisely did not wait on formal farewells and left a note for Mrs. McLaughlin.

Kitty wrote a brief note to Joseph McLaughlin. M. DuBois packed plentiful travelling hampers with cold meats, tarts, bread, and summer fruit. They enjoyed excellent tea and chocolate at the breakfast sideboard. Kitty sent Taylor down with special thanks and compliments for M. DuBois.

June 19, 1814

Dear Mrs. McLaughlin,

    We thank you for your hospitality, most especially the genius of M. DuBois. My sons wish me to convey their thanks to you and compliments to your stables. Sadly, "time and tide wait for no man." Please accept my apologies for our hasty departure.

        Yr. Humble &c.,
        Mrs. Pericles Tinsley

Kitty's note was certain to be read by the whole household should she leave it on the calling cards table as Mrs. Tinsley had left hers. She arranged to have her note delivered directly to Mr. McLaughlin. The boys' valet had no difficulty finding him, for he was at the stables, seeing to his cattle.

June 19, 1814

My Beloved Irish Giant,

    I shall always regret you. I most deeply wish society was truly Christian and based their opinion on individual merit rather than prejudice. But that is not to be. I most ardently pray you will find happiness and prosperity wherever you go. Do not renounce women for my sake but marry as soon ever as you find a woman strong enough to bear giants! If it is any consolation to you, I shall pray for you always. Fear not to write, for I shall reply.

> *Be Well & Happy,*
> *Yr. Heart-broken Friend, Kitty Otis*

Kitty posted a note to Marianne, whilst Mrs. Tinsley informed Mrs. Abernathy and her own household to expect them back early.

June 19, 1814
Gleannri Manor, Ireland

My Dearest Marianne,

> *I write you now a brief note, for we are leaving Gleannri and coming home as quickly as possible. My heart is breaking in two, for I cannot marry my beloved Irish Giant, and thus must flee Ireland. The McLaughlins do not approve of the match, and disdain and disapprove of me in particular. The Tinsleys and I shall be back home within the week. I shall write you all the details as soon as I have collected myself.*

> *Pray for me,*
> *Yr. Loving Friend, Kitty*

The weather was fine and the roads largely dry, so the party made excellent progress. However, it felt like a much longer journey than their arrival. Instead of sightseeing, conversation, and word games, Kitty was silent and grave. Attempts to introduce conversation garnered absent-minded and mechanical replies. Kitty dwelt entirely in a world of her own.

They encountered showery weather and mud that afternoon, which delayed them significantly. They arrived in Dublin and had to wait there because the skies opened. The seas were quite rough, which put Mrs. Tinsley off attempting the crossing.

On their third day at the inn, Mr. McLaughlin found them in the common parlour, partaking of coffee. After the usual civilities, Mr. Tinsley inquired, "And to what do we owe the pleasure of your company, Mr. McLaughlin?"

McLaughlin fiddled with his coffee cup and explained, "I've come to test my cattle on the waters, this choppy sea being ideal for the experiment. Some horses don't mind, but some do. And those that do die on long voyages. So, I reason to take them out on short, non-lethal local voyages and only take those as are fit for the longer voyage."

"Ah, the longer voyage?" Mr. Tinsley probed.

"I make my way with a herd of breeding stock to the Sidney colony, Australia. As the servants no doubt told you, I demanded my inheritance from my parents. I've culled breeders for hunting, carriage, leading, and hacks. I understand the need is great there." Mr. McLaughlin elaborated, "There's a fortune to be made, and I intend to be the one to make it."

Kitty felt this was one last plea for her to change her mind, and she blushed to the roots of her hair. As she had been thinking of nothing else for the past four days, she knew her own mind and heart very well. If she listened solely to her heart, she was torn between McLaughlin and her family. If she listened solely to her head, England won easily. So, on balance, she was resolved to cleave to her original decision, however deeply it grieved her.

"I also come bearing parting gifts," he said as he presented small packages to Kitty and Mrs. Tinsley. Kitty thanked him and chose to wait until she was in her room rather than risk embarrassing tears in the public parlour. Mrs. Tinsley opened hers, which was a small charm in the shape of Ireland, fashioned from the famous red gold of the island. Kitty then turned the conversation to the horses, discussing the breed herd. McLaughlin took the hint, and they escaped an embarrassing scene.

After tea, they parted with decent calm, but it was the last time Kitty would ever set eyes on Joseph McLaughlin. When she opened his gift in the privacy of her room, it proved to be an old-fashioned Irish cross, fashioned of Irish red gold, attached to a delicate chain. Kitty, in tears, had Taylor fasten it on, and cried herself to sleep.

Their return voyage, hastily arranged by Mr. Tinsley, was grey and rainy, but otherwise uneventful. Kitty found herself bewildered by loss and feeling a bit croupy. She was home again at the end of the week. In the scant month she had been away, Mac and Mary had posted the banns. Kitty expressed her felicitations, but in her heart she knew not what to feel. She felt envy of their happiness and remorse for her envy. Her heart (and mood) wavered between true joy for the couple and irritation she had not known about the banns. Overall, their happiness only sharpened her grief. So, to soothe her heart, she wrote to Mr. Tinsley.

June 28, 1814
Dixon Cottage, Threlkeld

Dearest Uncle,

I take up my pen to impose upon you once again. My farm manager, whom you shall recall is Robert MacDonald, is to marry my housemaid, Mary Hart. I wish to make a wedding present to them of a scant half-acre plot with lovely prospects but that is virtually useless for farming.

I shall have the surveyor out and would appreciate it if you could draw up the necessary deed of partition or whatever other legal documents may be required. The survey and boundary markings should be in place within a week. Please come to visit any time after that at your convenience to attend to the business.

Yr. Loving Niece, Kitty

Her inspection of the home farm elevated her spirits. Although slightly feverish and tired, she felt obliged to admire Mac's handiwork. Rarely had she seen such lush, abundant fields. Kitty's new draft horses, Mickey and Molly, were vast, amiable creatures. Kitty was quite pleased with the three new milk cows and young bullock Mac had acquired for her. Mac had completely repaired and improved the housing above the stables for himself and the benefit of Pike, Davey, and the farm labourers. Kitty hired Harriet permanently as scullery maid and laundress, and hired two full-time farm hands on Mac's recommendation. Mac reported Davey was coming along well.

"Aye, Miss." Mac grinned as he managed the ribbons on their tour of the property. "Davey calls Othello 'Old Fellow,' Castor is 'Cast-off,' and Pollux is 'Bollocks.' Err, yer don't want to hear what he calls the cows!"

Kitty chuckled, which died off in a cough. "I am glad to hear he has mastered his letters and numbers and now thinks of this as his home."

June 20, 1814
Loch Leven Cottage, Ballanchulish

Dearest Kitty,

> *Your last letter was so curt, so obviously written in distress, that it wrung my heart. I have included you in my prayers faithfully ever since.*
>
> *I spent time in fearful speculation, trying to discern how the McLaughlins could ever have thought ill of you. Alas! I love you too well to see any great flaw in you. I cannot imagine any part of your character that would so alienate potential relations.*
>
> *I am uncertain whether good news would cheer you or feel like salt in the wounds, but I can contain myself no longer. I am with child! I will deliver in very early February, so Mr. Wallace and I are coming to stay with my parents at Christmas, and we shall remain for my confinement.*
>
> *I will not impose on you with rambling discussions of trivial news but do beg you to write with more particulars about your Irish expedition.*
>
> *Yr. Anxious Friend, Marianne*

Every conversation Kitty ever had with McLaughlin replayed in her mind. His every action, opinion, and idea were examined and re-examined until threadbare. Even though she knew full well the futility of an answer, she spent considerable time asking God 'why?'

She daydreamed about happy outcomes for her dearest Irish Giant, either living in retirement in Ireland or England. She dreamed about running away to Australia. Contrary to the facts that she already knew, the Australia of her fantasy became an Eden of freedom with no bigotry or prejudice. In her mind, she found a safe haven for their love. Then, rationality would re-assert itself. She would once again conclude that life in Australia would be more difficult and more dangerous—but no more just—than England or Ireland.

Kitty questioned her own motives, torturing herself by wondering if she had shown prudence or cowardice. If every person whom she admired deemed her choice excellent, did that make her a loyal friend and obedient ward? Or was she a craven opportunist seeking only the approval of others?

Even when diligently concentrating on something else, Kitty was ambushed by her own mind. She relived that horrible moment behind the yew hedge in the Gleannri garden several times a day. She grew tired of her own thoughts travelling down the same well-worn paths, re-thinking the same tired old thoughts. Like the echoes of loud bells bouncing off of hard streets, Mrs. McLaughlin's cold civility and cruel pranks recurred endlessly in her mind.

Kitty discovered reservoirs of rage within her heart and mind she had never before thought possible. Horrified by the depth of her feelings, every pride-driven tale of vengeance from history and fairy-tales suddenly made perfect sense. She slept poorly and spent many of the small hours of the morning sitting at her bed-chamber window, staring into the night but took no comfort from the twinkling stars or the soft silver of moonlight on the fells.

Kitty thought she was behaving normally. The household and all of her acquaintance knew better. Her rage at the injustice of her situation leaked out, despite valiant efforts to command it. She spoke in uncharacteristically sarcastic tones and barked out curt orders that sent her staff scurrying. Soon, the entire household began avoiding her when she was "in her mood."

However, anger and resentment were her greatest shield against despair. Whenever rage waned, Kitty lost all motivation. Apathetic and humourless, she became a lost soul wandering through her life instead of actively living. Withdrawn and silent, she undertook no drawing or painting. She dutifully took up her needle-work, but let it sit idle in her hands whilst she stared vacantly out of the window. She even sent Pike out to exercise Othello. She answered inquiries absently or not at all. Her dress and grooming were careless, and she ceased issuing invitations.

When her friends paid morning calls, she did her best to maintain appearances, but all her lively humour had vanished. She offered no conversation and had no interest in anything anyone had to say, staring glassy-eyed when her guests spoke. Mrs. Warden and Mrs. Fletcher were united in their concern and discussed it with Mrs. Sumner, who suggested they leave it to Mr. Sumner to counsel her.

June 20, 1814
Dixon Cottage, Threlkeld

My Dearest Marianne,

I am so bewildered by the loss; I hardly know how to begin. I suffered so many slights from Mrs. McLaughlin! When she first greeted us, she was so taciturn; I took it that her character is reserved. But she was an amiable hostess with others, graciously conversing on a wide variety of subjects.

The first day we were there, we were not called to dinner. Taylor was situated as inconveniently as possible in that huge, ostentatious house. None of the house servants would lift a finger to help any of our servants, and none would attend even the slightest order any of us made.

I was given a mare known for throwing her riders. Another time, I discovered a burr under my saddle. I was furious someone would stoop to tormenting an innocent animal in the hopes of injuring me.

Always, I made excuses for his family. I attributed their behaviour to anything other than what it was: a calculated series of insults. McLaughlin's parents deeply resent all things English. Even though the English Admiralty founded their fortune! The family does not despise me for any characteristic I own, but only for being English.

I discovered this when I accidentally overheard two of my dear McLaughlin's brothers abusing me in the most vulgar terms imaginable. That is when I knew in my heart there was no hope for my Irish Giant and me.

McLaughlin soon discerned the problem, and I broke it off with him. It was terrible to see his face. He offered to take me to Australia, "And to Hell with all of them!" But, paltry as this may seem, I could not leave my father, my mother's grave, my fortune, my friends, everything I have built at Dixon Cottage, and my beloved homeland, and told him so.

He was so enraged by his family's actions that he beat his two brothers who were vile to me, then had a screaming match with his parents. Their shouting could be heard throughout the house. <u>That</u> house, as large as it is! They all swore terrible oaths. I am glad I am not closely connected with that family.

Oh! How I regret Joseph McLaughlin! Hardly a day has gone by that I have not cried myself to sleep. I am so overwhelmed with longing. I long for the McLaughlins to see me for who I am. I long to *run away to Australia. I long for my Irish Giant to be able to make a home in England. Most of all, I long for your company, if only to cry on your shoulder.*

Mac is a genius, and the home farm is returning excellent profits. Aside from that, the one ray of sunshine in my life is your expectations. I wish you joy, and I am counting the days until you arrive here.

Yr. Loving Friend, Kitty

MISS OTIS SUFFERS A CHEST COMPLAINT

Kitty had definitely come down with a terrible chest cold. Her fever was low but persistent, peaking in the afternoons. Always, she coughed, and her chest burned like fire. She could not sleep lying prone and had to be propped up on pillows.

Finally, at Taylor's urging, she took to her bed. Taylor wrapped her chest in warm flannels and fed her tea, toast, and nourishing beef broths. Mrs. Abernathy supplied an herbal tisane with liberal amounts of honey and dried lemon rind to disguise the bitter flavour. The tisane was of material help in soothing her sore throat but did little to mend her cough.

As the week wore on, Kitty became much worse, in spite of the constant, tender nursing of Taylor and Mrs. Abernathy. They carefully protected her from any drafts. They kept her on a low but nourishing diet and had the apothecary bleed her twice. Still, she worsened.

Her feet and ankles began to swell. She was sleeping most of the day and night. Mary, Mrs. Abernathy, and Taylor took turns sitting with her and propping her up to cough as she grew weaker. Every handkerchief and flannel in the house was pressed into service and kept Harriet busy laundering them all every day.

Almost three weeks after exhibiting her first symptoms, Kitty awoke one morning with the faintest blue tint around her lips. Taylor anxiously pressed her ear to Kitty's back, listening for the sounds of water in the lungs. Although she detected no signs of water, she was sorely troubled by Kitty's turn for the worst. In tears, she called for Mary to take her place and went to the kitchen to consult Mrs. Abernathy.

"She's blue about the lips, she can't breathe, but I hear no sound of water in her lungs. The inflammation seems to be only her chest, but her feet are swollen, just like her mam 'afore she passed. I'm sore troubled, Mrs. Abernathy. Someone so young shouldn't be so ill for so long! What'll we do?"

"We'll write to her Uncle Tinsley an' see what he has t' say," Mrs. Abernathy replied. "I'll send Pike over on Othello straightaway. We should have a reply by supper time."

July 14, 1814
Dixon Cottage, Threlkeld

Dear Mr. Tinsley,

> *It is my Sad Duty to Report that Miss Otis has been Struck Low by Illness—an Inflammation of the Lungs with Ague and Catarrh, and is Coughing so Badly she Loses Breath. In spite of me and Mrs. Taylor's best efforts, Miss Otis continues to Worsen, we had the local Apothecary, Mr. Wilson, in to see her Twice, but with Very Little Effect. Mr. Wilson says her Heart is Weakening due to the Pressure from her Inflamed Lungs. She can hardly Breathe, and her lips were Blue this morn. We are Deeply Worried for her, as we Believe she may have got Weak Lungs from her Mother (may God rest her Soul). Please Advise me and send what Aid you may as Soon as Ever You Can.*

> *Awaiting yr. Reply, Yr. Obdt. &c.,*
> *Mrs. Timothy Abernathy*

Better than a letter of advice, Mr. and Mrs. Tinsley and the eminent Doctor Jones arrived after luncheon. Although the servants had done their best to shield him, Mr. Otis was also deeply concerned. Indulging in no civilities, the visitors rushed up to Kitty's bed-chamber.

"Oh! Hallo." Kitty attempted a weak smile. "Please excuse me." She was halted by a racking cough from just that short speech. "I was not expecting you," she finished in a whisper.

"Hush, Kitty," Eliza Tinsley commanded. "You will only make your cough worse. This is Dr. Jones, who shall attend you now."

Dr. Jones, a man of some forty years, wearing a conservative, old-fashioned suit and short pig-tailed wig, smiled reassuringly. Mr. Tinsley withdrew, so Dr. Jones could examine Kitty with Taylor and Mrs. Tinsley in attendance. Mr. Tinsley belatedly greeted Mr. Otis, his cousin and oldest friend. He relayed the news of Kitty's condition to him, offering many reassurances about Dr. Jones's qualifications.

"I could not bear to lose her, too," Mr. Otis declared tearfully. Mr. Tinsley instantly saw the truth of it.

"I have a proposal," Tinsley volunteered. "Let us call together Kitty's friends and Mr. Sumner and have a prayer service for the sick. We can hardly do better than to ask for His mercy."

"Splendid notion, Tinsley. Yes!" Mr. Otis agreed enthusiastically.

Within moments, Hart, Pike, Mary, and little Davey, were dispatched with invitations to various households. After an endless anxious wait, Taylor and Dr. Jones appeared.

"I am relieved to report that Miss Otis has no water in her lungs, but quite the opposite problem. The phlegm in her chest is so dry that all her coughing will not expel it. This congestion is, as your excellent apothecary pointed out, weighing heavily on her other organs. It is causing much weakness and an erratic pulse," Dr. Jones began.

Mrs. Tinsley interrupted, "But what can be done for her?"

Taylor and Abernathy, having been relieved by Harriet, came into the hall. "Come in, you two, come in," the doctor commanded. "She is not got so low from poor nursing! I highly approve of the flannels and tisanes. No, I desire to hear a more complete history of the case."

"Well, sir, I think, beggin' yer pardon, she got ill 'cause she broke her heart for the Irish giant," Taylor began somewhat timidly.

The doctor looked mystified, and Mrs. Tinsley supplied, "She fell in love with a Mr. McLaughlin, and they desired most ardently to marry. However, a visit to his family's home revealed the unsuitability of the match, much to her distress."

"Aye, and then a return journey plagued by rainy weather, and a damp brine crossin'." Taylor clutched her hands together in front of herself. "When she began to fall ill, over two weeks ago, Tuesday it was, I tried to get her to rest. But she would'n listen to me. She says, 'Do not fuss, Taylor, it is but a cold.'"

"Ah, now all becomes clear. A severe disappointment, an insalubrious journey, refusing to heed the first sign of illness. Yes, yes, that would explain why the infection has taken so strong a hold in one so young." Dr. Jones trailed off, obviously deep in thought.

After a few tense moments, as everyone waited for the doctor to collect his thoughts, Mr. Otis broke in, "Is there anything that can be done for her, Doctor?"

The doctor sighed. "I cannot pretend her condition is not very grave. She is quite weakened. The usual recommendation is Calomel to purge the body of the toxins of infection. However, as weak as she is, I fear that the cure just might kill. No, I shall recommend an entirely new course of treatment: Hydropathy."

"Never heard of it," Mr. Otis interjected.

"Ah, but I have seen excellent results from it." Dr. Jones grabbed his own lapels and began to explain. "One forces fluids. She should have Mrs. Abernathy's excellent tisane, weak tea, and broth every half hour during the day and then every other hour at night. I shall dose her with Laudanum to ease her breathing. Tomorrow, we shall plunge her into a very hot bath, heavily tinctured with mint and marsh mallow with a few drops of camphor. The bath will draw the infectious toxins forth from her. The vapours shall soften and loosen the phlegm and help her to cough and expel all the infected matter from her lungs."

"Bathing her, as weak as she is!" Mrs. Tinsley cried appalled.

"Yes, Mrs. Tinsley." The physician resumed his explanation. "We are in luck, for it is the warm summer months. We can build a brisk fire in her bed-chamber, keep all drafts from her with screens, and plunge her into the bath without chilling her. I am confident that Taylor can wrap her up in flannel and a fresh shift in a trice and prevent any insalubrious air from interfering with her recovery. Once the bath has worked on her, she will only need a few more treatments. I believe hydropathy, as radical as it seems, is her best hope of recovery."

Mr. Tinsley turned to the servants. "Mrs. Abernathy, please prepare tea for us all." Taylor and Mrs. Abernathy curtsied their way out of the room.

Mr. Tinsley continued decisively, "If you will excuse us, Doctor, we shall consult together and let you know our decision." Mr. Tinsley guided him to the library and ordered tea be served to him there. "I invite you to avail yourself of Mr. Otis's excellent library."

"I thank you kindly, sir," Dr. Jones replied.

At that moment, Mrs. Warden and Marianne's younger sister, Jane, arrived. Soon thereafter, the Sumners and Mrs. Fletcher followed. Mr. Sumner led the group in prayer. The servants followed along from the hallway, and Mrs. Abernathy assembled a respectable tea for the assembly.

Oh, Almighty God, who in thy wrath did send a plague upon thine own people in the wilderness; have pity upon us miserable sinners, who now are visited with great sickness; that like as thou didst then command the destroying Angel to cease from punishing, so it may now please thee to withdraw from thy servant, Katherine, this grievous sickness. Oh, Almighty God, whose nature and property is ever to have mercy and to forgive, receive our humble petitions; through Jesus Christ, our Lord. Amen.

Mrs. Tinsley and Mrs. Warden were of the opinion this radical new therapy was too dangerous. Mr. Tinsley disagreed and pointed out that traditional therapies had been to no avail. Mr. Otis finally settled the matter. "God would not send us a bad physician in our greatest hour of need. We should heed the doctor's advice, I think."

The rest of them readily bowed to Mr. Otis's manifest faith and authority as her father. Dr. Jones was summoned to begin his prescribed course of treatment. Under the influence of laudanum, Kitty's coughing eased.

The next morning, whilst sitting in a steaming bath, pink as a boiled lobster, the intense herbal fumes had their intended effect. She coughed and coughed, bringing up enormous quantities of phlegm. Kitty then slept peacefully, her breathing much eased.

By evening, she was quite evidently better, for she started to complain at having to force fluids and use the chamber pot nearly hourly. Her lips were no longer blue, and the swelling in her legs started to recede. Still, the therapeutic bath was repeated twice more on subsequent days, with excellent results. Finally, on the fourth day of her treatment, Dr. Jones pronounced her out of danger. Mr. Tinsley left Kitty in Mrs. Tinsley's care and returned home.

Kitty's pulse continued to strengthen, the swelling in her legs abated completely, and she complained of hunger. The doctor allowed some coddled eggs, milk pudding, toast with black tea, and discontinued forcing fluids at night. In another day, he discontinued dosing her with laudanum at all. He permitted her to indulge in a "light diet" and permitted Mrs. Abernathy to add boiled chicken, soft vegetables, and strong broth.

Although she still coughed, it was not the desperately painful, unproductive cough of the height of her illness. Within a few days, Kitty succeeded in her campaign for "real food." She was rewarded with beef and cheese, with the promise of fruit the following week if she continued to mend. A very grateful Mrs. Tinsley dismissed Dr. Jones after paying for his services. A week later, with passionate lectures to listen to the greater wisdom of Abernathy and Taylor, and repeated promises from Kitty to take care of herself, Mrs. Tinsley went home to allow Kitty to complete her recovery.

July 20, 1814
Loch Leven Cottage, Ballanchulish

My Dearest Friend,

> *I pen this brief note in response to Mrs. Tinsley's ult. to let me know of your illness. I have been praying for you ever since. I hope this letter finds you much recovered.*
> *Construction on dear Wallace's section of the canals is coming to a close. My darling husband is casting about for other opportunities— especially opportunities to design and build residential and commercial buildings. We are planning on making our way to Keswick on December eighth, and expect to arrive in time for Christmas week, depending on the weather. Please do not write until you are well enough!*

> *Yr. Worried Friend, Marianne*

Kitty did not keep her dear friend in suspense and penned a note via return post to the effect:

July 23, 1814
Dixon Cottage, Threlkeld

Beloved Friend,

> *I am recovering rapidly and expect to be well in time to shop in Leeds with Mrs. Tinsley for my fall wardrobe. I long to see you again and eagerly await your return to Keswick. I shall not go to London until late in the Season, so I can be with you for this most joyous occasion.*
> *I have long yearned to erect a terrace across the back, southern exposure of Dixon Cottage. Would dear Mr. Wallace be willing to design and build it for me? It is a very modest commission, but I hope not beneath his notice.*

> *Yr. Friend, Kitty*

From Kitty's point of view, though her life had been spared, it seemed meaningless. She read her Bible but drew no comfort. She felt swathed in thick wool fleece, no longer perceiving or feeling anything acutely. It was as though a giant hole in her heart had swallowed all real purpose and meaning from her life.

She diligently read to her father and amused him with card games and backgammon, and reassured him frequently that her health was improving, but did not confide her heart was broken. Finally, a month after her return from Ireland, the walls came tumbling down during confession.

"Why is God so intent on breaking my heart and spirit? What have I ever done to deserve any of this? I am deprived of all my siblings, my mother, my father, my home, and now the man whom I love and most ardently wish to marry! My dearest friend is married and is now expecting; my housemaid is happily married. Even that presumptuous little mushroom, Mr. Peale, is now married and about to become a father! Yet, here I am, unwed and barren, and likely to remain so. I *hate* God, and I am so ashamed to say so! But it is true. I can find no comfort in the Bible. God seems **bent** on making me hate him!"

Kitty was embarrassed to be shouting at Mr. Sumner, but Mr. Sumner was relieved. He knew, like an infected wound, Kitty's doubt, grief, and anger must pour forth to be cleansed, and restore the sad ghost of recent weeks to the vital young woman she had been. Kitty continued in this vein for many minutes, with Mr. Sumner encouraging her by saying, "You may be angry at God, for His love is incomprehensibly vast."

When Kitty had finally shouted and cried herself to a stand-still, Mr. Sumner counselled her. "My child, do not despair. None of us knows what God has in store, and He only sends us trials in order to strengthen us. I do not believe you are destined to hate God forever, Kitty. I believe you are destined to become stronger and gentler than you ever imagined possible, and you will share your strength. Do you now repent of your anger and doubt?"

"Oh, Father, I am sorrier than I can say!" Kitty replied.

"Then, let us pray," said Mr. Sumner.

Almighty God, the Father of our Lord Jesus Christ, who desireth not the death of a sinner, but rather she may turn from her wickedness and live; and hath given power and commandment to his Ministers to declare and pronounce to his people, being penitent, the Absolution and Remission of their sins: He pardoneth and absolveth all them that truly repent, and unfeignedly believe his holy Gospel. Wherefore let us beseech Him to grant you true repentance, and his Holy Spirit, that those things may please Him, which we do at this present; and that the rest of our life hereafter may be pure and holy; so, at the last, you may come to his eternal joy; through Jesus Christ our Lord.

"Amen," Kitty and Mr. Sumner intoned together. And, as Mr. Sumner had predicted, Kitty went away feeling much better. Months passed before she forgave God for His 'slings and arrows.' Kitty struggled with resentment daily, striving to abandon her resentment against God and forgive the McLaughlins and society. Each week she confessed, and each week, another little bit of anger and grief left. Slowly, hesitantly, and with many setbacks, Kitty once again began to participate in her own life.

As Kitty healed her heart, the home farm proved fruitful, and the harvest was abundant. Her profits amounted to two hundred fifty pounds, far more than her parents' larger parish farm had ever returned. Kitty thanked God for sending Mac to her.

Mr. and Mrs. Tinsley arrived, and Kitty handed over the deed to a dazzled and grateful Mac and Mary, together with his twenty-five-pound share of the farm profits. She improved his salary to sixty-five guineas per year. After she distributed gifts to the staff as she had the year before, Kitty still felt authorized to award herself sixty pounds to renew her wardrobe. That amount enabled her to hire seamstresses and spare Taylor and herself much labour. She arranged to shop once again with Mrs. Tinsley in Leeds.

A Hunt Breakfast

While the seamstresses in Leeds worked to provide her with the latest London fashions, Kitty and Taylor worked to trim up hats and bonnets and refurbish her existing wardrobe. Kitty could now claim, between her father's estate and her own, a fortune of over eight thousand pounds. Kitty dipped into the home farm income and set about establishing an excellent wine cellar with the view of entertaining more frequently this hunt season.

Kitty organized an elaborate hunt breakfast to open the local season. She ordered everything at the *Horse and Farrier* with the understanding that Mrs. Abernathy would be lead cook. Finally, all was in readiness.

Kitty took special care of her hair and grooming, electing to wear her new rose riding habit and a dashing new hat with a ridiculously expensive veil of cream *point d'esprit* lace. When Kitty was fully outfitted, she was pleased with the effect. After the hunt, she made her way through the crowd of mounted hunters in front of the *Horse and Farrier*. She ran into Lady Margaret, and again, had a delightful conversation as they led the way to breakfast. Suddenly, Mr. Blanchard stood before her.

"Oh! Mr. Blanchard, how delightful to see you again." Kitty dropped a curtsey as Mr. Blanchard bowed. "I did not know you kept a hunting box in these parts."

"The pleasure is all mine. You did not know of it because I keep no box. I am here at the invitation of Lady Margaret," Mr. Blanchard replied. "I hope your duties as hostess do not preclude you from indulging in a bit of hot chocolate or tea. Shall I fetch some for you?"

"So very kind of you. Tea, please; no cream or lemon; just a lump of sugar." Kitty turned to greet her guests as Mr. Blanchard turned to fetch the tea. Kitty was very busy greeting and seating guests, placing orders with the kitchen, and acting hostess for the next few minutes. But, soon enough, the hubbub died down.

Once again, Mr. Blanchard was beside her, offering a beautifully composed plate with half a game bird galantine, a delicate slice of beef, and a bit of the side dishes, including one of Mrs. Abernathy's excellent tarts.

"I believe it is proper for the hostess to eat at her own breakfast, Miss Otis." Mr. Blanchard offered her the plate. "So, I took the liberty." He escorted her to a table with one dish already laid.

Kitty smiled in return. "How very thoughtful of you."

Once he had seated her, he indicated the already laid dish. "May I?"

"Please do." She smiled before falling on her food with less than ladylike eagerness. After her exertions of the morning, Kitty was famished and more grateful than Mr. Blanchard knew for his kindness in provisioning her.

Mr. Blanchard, for his part, was admiring the brilliance of her complexion, her colour heightened by the crisp air and the morning's exercise. Mr. Blanchard's intelligence about their mutual acquaintance in London was more recent than her own, and they spent an agreeable half-hour discussing news of London and the Royal Society's latest gatherings. Then, Kitty appeased her curiosity about a very salient issue.

"Have you known Sir Richard long?"

"Yes. Indeed, we were schoolboys together. We have grown apart since those days, however," Mr. Blanchard returned, fully alive to the implications of her inquiry.

"Oh?" Kitty encouraged him.

"Yes, we have very different tastes. I am interested in theatre, ballet, science, and antiquities; Sir Richard favours dog fights, gambling, and ... erm"—Mr. Blanchard coughed with embarrassment—"'wine, women, and song.' I am afraid I am a terribly dull, rusticated, old widower." Mr. Blanchard smiled modestly.

"Old! Why, you are not even thirty!" Kitty interjected.

"Twenty and seven, actually; but dull and rusticated, nonetheless."

Kitty reassured him, "Well, that is a fortunate circumstance, as I tend to be dull and rusticated, myself. Although, are you quite certain you wish to be so rusticated that you still use your father's tailor?"

Blanchard laughed. "That obvious, eh?"

"Mmm." Kitty cocked her head. "While I do not advise emulating Sir Richard in any other way, he does employ a brilliant tailor."

"How can a woman with such unerring taste in fashion count herself rusticated?"

"Oh, I thoroughly enjoyed London's diversions when I first arrived for the Season. But I found myself yearning for the country again after only a few short weeks."

"I have a similar experience, although my tolerance for London is greater than your own," Mr. Blanchard replied. "I manage to enjoy myself for a full ten or twelve weeks before I find myself yearning for my estate. I rather suspicion one's tolerance for idleness varies with the company one keeps."

"Point taken. It is certainly no punishment to enjoy a round of whist with my Aunt Emma's talented circle of friends. They are card sharps, the whole lot of them. My game has improved considerably under their somewhat brutal tutelage." Realizing her party was on the wane, Kitty arose from her seat. "I must not monopolise you, Mr. Blanchard. No doubt, Lady Margaret needs attention. If you will excuse me?"

Mr. Blanchard leapt up and, making a perfectly correct bow, pulled back Kitty's chair for her. "Wonderful breakfast, Miss Otis, sure to set the standard for all subsequent social events."

Kitty, pink with pleasure, replied, "So kind of you to say so," before she hurried to bid her guests *adieu*.

DAVEY FALLS OUT OF A TREE

The next day, Mr. Blanchard paid a morning visit. Mrs. Fletcher's visit was drawing to a close, and Mr. Hart invited him to wait in the library. When Mrs. Fletcher had been seen out, Kitty discovered her guest engrossed in a back copy of the *Proceedings of the Royal Society*. As she stepped into the room, he immediately rose to greet his hostess.

"How do you do, Miss Otis?" he inquired as he set aside the publication.

"Quite well, I thank you," she replied. "Please feel free to carry off Papa's old copy. I know I would suffer terribly from an itch of curiosity were I not allowed to finish an article I had begun."

Mr. Blanchard tucked the copy under his arm. "Most kind of you."

"Shall we adjourn to the drawing room?" Kitty offered.

"Certainly. However, I come bearing gifts." Mr. Blanchard smiled and darted into the hall to retrieve a small parcel from the card table. He followed Kitty to the drawing room and presented it to her.

"Oh! Some tea! How lovely!" Kitty exclaimed.

"My own particular blend with red Siam and black Chinese teas mingled with dried lemon and orange peel. I do hope you approve," Mr. Blanchard replied.

"It smells lovely. I shall have Mrs. Abernathy make up a pot for us straight away." Kitty rang the bell to make good on her promise. "Father, may I present to you Mr. Blanchard of Eynsham House, Oxfordshire. Mr. Blanchard, my father, Mr. Merit Otis."

Mr. Blanchard made his bow, and Kitty continued, "Do sit down."

As soon as they were seated, Mary MacDonald, panicked and tearful, rushed into the room. "Miss Otis! Davey's fell outta tree and broke his back!" Then, belatedly focusing on the remaining occupants of the room, she turned beet red and dropped a curtsey. "Beggin' yer pardon, Miss ..."

Kitty immediately rose and took both of Mary's hands in her own. "Where is Davey?"

"Mac's bringin' him to kitchen," she replied tearfully.

"Excellent! Mrs. Abernathy is the best nurse I know. You must stay here and calm yourself, Mary. Pray with Mr. Otis. Can you do that?"

Mary nodded, and Mr. Otis reached for his prayer book.

"I have some modest field surgery skills and may be of assistance if you will allow me," Mr. Blanchard offered.

"I would be most grateful. Davey is my nine-year-old groom."

Kitty and Mr. Blanchard hurried toward the kitchen. Mr. Blanchard and Kitty were greeted by the sight of a chalk-faced Mac gently laying Davey on the hastily cleared table.

"He's fainted," Mac explained.

"Excellent! It will be much easier to find the break without hurting him," said Mr. Blanchard. "We shall need to strip him to the waist. You there," he continued, indicating Hart, "help me with my coat."

Hart immediately obeyed, and Mrs. Abernathy and Mac gently relieved Davey of his shirt and short jacket.

"We shall need him on his stomach. Try to turn him without twisting his back," Mr. Blanchard directed. Hart eased him out of his coat. Mr. Blanchard bent to a minute examination of Davey's back, gently poking and prodding before announcing, "He has not broken his back. He seems to have done in his shoulder blade, instead." Everyone sighed in relief.

"Harriet, fetch my Laudanum from upstairs," Kitty ordered before turning to Mrs. Abernathy. "Please fetch some of your arnica liniment."

"We shall also need a back-board and a towel or cloth to pad it with. The lad will need to be splintered for at least two weeks and in a sling for another month after that. This type of break is slow to heal," Mr. Blanchard said. "Can anyone think of anything to use as such?"

"Aye," Mac, who was rapidly regaining colour, replied. "I've some light lumber I was goin' to use fer a tray fer Mary. Be right back."

Everyone was much relieved to be useful. Davey, who was already reviving, was soon anointed with liniment, dosed with Laudanum, padded, and splintered. Mr. Blanchard gave explicit instructions on changing the splint bandages and Laudanum dosing. Then Mac carried Davey up to bed, and within minutes, the boy was fast asleep. Hart eased Mr. Blanchard's coat back on. Mrs. Abernathy resumed preparing tea, and Kitty and Mr. Blanchard repaired to the drawing room.

"Davey did not break his back. He is all doctored up and is resting comfortably," Kitty announced as they entered. "The hero of the hour is Mr. Blanchard, whose surgery skills saved the day."

Mary hastily rose from kneeling by the fire and spoke a heartfelt, "Thanks be to God! And to you, sir," and curtseyed herself out of the room.

"Well! That was hardly what I had in mind as entertainment for my guest! I do apologise for imposing upon you and wish to thank you for your timely and obviously expert assistance. However did you become a surgeon?" Kitty inquired.

"Pressed into service as surgeon's assistant when I served as midshipman under Captain Edwards aboard the St. George," Mr. Blanchard explained.

Mrs. Abernathy appeared with the tea. Kitty locked up her newest treasure in the tea cupboard and poured out.

As she handed her father his tea, Mr. Otis suddenly burst out querulously, "Why another suitor, daughter? I thought you were over the moon about that Irish fellow ... whatever happened to him? It is not like you to be fickle."

Kitty blushed from toes to top and stood absolutely rigid. "Recall, Papa, Mr. McLaughlin's family would not permit him to marry me, and Mr. McLaughlin has taken himself off to Australia." Kitty avoided characterizing Mr. Blanchard's visit in order to avoid worsening an already profoundly embarrassing moment.

Mr. Blanchard paid very acute attention to this exchange. He twisted his signet ring and fiddled with his cuffs before extricating Kitty. He began with, "I was very ambitious to succeed in the Navy and passed the Captain's examination. But I had not even taken up my commission before I succeeded to my estate."

Kitty cast a grateful glance his way. "Your father must have been very young."

"Yes, only forty-nine. A carriage accident in bad weather on a poorly maintained bridge. We lost all of the horses and most of the equipage. By a miracle, the coach driver and groom escaped alive.

Our coachman dove into that raging torrent three times, trying to rescue my father. I shall always be grateful to him. But too late. My father struck his head in the accident and could not be revived. I inherited when I was only two and twenty."

"How tragic!" Kitty sympathized.

"Yes. My mother took his death hard. Very hard, indeed. She now lives in the Dower House. Claimed she could not bear to sleep in the room they had shared. Spends most of her time at the main house with my youngest sister, Georgina. My older sister is properly now Lady Leyton," Mr. Blanchard explained.

Mr. Hart came in with Mrs. Warden's card. Mr. Blanchard excused himself very gracefully; Kitty introduced them in the hallway. "Mrs. Warden, may I present Mr. Blanchard, our hero of the day. Davey broke his shoulder, and Mr. Blanchard doctored him."

"Well, bless you, Mr. Blanchard! I hope little Davey is going to be all right," Mrs. Warden responded.

Kitty smiled. "Oh, yes. He is resting comfortably, now."

Mr. Blanchard bowed. "We are all fortunate Davey's case was so simple. He should be complaining bitterly about his confinement in a week and out of his sling in a month. I shall not keep you. Hope to meet with you ladies again quite soon, Mrs. Warden, Miss Otis." Mr. Blanchard bowed. Mrs. Warden and Kitty both dropped curtsies, and they parted amicably.

As soon as Mr. Blanchard had exited, Mrs. Warden turned to Kitty. "My goodness, what a handsome young man. Such lovely manners, too. I hear he has a substantial estate in Oxfordshire. Come now, you must tell me all about him."

"Well, he is staying with the Raleighs, and is Sir Richard's life-long friend," Kitty began, voicing her greatest concern.

"Ah. Well, I admit, that is a troubling circumstance. However, I would not wish to tar him with the same brush," Mrs. Warden advised. "I think it wise to withhold judgement until we know him a good deal better." The talk turned to other topics, and their visit passed away pleasantly.

* * *

Mr. Blanchard got his wish, and Kitty encountered him two days later after services. Mr. Blanchard offered to fetch tea for her. "Black, one lump, as I recall."

Kitty was flattered his memory was so exact, and nervous as well. She was certain Mr. Blanchard was courting her and fully alive to the compliment he was paying her.

She could not conceive giving her heart away again, bruised as it was. She was thinking of how best to extricate herself without hurting him. For it seemed to her he was an honourable man, not a mushroom like Mr. Peale or a self-absorbed schemer like Sir Richard, and deserved tactful handling. With these thoughts uppermost in Kitty's mind, Mr. Blanchard returned.

"Your tea, Miss." He smiled.

"Thank you." Kitty accepted. "You told me in London that you are a widower. If you do not mind, what happened?"

"Ah." Mr. Blanchard cleared his throat. "When I married Alice, she was but nineteen years of age, and I was only twenty-four. She died in childbirth—she and the baby both—less than a year later."

"What a tragic blow for you!" Kitty sympathized.

"Yes," he confessed. "It was ages before I could look upon a woman with a baby in arms and not feel grief. I am ashamed to allow, but it was even longer before I abandoned resentment against every young couple with a baby."

"I understand perfectly," Kitty said. "I was prevented from marrying Mr. McLaughlin only a few months ago. Like you, I find I am deeply envious of my farm manager and housemaid who married where they liked." Kitty was once more struck by his acuity, for his face expressed his immediate comprehension of her hint.

"It is fortunate that God did not create us out of porcelain. It is not a case of 'once chipped, always chipped.' Human hearts do mend. Eventually." Mr. Blanchard immediately changed the subject, and they talked on indifferent matters, parting soon thereafter.

Kitty continued to dance with Mr. Blanchard at local parties, sat with him for local musical entertainments, and laughed at his jokes at the Custom House after services. However, he never brought any more gifts and did not pay any more morning calls. Kitty was a little bit saddened but also relieved by this development. The hunt season passed quickly, and Kitty's thoughts turned to Christmas and the Wallace's visit.

ANOTHER CHRISTMAS

When Marianne presented herself at Dixon Cottage for her first morning visit, Kitty and Marianne greeted each other ecstatically. They embraced, with Kitty leaning rather far over Marianne's now distended abdomen. After the first flush of excitement, Kitty laid her hand on Marianne and felt the little one kicking within her.

"Are you buttering your belly every day?" Kitty enquired anxiously.

"Oh, yes," Marianne replied. "And it eases the discomfort of my stretched skin."

The ladies discussed the layette, Marianne's maternity wardrobe, and choices for midwives. In short, they had a lovely time whilst ignoring poor Mr. Wallace, who spent his time tolerantly bemused and making conversation with Mr. Otis, who reminisced about his wife's pregnancies.

At long last, the ladies awoke to the fact they were rudely ignoring the men, and general conversation ensued. Kitty renewed her offer of a commission to build a terrace, and Mr. Wallace paced out the back of the house and made sketches to "prompt his thinking."

The visit wore away amicably, and the ladies once again fell into the habit of daily social calls. Kitty more often called on Marianne than the other way around. The weather was so often very bad, and Marianne dared not expose her baby to such dangers.

Kitty issued invitations for a St. Stephan's Day party just before Christmas, with dinner to be followed by a private dance. She invited the whole Tinsley family, all of the Wardens, the Wallaces, the Sumners, and their niece and house guest, Miss Melissa Morely, Lady Margaret, since her son was in London, and of course, her house guest, Mr. Blanchard.

The drawing room furniture was re-arranged, and extra chairs were crowded around the dining table. Everyone was in their best looks, and Dixon Cottage appeared to advantage with liveried servants and fresh new wall-papers. The older couples played cards in the library, and the younger couples danced with every sign of enjoyment. During a break in the dancing, Kitty suggested that she and Mr. Blanchard repair to the library, where they interrupted the close of a round of cards.

"Oh, there you are!" Mr. Tinsley rose and smiled a greeting to Kitty and her escort. "I have no taste to go down to yet another defeat at the hands of my wife and her very able partner, Lady Margaret." He bowed in their direction, and general laughter ensued. "Your interruption is most timely, as I wish to present an investment opportunity."

"What is it, Uncle Tinsley?" Kitty enquired.

"A Lloyd's syndicate. Since the musicians are resting, shall we adjourn to the punch bowl to discuss it?" he responded.

Everyone consented, and after obtaining refreshments, Mr. Tinsley began. "I have come upon an interesting Lloyd's syndicate. A risky investment, and I would not advise anyone to place any substantial amounts in. It is very possible to lose more than your investment. Howsoever, the profits are so attractive. I thought I should mention it to you."

Mr. Blanchard opined, "I have always steered shy of Lloyd's syndicates because they too closely resemble a blind wager."

Mr. Tinsley responded, "Ah, but in this case, I know the vessel and the captain and am impressed with them both. So, this syndicate wager is not entirely 'blind.'"

Kitty asked, "What are you recommending?"

Mr. Tinsley explained, "I would not want you to risk your settlements, but a hundred pounds from the home farm proceeds would be appropriate."

"What profits can I hope to gain?" Kitty persisted.

"Typically, a five-to-eight hundred per cent return with reasonable luck. Otherwise, you may lose all of your investment. Additionally, you may be required to pay the ship's owners an insurance settlement up to five times your original investment."

Mr. Blanchard asked, "If this is so risky, why is it a suitable investment?"

Mr. Tinsley explained, "Because I believe in Captain Jackson. He is a very experienced mariner. He intends to import tea, spices, and silk. The captain plunges the merchandise into barrels of rice and then wraps the barrels in oilskin. Thus, the rice absorbs any moisture and prevents the stench of the oilskins from contaminating the cargo. I have seen Captain Jackson's packaging and am therefore optimistic for his success."

"I see," Mr. Blanchard replied. "I may be interested in this syndicate. What is the minimum investment and time of return?"

"A hundred pounds. We should expect to see Captain Jackson back in eight months, more or less. Lloyd's will write the venture off as a loss at twenty-four months, should he fail to appear."

Within a few moments, Mr. Blanchard had pledged to buy five shares, and Kitty pledged to buy one. An appointment to meet at Lady Margaret's home to finalize the transaction was soon agreed upon, and they resumed their Yuletide merriment.

Kitty and Mr. Tinsley arrived at Lady Margaret's at the appointed hour, and they were seated in the foyer to wait for their hostess. They heard shouting from behind the closed doors of the library, which was situated across from the drawing room. Kitty and Mr. Tinsley eyed each other uneasily, more embarrassed than anything else.

"Should we come back at another time, Uncle?" Kitty asked nervously.

"No, I think it were better we feign deafness," her uncle advised. Sir Richard marched out of the library at high speed, red-faced and angry. He ignored them completely and stormed out of the house.

Mr. Blanchard descended the stairs and greeted them in the hall.

"I trust you survived the recent invasion unscathed?" he inquired.

"Yes," Tinsley replied with asperity.

Mr. Blanchard fiddled with his cuffs, glanced at the ceiling as he collected his thoughts, adjusted his waistcoat, and sighed before replying, "I believe I can trust in your discretion; Sir Richard always arrives when he is least expected, invariably prompted by pressing financial need. Lady Margaret's man of business and I have been united in our warnings to her to resist her son's demands for money. So far, Sir Richard has been no more successful than Bonaparte was in Russia."

Turning to Kitty, Mr. Tinsley said, "In retrospect, your campaign to save Marianne from him shows some acuity of thought." Turning back to Mr. Blanchard, he continued. "Let us all hope that, with your excellent advice and the support of friends, Lady Margaret continues to be the Russian winter towards her son."

The conversation turned to indifferent subjects. After a few moments chatting in the hallway, during which Lady Margaret's guests conjectured, she composed herself. The butler ushered them into the drawing room. The gentlemen withdrew to the library to finalize the Lloyd's syndicate paperwork. Kitty and Lady Margaret settled in before the fire in the drawing room.

Whilst eaten up with curiosity, Kitty could not ask what had transpired and so, struck on an indifferent topic.

"How did you enjoy this past hunt season, Lady Margaret?"

"Well enough," Lady Margaret replied. "But I fear it is my last, or very nearly my last. I have grown weary of the long travel required. And I am a bit beyond actual hunting."

"I am sorry to hear that," Kitty returned.

"I shall sell this and buy a little *pied-à-terre* in London or Bath in which to retire. I have not yet decided which," Lady Margaret continued.

"I hope you select London, for then, we shall be able to continue our acquaintance," said Kitty.

"What a sweet thing to say." Lady Margaret smiled. "Are you not concerned associating with me will damage your reputation?"

"Certainly not," Kitty said without pause for thought.

"Ah, but my son is another matter." Lady Margaret sighed, her fists clenched and tears in her eyes. "He is *just* like his father. I am afraid my son has ruined his life, all because he has no real sense of honour. In fact, although his income is three times my own, he was just here demanding a loan drawn from my settlements. I refused." This outburst had obviously been pent up for some time and was only now escaping.

Kitty was appalled to hear such severe criticism from the man's own mother, even though she knew the truth of it. "But surely, he has some good qualities?"

"Well, if they extend beyond a handsome countenance and superficial charm, I have yet to discover them," Lady Margaret replied sourly.

Seeing Kitty's expression, she continued, "Do not be shocked, Miss Otis; my son has earned my every criticism. His father *ruined* him—taught him that all restraint and self-discipline was a waste. Never once did either of them understand the difference between ephemeral pleasure and true happiness. And now my son is ruined in all decent society."

"To see someone I love wreak his own ruin would break my heart! Oh, how awful this must be for you," Kitty sympathized.

"Thank you," Lady Margaret replied quietly. "I am so mortified. I apologise for having burdened you, but so many of my friends are now gone, I could not withstand the temptation."

"No burden at all; perfectly understandable when you are still upset from your interview with your son. Now that I understand your vexation, I am determined not to let your son influence my judgement of you," Kitty promised stoutly.

"You are a very great comfort, dear," Lady Margaret said with tears in her eyes. "Have you seen Hal Warden's new colt? It should be fit for hunting soon."

Kitty took the hint, and they discussed horses and hunting amiably for the remainder of the visit.

Only two weeks later, Kitty bade goodbye to Mr. Blanchard at the Chapter House before he left for London. She was surprised how much she missed him. To counter her sense of loss, Kitty plunged into preparations for Marianne's child, and finalising her plans for the terrace.

December 27, 1814
Dixon Cottage, Threlkeld

My Dearest Aunt Williamson,

I raise my pen to share joyous news. My dearest friend, Marianne Wallace, is with child and has returned to her mother's house, which is very nearly next door to me, for her confinement.

I should very much like to be here to share her joy. Mrs. Wallace is expecting in early February, and I calculate to be in London at the beginning of March. I hope that is not too late in the season, nor any inconvenience to you.

In other news, your sister is well, as are her boys. Alexander did very well on his examinations and is attending Oxford. He is as ambitious as Phillip and has chosen to read the classics with the intent of following his father into the law rather than avoid rigorous study and merely keep his term there.

You may be amused to know we discovered a warehouse in Leeds which announces itself "as good as Grafton's of London." I found many lengths of cloth at a good price, so I could afford to indulge in hiring a local seamstress.

I have engaged Mr. Wallace as architect for the terrace across the back of Dixon Cottage. He has advised we excavate and lay the gravel course now, during winter, so any sink holes will become evident during the spring rains. Thus, they may be shored up and made whole before laying the final stone this spring.

Always Yr. Affectionate Niece,
Kitty

THE BLESSED EVENT

After extensive consultation with Mrs. Warden, Marianne declined the services of the local midwife. She hired Mrs. Abernathy, the mother of four children and midwife to her daughters, to attend her birthing. At last, the night arrived, and Mrs. Abernathy was sent for. Kitty hastily dressed to accompany her.

Even though they had taken care to keep the path between the houses clear, they rode, with Kitty on Othello and Abernathy on Castor, rather than risk the carriage foundering. Kitty wore her very warmest clothing and boots, and bundled up in a coat topped with a riding cloak. Mrs. Abernathy, equally warmly dressed, was more prosaically wrapped in a blanket.

They found Marianne dressed in nothing more than a shift and slippers, reclining on the drawing room setee, rubbing her hugely swollen belly and perspiring freely. Vastly relieved, Mr. Wallace promptly handed his wife over to the care of the ladies and withdrew to undertake his duties as a first-time father. In other words, drink tea and fidget in the drawing room.

Mrs. Abernathy admonished Marianne, "Up with ye, lass. Walk 'till yer water's broke, and it'll go easier fer ye."

Kitty helped Mrs. Abernathy support Marianne's progress up the stairs. Once in the upstairs hall, Mrs. Abernathy briskly rolled up the carpets. "Easier to mop up the waters from a wood floor than it is to clean a carpet," she explained. Under Mrs. Abernathy's capable supervision, while Marianne paraded up and down the hall, Kitty helped stretched oilskin over the bed and folded up a heavy pad of an old quilt.

As they paraded up and down the hall together, Kitty asked, "Are you in much pain, dearest?"

"No, not exactly." Marianne panted. "It is deucedly hard work, and I am quite hot. The hardest part is, I have no choice in the matter at all! This is not volitional, I assure you."

"Aye, and a blessing it is. Or mams'd never bring themselves to get started at all!" Abernathy smiled. "Ah, there goes yer waters, ma'am, time for the bed."

They piled pillows behind Marianne, so she was semi-reclining. Mrs. Warden called down the stairs to alert Mr. Wallace of Marianne's progress. She requested the chambermaid come and mop up the mess and roll out the carpet again.

For two more hours, Marianne laboured in increasing pain, with Mrs. Warden, Mrs. Abernathy, and Kitty alternately bathing her temples with lavender water. They gently massaged her stomach after contractions and supported her back with their arms during contractions. Mrs. Warden, somewhat grey with lack of sleep, had gone downstairs to snatch a sip of tea and deliver news that the baby's head could be seen to Mr. Wallace.

Meanwhile, upstairs, huffing and puffing, sweat pouring off her brow, Marianne finally produced a perfect, tiny, still baby. Mrs. Abernathy gasped and snatched the child up, chafing his belly and back, but no life nor breath was to be discovered.

"Oh, oh, oh ..." Marianne could barely speak between her anguish and the continuing spasms of her body attempting to throw off the afterbirth. "What happened? What is wrong?"

Mrs. Abernathy wrapped up the tiny body in the receiving blankets and was going to thrust it under the bed, out of sight, when Kitty intervened.

"No! No, Mrs. Abernathy. Lay him in her arms, so"—gulping to control her own tears, she continued—"so she may bid him farewell. She will never feel right if she does not."

Dubious but obedient, Mrs. Abernathy laid the tiny still form in its mother's arms.

"Where did I go wrong?" Marianne whispered.

"You did nothing wrong!" gasped Kitty, appalled. "You loved your son as no other! I would testify before the bar to it." She attempted to wipe her tears and Marianne's, now flowing freely, and fiercely clutched Marianne's hand. "I shall fetch dear Wallace."

Blinded by tears, Kitty staggered to the top of the stairs. Mr. Wallace was standing in the doorway with his mama-in-law, who was evidently making her way back upstairs. Mrs. Warden did not immediately perceive Kitty's expression in the candlelight and called out gaily, "Alice or Angus?"

"Angus, ma'am ... and Marianne is as well as can be expected ..." Kitty, now completely overcome, could not continue. James Wallace went absolutely still. Kitty was certain he knew already and had only to confirm his dread presentiment.

"I heard no cry," he said in a low, strained voice.

Kitty took in a long shuddering breath and forced out, "Nor shall you."

Mr. Wallace's face drained of all colour. Mrs. Warden fainted dead away. Mr. Wallace caught her, laying her gently on the floor.

"Oh, I will see to her," Kitty volunteered, "Go to Marianne!" Kitty bustled down the stairs to tend to Mrs. Warden as Mr. Warden dashed past her going up the stairs.

※ ※ ※

February 15, 1815
Dixon Cottage, Threlkeld

My Dear Aunt Williamson,

It is my sad duty to report that Mrs. Wallace's son was stillborn. I cannot, in good conscience, abandon her to her grief. So, I must not just postpone, but rather, decline your generous invitation to visit London this year. Please accept my sincerest apologies for rebuffing your liberality so abruptly. Sadly, I have no taste for dancing at present.

Aside from the Wallace's tragedy, we are all well here. Mac is making ambitious plans to expand the acreage under cultivation. Mr. Wallace is distracting himself by proceeding with the construction of the back terrace.

Please accept my apologies for my abrupt, and I fear, churlish, note. I am called now to attend that poor babe's funeral.

Yr. Obdt., &c., Kitty Otis

The funeral, with its tiny coffin, was hardly bearable. The family stood grieved beyond tears, stiff and waxen-faced. Afterwards, Mr. Warden launched a completely unjust accusation that some lack of care on Mr. Wallace's part had led to disaster. Marianne began offering nearly hourly heart-rending prayers seeking to know *why*.

Suffice it to say it was months before Mr. or Mrs. Wallace smiled, and more months still before either laughed. Even then, they looked conscious, as though laughter were an insult to their son's memory. But slowly, and very slowly, they healed.

During one afternoon tea about a month after little Angus's funeral, Marianne compared the loss of her child to a martyrdom in Mr. Otis's presence.

Mr. Otis emerged from his fog and replied gently, "Martyrdom? Oh, I think not. Think upon the sufferings of St. Catherine. Or consider my own dear wife, who lost all four of her children to smallpox. All four at once! Little John was horse-mad and had already shown a decided gift for Latin. And to lose him and his brother, no male heir to carry on my family name? No, no, I will allow losing Angus was a painful blow, the *most* painful blow a mother can sustain. Remember, death is a grief even to God. Our Lord wept at Lazarus's tomb. Tears are appropriate. To quote from one of St. Paul's epistles, 'Do not grieve as one who has no hope.' So not martyrdom, I think, eh?"

Marianne blushed to the roots of her hair, and Mr. Otis continued, "There, there, my dear. Nothing to fret about. Time is needed to gain perspective. Years passed before I could feel grateful for the few short seasons I had with my children and recall I shall be with them again, in the end. You too will doubtless gain perspective in time."

Mr. Wallace, who had been anxiously hovering about his wife, caught up her hand and peered into her face.

"Do not worry, my dearest; Mr. Otis is right," Marianne assured her husband, with tears in her eyes, "I *do* lack perspective."

Mr. Otis reassured her, "Do not study so hard to be brave, Mrs. Wallace. Now is your season for grief, and this too shall pass. You are young yet, and though grief seems very dark right now, the light comes again."

An Invitation

Work progressed on Kitty's terrace as the weather improved. Mr. Wallace was eager to distract himself with his labours. The library window was enlarged into a double French window. Despite all their care in rolling up the carpet, moving furnishings, and shrouding the bookcases, a powdery fine stone dust penetrated every corner of the room. Much to Harriet's disgust, though the grit was fine as dust, no amount of sweeping would clear the stone away. The heavy, gritty powder had to be scrubbed off.

She had just finished throwing open the windows and wetting down and soaping the floor when she broke the back of the floor-brush and left to fetch another. Kitty and Mr. Wallace were on the southern side of the terrace, discussing the work in progress. Mr. Blanchard presented himself for a morning visit wearing a faultlessly tailored, fashionable new suit.

"Why, if it's not Mr. Blanchard," Hart said, beaming, upon opening the door.

"Yes, indeed, Hart. I decided to stop in at the *Horse and Farrier* and pay compliments to some of my acquaintance hereabouts," Mr. Blanchard replied as he handed over his calling card.

"I shall convey this to Miss Otis this instant, sir. If ye'll make yerself comfortable in the drawing room?" Hart departed immediately to deliver the card.

"Thank you," Mr. Blanchard was about to sit down when he spotted the ongoing work at the rear of the house through the open double door connecting the drawing room and the library. He wandered over to the opening in order to see more when he heard a terrible sound.

Davey, despite many warnings, was playing on the stacked stones awaiting installation out back. He fell, and his shriek of terror resounded through the house. Unthinking, Mr. Blanchard ran at high speed toward the sound of the child's distress. The wet, soapy floor entirely escaped his notice.

As soon as his foot landed on the slippery surface, his feet went out from under him, and he sat, quite abruptly, his legs straight and splayed out in front of him. His attempt to catch himself by thrusting his hands behind him had the unfortunate effect of accelerating his progress. So, he proceeded at high speed across the room toward the open French windows, his mouth hanging open in sheer astonishment.

The entire household was turned towards the sound of Davey's voice directly opposite the open French windows. Thus, they were treated to the sight of Mr. Blanchard as he shot out of the side of the house at high speed, landing square on his wet, soapy arse in the freshly laid terrace sand, before collapsing spread-eagle on his back.

Davey, who was entirely unhurt, was the first to respond. He laughed wholeheartedly, crumpling in mirth upon the turf. The household staff instantly retreated to the kitchen, where gales of laughter were ringing out. Kitty, Mr. Wallace, and Hart, who had approached to deliver his card, all rushed to Mr. Blanchard's aid with ill-concealed merriment. Hart was the more successful of the three and merely quivered violently with suppressed laughter.

"Oh!" Giggles escaped. "Poor Mr. Blanchard." Harder mirth followed. "Are you hurt?" Giggles returned. "Oh! I am so sorry! And in such a handsome new suit!" Kitty gasped as she worked valiantly to overmaster her laughter.

"Well," Mr. Blanchard said in a very dry tone as Hart helped him up, "So much for gallantry."

Thus, Kitty, Mr. Wallace, and Hart were entirely undone and laughed uproariously. When they were finally laughed out and had caught their breath, Kitty offered, "Shall we repair to the drawing room?"

"Ah, no," Mr. Blanchard said whilst attempting to brush sand out of his hair. "I thank you. Actually, I wish to return to the *Horse and Farrier* to repair my wardrobe. But more importantly, I am come to issue an invitation. I would be delighted if you and your father, and you, Mr. Wallace and your lovely bride, would consent to join me at my estate in Oxfordshire for the month of June. I have already spoken with Mr. and Mrs. Tinsley, who have accepted and will be coming to my estate with their boys."

"Thank you. I would be delighted," Mr. Wallace accepted with dispatch. "I believe a repairing lease would do Mrs. Wallace a world of good."

"I am not sure I should accept on my father's behalf," Kitty replied. "I am concerned for his health on such a long journey."

"Understandable," Mr. Blanchard replied. "However, I generally make the journey in ten days; eight days, if I am in a hurry. I would think stretching the trip out to twelve days, with a full day of rest on the Sunday, should make the journey easier. The roads past Lancaster are excellent. I will, of course, not wish your excellent farm manager to be deprived of the farm wagon. I intend to drive up here in my own *barouche-sociable*. Thus, with the valets riding postillion, we shall have ample room for everyone and all the luggage."

"An excellent scheme," said Mr. Wallace, who turned to Kitty. "Come now, in the mild weather of May; the excursion will be excellent for Mr. Otis."

"I cannot in good conscience accept on my father's behalf," Kitty said. Then she offered, "Why not return for evening tea after your valet has seen to you? Mr. and Mrs. Wallace will be here, and I shall apply to Papa in the meantime."

Mr. Blanchard agreed, excused himself, and re-appeared in a handsome new suit with freshly washed hair at the appointed hour.

"Ah, Mr. Blanchard, welcome," Kitty greeted him. "Do sit down." Kitty turned to her father. "Papa, you recall Mr. Blanchard has invited us to visit his family home, Eynsham Hall, just seven miles to the west of Oxford. We are to depart in the middle of May, stay for the month of June, and then return here in July."

"Oxford!" Mr. Otis exclaimed. "Why, that must be three hundred miles."

"Very nearly," Mr. Blanchard confirmed. "It is two hundred sixty miles distant."

"We would be passing very near Shipston-on-Stour and be able to visit with dear Aunt Shackford. Her health will not allow her to travel, and she would be glad of the company. I feel I owe her that much for all of the help she offered for my come-out. Will you not consider making this journey with me?" Kitty asked.

"Well, well," Mr. Otis replied. "You seem to have your heart set upon this adventure; who am I to deny you? Shall we take Biddle with us?"

"No, Papa," Kitty corrected him. "Biddle has retired. We shall take your new valet, Hart."

"Yes, yes, Hart," Mr. Otis said, slightly irritated. "That is who I meant."

"We shall be travelling with the Tinsleys," Kitty added.

"Tinsley is coming?" Papa seemed surprised, although Kitty had told him about the Tinsleys several times. "Then it must be all right. We shall accept then, shall we?"

"Oh, thank you, Papa. I shall write to Aunt Vivian straightaway." Kitty planted an affectionate kiss upon her father's cheek.

"Thank you, Sir," Mr. Blanchard added. "I sincerely look forward."

The next day, Kitty once again bid Mr. Blanchard goodbye as he made ready to return to his home, and they made final arrangements regarding the journey. Kitty was rather sad and slightly annoyed by his departure. She was deeply flattered that he had attended her hint and outfitted himself with smart new clothes. The thought occurred to her that prior to her thwarted *affaire* with McLaughlin, she would have been thrilled by Mr. Blanchard's attentions and already imagining her wedding day.

But now, as much as she liked him and missed him when he was gone, his attentions made her nervous. Her experience had made her shy in matters of the heart. Kitty reached up to touch her Irish cross, as she did many times each day, and said a little prayer for Mr. McLaughlin.

How could she bestow her hand on any man when she still thought about and prayed for her Irish giant every day? It would hardly seem just to her new husband, and she conjectured her habit would provoke jealousy in even the most amiable of men. So, she determined not to think on it too much as she was certain McLaughlin was a permanent fixture in her heart. She had a neat, comfortable house, excellent staff, a productive farm, and investments. She was not in any great need, and therefore, in no great hurry.

The next week, as Marianne and Kitty were on their usual daily ramble about Warden Grange Park, Marianne burst out with, "Oh! I am so put out. My father has now decided my dear Wallace is incompetent to care for me. Papa is ever critical, and my dearest husband bristles up and looks the bull-dog, and I can do nothing to restrain Papa or soothe my dear Wallace. But, oh, I shall be so glad to quit my parent's house this summer!"

"I perfectly understand," Kitty replied. "Let us just hope you can survive the next five weeks. Wait, I have an idea. What if we leave three weeks early? That advances your day of relief and still leaves enough time for Mr. Wallace to finish the terrace. I shall write to everyone and discover whether they can conveniently accommodate our change of plans."

Mr. Warden, bereaved of his first grandson, was eager to lay blame upon someone. He was also suffering from headaches, and much to his annoyance, was beginning to suffer palsy and weakness on his left side. Between grief, pain, and medical woes, Mr. Warden had, in his wife's phrase, "completely lost the plot."

Mr. Warden had trapped Marianne in the library. Mr. Wallace sat in the adjoining drawing room, able to hear their conversation as the door was ajar. Mr. Warden was delivering a terrific scold to Marianne. Marianne replied quietly and gently and attempted to soothe Mr. Warden into being reasonable. Mr. Wallace had a different response as he listened to Mr. Warden's irrational abuse of Marianne's character.

The newspaper he held was mercilessly mangled. With each passing moment, his brows lowered, and as though connected by a wire, his jaw jutted dangerously forward by an equal degree. Soon, Mr. Wallace did 'look the bulldog.' Finally, he could stand it no longer and hurled the newspaper to one side. He marched into the library peremptorily, startling Mr. Warden into silence.

"With all due respect, sir, I recognise you are addressing your daughter. But I would thank you to remember you are addressing *my wife!*" Mr. Wallace declaimed passionately through clenched teeth. Mr. Wallace then firmly threaded Marianne's hand through his arm, and in much gentler accents, said to her, "Come along, dearest."

Relieved, Marianne smiled up at her rescuer. They promptly quitted the room while Mr. Warden was so surprised as to be bereft of speech and watched them go. Mr. and Mrs. Wallace made their way to the stable-yard and waited there whilst Grandee was harnessed to their *cabriolet*. They quickly found themselves at Kitty's house, spilling out their tale of woe.

"You must stay here until we make our way south," Kitty offered in response to their plight. "I shall invite your mother and sisters over daily, Marianne. Please do say yes."

It was soon agreed. Pike was sent to Warden Grange in Kitty's carriage with notes directing the servants to pack up and present themselves as soon as possible. Within hours, the Wallaces were reunited with their servants and possessions. They had a lovely time visiting Dixon Cottage whilst Mr. Wallace supervised the last of the construction of Kitty's new terrace. In honour of the completion of the terrace, Kitty hosted an evening pic-a-nic on the newly completed terrace. Mrs. Warden and all of Marianne's sisters were invited for morning calls, luncheons, and pic-a-nics daily. The Wallaces arranged to meet with Marianne's brother, Hal, at the *Horse and Farrier* on several occasions and for a farewell lunch.

Mr. Warden's agitation and resentment only increased along with his palsy, and he developed the *idée fixe* that James Wallace was *beating* Marianne. Mr. Warden never actually told a lie or directly accused his son-in-law of any impropriety. He expressed 'deep regret' over having allowed a 'cad' into the family. He 'speculated' or 'conjectured' about Mr. Wallace's behaviour; he 'expressed deep concern' and 'anxiety' to anyone who would listen. Within a week, it was common knowledge throughout the parish that Mr. Wallace was a monster who abused his lovely young wife. All those who knew the couple did not believe a word of it.

Mr. Sumner attempted to intervene. "Mr. Warden, Mr. Wallace, as we well know from our inquiries, is an officer and a gentleman. He is a faithful son of the Church, and most significantly, Mr. Wallace is the very model of a doting husband!"

"Nonsense!" Mr. Warden replied. "A Banbury tale if I ever heard one. You do not know him as I know him. He is a cad, and he is the reason my dear daughter lost the baby!"

"Not at all, Mr. Warden," Mr. Sumner assayed again. "Marianne's doctor is certain she lost the baby because of her delicate frame and youth. Besides, I am Marianne's confessor, and she has made not one restraint—er—*complaint*."

"Bullied her, I reckon," Mr. Warden averred, stubbornly clinging to his *idée fixe*. "She is too afraid of him to say anything, but I see the signs!"

"But Mrs. Wallace goes smiling through the day!" Mr. Sumner attempted again but to no avail. Mr. Warden could not be moved, and Mr. Sumner could not convince him any more than his wife had been able to convince him, to be quiet or discrete.

So, with sorrow, feigned or real, all of the Wardens' acquaintance snubbed him. Whilst Mrs. Warden received sympathetic treatment and was invited to various ladies' events, she was of necessity excluded from any invitation that would normally include Mr. Warden. Mrs. Sumner felt so badly for him; she could not bring herself to snub him. She found herself ducking into the local blacksmith's forge for the first and *only* time in her life, to avoid him in the street.

JOURNEY TO OXFORDSHIRE

The Tinsleys, the Wallaces, and the Otises prepared for their journey. Mr. and Mrs. Tinsley were ready early, as was Mr. Blanchard. The Wallaces heavier luggage was consigned to Kitty's larger coach as their light *cabriolet* could not hold the weight. The abigails and Hart, due to his seniority, rode in Kitty's coach with the Tinsley boys, whilst the four other valets rode postilion, changing places with the grooms from time to time. The rest of the party were grouped in Mr. Blanchard's *barouche-sociable*.

So, bright and early on a Monday, a sedate expedition made its way through the fells of Cumberland. They only made twenty miles in the first two days. As they left the mountains for more gently rolling countryside with better roads, they were able to pick up the pace and averaged almost thirty miles per day.

The Wallaces spent most mornings in their own *cabriolet*, and gave it up most afternoons to the Tinsleys or their sons, so they could remain sociable with the rest of the party. Mr. Otis slept most afternoons, although Kitty made sure he walked every time they stopped to water the horses or for a meal.

On the third day of their travels, the entire entourage left in fine weather. But as they moved further south, the sky grew drearier and drearier. By the time they reached Stafford, the skies opened.

They arranged accommodations at the *Swan* on High Street to wait out the rain. The next morning, it was still raining. Coach drivers from further south reported it was clearing in that direction, so they set forth once more. Although they did not make particularly good time in the morning, the weather ultimately cleared. They made it past Birmingham to Cotteridge and counted it a good day's travel.

On Thursday, May 12, they arrived at Lady Vivian's house early enough to take supper at four o'clock and were quickly installed in their guest rooms. Kitty was saddened to see how pale her beloved Aunt Vivian seemed and how cruelly arthritis had twisted her fingers. But Aunt Vivian was as acute as ever and could still hold a hand of cards. She demonstrated her skill by teaming with Mrs. Tinsley, and trouncing Mr. Blanchard and Kitty during a double rubber of whist.

On Friday, whilst Kitty and Marianne were walking in the pleasure-garden, Mr. Blanchard was able to converse with Lady Vivian alone. Lady Vivian divulged many of Kitty's childhood stories.

"Oh! Kitty was an absolutely terrifying child," Lady Vivian declaimed with a chuckle.

"How so?" Mr. Blanchard inquired.

"She was a neck-for-nothing rider, even then. She threw her heart over the fence before her horse was even set for the jump. My poor sister had nightmares about her breaking her neck. Kitty was quite the tomboy in her time as well.

"I recall she came home one day scratched, bruised, torn, and muddy. Well, it was discovered some of the servants' children were cruelly teasing a little downy chick. She was horrified and rushed in to save it. The boys beat her off. When they were discovered, it took the boys a long time to recover from that whipping! But it was too late, the boys had set the little chick on fire, and it was dead. Kitty wept for days.

"Kitty could also be quite the dare-devil. She climbed into a bull paddock on a dare and fled into a nearby crab-apple tree when the bull objected. When the gardener rescued her, Kitty declared she had not, until that moment, realized she had the power of *levitation* at her command.

"That is so like my sister, Anna, now Lady Leyton," Mr. Blanchard reminisced. "When she was little, she was determined to be like Mama. When she was only five years of age, she managed to drag out Mama's presentation *saque* and draped it about herself. To this day, none of us can imagine how she contrived it. She was so tiny and the dress so cumbersome. Nevertheless, she managed to put it on and promptly became so tangled in it that she tumbled down the stairs. Our steward found her in a crumpled heap at the foot of the stairs. She was largely unhurt; we believe the dress cushioned her fall."

"To be a parent takes nerves of steel," Aunt Vivian declared. "That puts me in mind of the time that Kitty played at being Princess Pocahontas. She braided her hair and put feathers in the braids, and very nearly burnt a cornfield with her 'Indian Fire.'"

"I, too, went through an Indian phase," Mr. Blanchard recalled fondly. "Assembled my own bow and arrow set."

"No serious injuries, I hope?" Lady Vivian inquired.

"No, just a broken flower vase," Mr. Blanchard revealed with a grin. "I was made to write letters of apology to my mother and the housekeeper, and sent to bed without supper. My mother rather spoiled that last bit by smuggling a roll and milk up to me in my solitary confinement. But I eventually learnt my lesson. Now, I rarely repeat an error; instead, I devise novel ways to make mistakes!"

"Kitty's mother despaired of ever turning her into a lady. However, I believe she succeeded in the end. Except for lack of musical talent, and an unfashionable interest in science and politics, I hold Kitty can lay claim to the title."

"She most certainly can," Mr. Blanchard agreed, smiling. They arrived back at the house and joined Kitty in the sitting room.

Aunt Vivian exclaimed, "Oh! Kitty, there you are. Hallo, Marianne. I have just been revealing Kitty's youthful indiscretions to Mr. Blanchard. Please, won't you join us?" Kitty and Marianne accepted, and a cheerful party resulted, which lasted until it was time to dress for dinner.

At dinner, Kitty mentioned Mr. Blanchard's doctoring of little Davey. They soon discovered Captain Edwards of the St. George was Lady Vivian's son-in-law. A pleasant hour was spent establishing connections. Mr. Blanchard spun several fascinating sea-tales.

Later that evening, when they were teaching Mr. Blanchard how to play a progressive gin game, it was Kitty's turn to deal.

"Now, on this round, we have progressed to eleven card hands. The object is to assemble two four-card runs of consecutive cards in the same suite and one book of three cards of the same value; say, all eights. The runs of consecutive cards in the same suite are the trickiest; books are easier to come by, so I suggest starting with the runs," Lady Vivian explained.

"And I draw and discard by the same rule as the previous rounds?" Mr. Blanchard confirmed.

"Yes, and I believe you have first draw this round," Lady Vivian said.

Mr. Blanchard drew a card and grinning broadly, lay down two perfect runs and a book of fours, discarding a single card. The ladies all gasped.

"Two runs and a book, I believe you said?" he confirmed, smiling smugly.

"I have been playing this game for decades, and that is the first time I have seen a pat hand on the eleven-card round. I did not think it was mathematically possible!" Lady Vivian marvelled.

"Sadly, however, it does not count," Mrs. Tinsley said. "Kitty misdealt; I have only ten cards in my hand, not eleven."

"Oh! No!" Kitty exclaimed, blushing furiously.

"Oh, indeed, yes," Mrs. Tinsley insisted and counted out her hand on the table.

"Oh, Mr. Blanchard, I am so sorry," Kitty apologised. Mr. Blanchard's smug smile faded to a look of dismay before he rose to the challenge.

"Never mind, we are only playing for farthings," he managed as gracefully as he could.

Lady Vivian eyed him with wonder before turning to Kitty to say, "Well, if he offers for you *now*, we shall all be certain it is true love!" Which broke the tension.

As the visit wore on, Mr. Wallace overcame some of his shyness. One evening, he told anecdotes of his youth in Scotland, complete with voices and well-mimicked accents. Kitty was hugely relieved to see he and Marianne were overcoming their grief at last. Moreover, Kitty was surprised to learn she was growing to like James Wallace in his own right, not just as Marianne's husband.

On the last day of their visit, they once again attended services at Lady Vivian's neat, modern church. After services, her Aunt Vivian approached her. "I am sorry to see you go, Kitty. I wish to converse with you, as I shall not likely see you before you set out tomorrow." Aunt Vivian carefully navigated teacup and saucer to take a sip and just as carefully replaced it.

"Of course, Aunt Vivian," Kitty said as she settled into the chair next to her.

"I like Mr. Blanchard very well." Aunt Vivian took Kitty's hand and entreated her. "What is more to the point, I think he suits you. He is quite clever, with a lively and inquiring mind, and that is rare. I do understand you are still quite tender from losing your amiable Irishman. But I implore you to exert yourself to overcome. You are your father's only hope for grandchildren."

"I *have* been exerting myself," Kitty protested. "It is just ... as much as I work to master myself, I am not entirely the master of my own feelings and certainly not the master of my heart's desires. In short, the best I can promise is I shall continue to exert myself. But I cannot promise any result."

"Ah. Your desires. Well, my dear, it may surprise you to know companionship is a far better foundation for happiness than desire. Conversation endures longer than passion," Aunt Vivian advised her.

"Thank you, Aunt Vivian." Kitty promised, "I give you my word, I shall continue to exert myself and will try to attend your hints." Kitty kissed her aunt on the cheek in a rare instance in which such advice is accepted without insult.

"All we can do in this mortal life is exert ourselves, which is all I require of you, my dear," her aunt replied, obviously well pleased.

They had a spell of very fine weather and made excellent time putting up at the *Cromwell Lodge* for the night. Mr. Tinsley bespoke a private parlour for their supper, and they remained thereafter while Mr. Otis read out Chapter Eight of *Ecclesiastes*. The company bent their minds to a discussion of 'wisdom' and 'foolishness,' and its echoes of Aunt Vivian's advice was apparent to Kitty.

"Well, as we have all done good work and gained some small grain of wisdom, let us reward ourselves with tea and cards," Kitty suggested. Her suggestion was adopted, and the evening passed pleasantly.

The next day, they made their last twenty-one-mile trek to Eynsham Hall. They travelled through the bucolic landscape of the midland plains. Small villages and fertile fields presented themselves at intervals. They passed an occasional woodland, small pockets of the vast and ancient forest that had once blanketed the plains. The weather was sultry enough that every patch of shade was a relief. The landscape moved by so slowly and seemed so timeless that Kitty sometimes fancied they were floating through a Constable painting. There was little conversation, after a comfortable lunch in the heat, with the unvarying clip-clop of the horses' hooves and the well-known creaks of the vehicles lulling everyone to sleep.

The party brightened considerably when they turned from the toll road past impressive stone columns into the park surrounding Eynsham Hall. They proceeded south through thick stands of forest furnished with towering oaks, cedars, linden, ash, and plane trees, and continued past manicured open meadowland.

Mr. Blanchard acted as tour guide. "It is almost exactly one-third of a mile from the gates to the front door. Eynsham encompasses over 7,000 acres and supports forty-two tenant farmers, whose farms range from a scant twenty-five acres to nearly a hundred acres. The Hall was originally of Jacobean construction, built by Willoughby Lacey in the very early 1700s.

"My father acquired it in 1785, and vastly enlarged and modernised it in the following decade. As you can see, the original core of the house faces nearly due north, and the entrance is sheltered by the two wings of modern construction. Thus, it is rather shaped like a large "H," with the Jacobean part forming the cross-bar of the "H." The original house was only two stories but was enlarged to three stories when the wings were added," Mr. Blanchard explained. He spoke with pride and obvious love of place but did not appear to Kitty to be overly boastful.

"Goodness! It is every bit as large as Gleannri, do not you agree, Mr. Tinsley?" Mrs. Tinsley inquired.

"It certainly appears so! Do, go on," Mr. Tinsley urged.

"The southern wings at the back of the house partially enclose a terrace. There is a small formal garden at the entrance, as you can see, and a larger pleasure park to the south. The southern park has no water feature. I shall request Mr. Wallace present me with a proposal for one." Mr. Blanchard reigned in at the front door. "Shall we save the rest of the shilling tour until after everyone has had a chance to settle into their rooms?"

Mr. Blanchard's suggestion was met with enthusiastic approval, and they all alighted from the coaches. Before they could reach the front door, that vast slab of oak was thrown back. An obviously delighted butler in full house livery, complete with powdered wig and hose, greeted his master. A tide of dogs poured forth yelping, hopping, and wriggling with excitement.

The pack seemed to consist of an exemplar of virtually every canine known to England. There was one enormous mastiff and a small terrier-like dog. One dog had the obvious stamp of Spaniel ancestry, but the majority of the dogs were of no discernible breed whatsoever. Mr. Blanchard was soon occupied, pulling ears, fondling heads, slapping sides, and shouting out useless and disregarded commands. "Widgeon, get down! No jumping, Zeus!"

Once the first frenzies of greeting died down, Kitty realized that there were eight dogs. One of the terriers presented himself to Kitty by standing up on his hind legs and dancing in a circle.

"Oh, what a clever dog you are!" Kitty crooned, stroking his wiry fur. "Oh, hello, jealous!" she cried as a russet-haired Spaniel-like puppy attempted to nudge in under her hand. Then, the dogs fanned out and attended to the serious discipline of sniffing the guests.

"Mr. Blanchard, delighted to see you!" the butler cried out. "Your mother has equipped all of the guest rooms with tea and a light repast and bath-tubs, so your guests may refresh themselves. She desires me to extend her invitation to you all to meet in the library as soon as ever you may as Mrs. Blanchard is eager to meet you all." The butler stepped back from the door, bowing deeply again.

"Do come in," Mr. Blanchard invited them into his home. A well-ordered ballet ensued, with footmen appearing with luggage sorted as to owner, no doubt, instructed by the visiting servants. They were shown up a magnificently carved flying staircase that divided at the landing, with one-half of the stairs ascending to the left and the other half to the right.

They all trooped up the stairs, except for Mr. Otis and Hart, who were shown to a ground floor room. The little russet-haired Spaniel puppy attached herself to Mr. Otis, to his delight.

"Why, look, Biddle," Mr. Otis said cheerfully, "I have a new friend. I reckon she is hoping for some cheese, what?"

"It does appear she's adopted ye, sir," Hart responded.

"Yes, pretty little thing; reminds me of Glossy, our little Spaniel. We lost Glossy years ago, had not the heart to replace her. Then, with Mrs. Otis gone, well ..."

"I understand entirely, sir," Hart replied, coming to a halt. The footman politely held open the door for them, including the little dog, and they all entered.

Kitty had grown quite peckish. She was delighted to discover small meat pies, seasonal fruits, some nuts, fresh rolls, and Mr. Blanchard's personal blend tea awaiting her. Almost as soon as she entered, a soft knock landed on her door, and a footman and housemaid team brought in a large hot water salver to temper the cold water already served into the bath.

Kitty sank into the tub whilst Taylor freshened up her sprigged muslin gown. It suddenly occurred to Kitty she had worn the frock upon her first meeting with Mrs. McLaughlin. Abruptly seized by superstition, she bade Taylor to make her French-blue silk gown ready instead.

Taylor evidently apprehended the same memory and assured her mistress the blue gown was the better choice. Kitty emerged freshly bathed, gowned and coiffed less than an hour later, and stood uncertainly at the head of the stairs.

"Beggin' yer pardon, Miss." A housemaid approached her. "All of Missus guests are meetin' in the library."

"Oh. Thank you," Kitty replied, "Where exactly is the library?"

"Just downstairs, then turn diagonal through the entry hall, and continue on towards the back of the house. That'll be the library that overlooks the gardens out back."

"Thank you." Kitty followed the maid's directions and found herself fascinated by the house. The Jacobean origins of the place were evident in the simple oak wainscoting, now dimmed to black and carved flying staircase. Eynsham had been elegantly updated with plaster ceilings and modern light-toned wall-papers.

The furnishings were a blend of eras, some from the time of the original house, some more modern, and all coexisting happily together. Despite its size, there was much more charm and elegance and far less ostentation at Eynsham than at Gleannri.

"Ah, Miss Otis, welcome to Eynsham. Please allow me to present you to my mother." Mr. Blanchard hurried forward to meet her when she entered the room. He escorted her over to a comfortable group of settees. The Tinsleys and the Wallaces were already seated with an elegant, handsome woman of average height and frame, with light brown curls beginning to show some grey. Kitty was relieved she had chosen the silk gown, as it proved ideal for the occasion.

Mr. Blanchard introduced them. "Mama, may I present Miss Katherine Otis, of Dixon Cottage, Cumberland; Miss Otis, my mother, Mrs. Blanchard."

"Miss Otis, my younger sister, Miss Georgina," Mr. Blanchard continued. The young ladies curtsied.

Kitty would have known Georgina instantly, as she so closely resembled her brother. Although she appeared to be but sixteen or seventeen, she had the same soft auburn curls, the same elegant architecture of wide cheekbones and jaw, only more delicately moulded, the same arch to the brows and the same changeable blue-green-grey eyes. She was beautifully dressed, but not uselessly fine. Kitty found herself looking forward to her acquaintance.

"After being cooped up in a carriage all day, I expect you are all in need of some exercise. Would you care to join me for a walk in the garden?" Mrs. Blanchard asked. "Shall we wait upon Mr. Otis, then?"

"I would love to, but this journey has been very fatiguing for him, and I would be very much surprised if he were not sleeping. Let us summon Hart, shall we?" Kitty responded.

It was quickly done, and Hart presented himself with a very courteous bow.

"How is my dear Papa doing, Hart?" Kitty inquired.

"He's sleepin' peacefully after the exertions of our journey. I expect he'll awake and be eager for evenin' tea," Hart reported.

"Ah. Then, we shall leave him to his rest. I can always take him on his evening constitutional when he wakes up. Just let me dart upstairs for a parasol," Kitty replied.

"Oh, no need, I keep a ready supply here," Mrs. Blanchard informed them, whilst gesturing to a very practical brass stand holding several parasols. Kitty made a mental note to follow Mrs. Blanchard's efficient example at Dixon Cottage and fished out a parasol from the house collection.

A pleasant half-hour ensued with everyone chatting amiably and discovering each others' connections. Aside from the connection formed by Lady Vivian's son-in-law, Captain Edwards, Mrs. Tinsley, and Mrs. Blanchard had attended the same lady's seminary. Although they were in different years and had not known each other there, they were able to reminisce and chatted amiably.

"What are you doing?" Mr. Blanchard asked Kitty when they were turning from the garden towards the house.

"Oh." Kitty looked embarrassed. "I was mentally framing a painting. I am quite inspired by your park and wish to commit it to paper. Of course, I neglected to bring my water colours with me, so I shall have to create this study from memory and pencil sketches."

"Your talent lies more with paint and canvas than notes on a pianoforte?" Mr. Blanchard smiled.

"Did you not hear?" Kitty replied archly, smiling. "I said, 'commit to paper,' as in, 'to commit a crime.'"

Mr. Blanchard laughed. "You are too modest, Miss Otis; I have seen examples of your handiwork at Dixon Cottage."

"Too kind," Kitty replied, flattered he had that particular memory of her work. Mrs. Tinsley and Mrs. Blanchard enchanted the assembly with duets upon the pianoforte. Mrs. Blanchard announced she was hostessing a ball as soon as her cook, M. Colgate, had assembled enough white soup for the occasion. "I have already sent around the cards."

This announcement met with great approval from all the party. As Kitty prepared for bed, she announced the ball to Taylor, and they spent a few minutes planning her toilette for the event. Taylor had just finished running up a ball gown patterned after her trusty Russian-bodice gown. The silk was the palest blush, shot with deeper rose. Whilst the lines were very tailored, with no embellishments except for a modest demi-train, the elegant materials elevated the gown to sophistication, in Kitty's opinion.

"Time to break out them filigree and pearl hair pins," Taylor advised.

"Yes," Kitty replied. "I shall wear my double strand of pearls and Aunt Vivian's pearl ear-bobs as well."

"Aye," Taylor agreed. "I done up some velvet knots in a lovely shade of pink that's just a touch darker than yer silk, and that'll finish ye off proper."

"Oh! And my very newest cream kid gloves and my favourite fretwork fan." Kitty smiled and turned to catch Taylor's eye. "Taylor! You are on the verge of tears!"

"It's just that…" Taylor sniffled. "Well, this is the first time I seen ye gay since … ye know … since Ireland. And it's been most of a year, and it's only right to be a bit frivolous and happy at this season of yer life."

Kitty caught up Taylor's hands in her own. "Thank the Lord you are my abigail, Taylor. Whatever would I do without you?"

This effusion completely undid poor Taylor, who snatched up a kerchief and openly wept tears of joy. They comforted one another, and both went to bed happy.

The next day was filled with tours of the house and the perimeter of the estate in Mr. Blanchard's *barouche-sociable*. Tea followed and then fiercely competitive card play.

Miss Otis Undertakes a Painting

The next Sunday, the entire entourage headed north to attend services at St. Mary's church. Kitty was delighted to discover St. Mary's had harboured worshippers for seven centuries. It seemed perfectly able to do so for another seven. It was exactly what a church should be in Kitty's mind, and she was immediately at peace. She pronounced herself enchanted.

In the tiny run-down Chapter House, Kitty, Marianne, and Mrs. Tinsley were making the acquaintance of the local ladies. Mr. Tinsley and Mr. Otis reminisced together. Mr. Blanchard and Mr. Wallace conversed with the vicar, Mr. Norton, a young man of an age with themselves.

"I am pleased you are entertaining again, Mr. Blanchard." Mr. Norton smiled. "Especially the lovely Miss Otis. I hear rumours that she is quite clever as well."

"Yes, a true matrimonial prize. I must own, though, her preference for geldings is somewhat off-putting," Mr. Blanchard drawled. The other men laughed, as he had intended, and thus, he was able to introduce a new subject of conversation.

On Wednesday next, Kitty and Marianne were on a ramble in the pleasure gardens. When they were separated somewhat from the rest, Marianne suddenly announced, "I am again with child, Kitty."

"Oh!" An unreasonable fear clutched at Kitty's heart before she had the sense to offer her felicitations.

"Thank you," Marianne said in a small, controlled voice. "I do not know how to feel. I should be overjoyed, and yet, I am filled with dread."

After many jumbled thoughts, Kitty managed, "Have you seen a doctor?"

Marianne nodded. "Mr. Blanchard recommended his own physician, who was excellent."

"What does the doctor say, Marianne?"

"He says there is hope; I am older and stouter than I was the first time, so more able to bear a child. I weigh almost 115 pounds now. Oh! I know I should not be afraid, for God does not send the spirit of fear, but how can I not? Whatever was wrong with me then is wrong with me still."

"Stop that!" Kitty declared fiercely. "There was nothing wrong with you other than a delicate frame and youth! I've seen it in mares. The youngest ones, who are still not filled out, have the hardest time foaling. But after slipping the first time, go on to become proper broodmares, and so shall you." Kitty embraced her friend warmly, both of them in tears.

"What a wretched metaphor, Kitty. Broodmare, indeed!" Marianne sniffed into her handkerchief.

"You shall make an excellent milk cow, too, I wager." Kitty continued to briskly chivvy her out of her fears with an even *more* unsuitable metaphor. "Remember how painful it was for you to dry off after you lost wee Angus? You shall be a prodigy, my dear, just you wait." They embraced and continued their walk, with Marianne much comforted. When they re-joined the main party, they discovered Mr. Wallace fussing about with a sighting pole and transit level, making voluminous sketches of the gardens.

"Are we to know your artistic inspiration for the water feature, then?" Kitty inquired when they came even with him.

"Well, not particularly inspired today." Mr. Wallace shrugged. "The terrain is so level here, little can be done to create water pressure, so sprays are straight out. I am reckoning on a very gentle flow of water. It should also be restrained to compliment the Jacobean design of the house."

"There was one garden I visited with an urn at the end of a long shallow pool where the water just barely slipped over the lip of the stone vessel," Kitty suggested. "It was very slow-moving but enough to make the water dance."

"Oh, famous!" Mr. Wallace exclaimed. "Long and narrow is not good with this garden layout, but perhaps a circle."

Mr. Wallace resumed sketching furiously, obviously unmindful of the ladies before him. Kitty and Marianne smiled indulgently to see him so engrossed by the idea, which was obviously evolving before them. The ladies walked on without even so much as a by-your-leave, so they would not disrupt his creative fugue.

The day after next, Kitty took her breakfast on the terrace, enjoying the fresh morning air before the sultry heat of the day. Mr. Blanchard and the butler, Mr. Wright, approached, carrying bulky bundles.

"Good morning, Mr. Blanchard!" Kitty called out cheerfully as they approached.

"Good morning, Miss Otis," Mr. Blanchard replied.

"Miss Otis." Mr. Wright bowed.

"I come bearing gifts," Mr. Blanchard said, smiling, as he opened an artist's easel with a built-in tray. Mr. Wright opened a folding artist's stool and placed an abundant supply of water-colour paper and tins of paint upon it.

Mr. Blanchard explained, "I have procured for you brushes, pencils, rubbers, charcoals, sponges and pans of water-colours, all upon the advice of the artist's supply merchant in Oxford. So, I disavow all responsibility for any defects in the equipage."

"Defects? Why, this is perfect!" Kitty beamed. "Oh! Thank you! *Winsor & Newton* colours, too. This is lovely. Thank you."

"Ah, but my beneficence comes at a price," Mr. Blanchard replied, grinning.

"Oh?" Kitty returned, archly, with a prim little smile.

"Yes. I have no portrait of my mother," Mr. Blanchard explained, "Except for a miniature taken at her presentation, and I would be obliged if you would paint her. Perhaps a portrait of her in the garden?"

"Oho, the true depth of your cunning design is now known!" Kitty joked. "Thank God this is no barbaric court where the artist who produced an unflattering portrait paid for it with his head. What will you do if I fumble this particular commission?"

He smiled, then teased, "Obviously, I shall confiscate the supplies and send you home in disgrace."

"A dreadful punishment, indeed." Kitty laughed. "Quite enough to make me too nervous to perform at all!"

"I foresee very little chance of that, Miss Otis," he reassured her. "Perhaps we can tuck your equipment into a corner of the library, so you need not carry it up and down the stairs to execute your painting?"

Kitty agreed enthusiastically.

That evening, as they all assembled in the library before dinner, Mr. Wallace brought forth his sketches. Mr. Blanchard commissioned the project on the spot with the work to begin immediately. Mrs. Blanchard insisted on transplanting the existing bay laurels, peonies, and roses, rather than removing them. The ladies cheerfully entered into her garden planning. They scattered the transplants to various corners of the garden with good effect. By the end of the week, work on the water feature had begun in earnest.

Kitty made excellent progress on the portrait. By replacing the strands of grey with honey gold and ignoring a certain laxity along the jaw line, Kitty produced a lovely painting of Mrs. Blanchard in her prime, or as near to it as anyone could recollect.

Mr. Blanchard enthused, "Why, that is a wonderful likeness!"

"I am so pleased you approve," Kitty replied. "But you really should have one executed in oils for a permanent record. Water-colours fade so quickly."

"Done and done," Mr. Blanchard replied. "I now see your cunning design: to acquire even more art supplies."

"Yes, of course. I came into Oxfordshire with no other view." Kitty smiled back.

"I am afraid I must excuse myself; I am late making my rounds of the tenant farmers," Mr. Blanchard apologised.

"Oh," Kitty said. "I so envy you! I dearly long to interview farmers, so I may learn to improve the management of Dixon Cottage farm."

"You wish to accompany me?" Mr. Blanchard asked, surprised.

"Please excuse me." Suddenly shy and flustered, Kitty blushed. "I did not intend to beg an invitation, but I most ardently desire to learn more of farming."

"I can think of nothing so delightful as your companionship whilst performing my duties," Mr. Blanchard replied.

She collected her parasol, and they were soon seated comfortably in his *curricle*, making their way to visit the most important of his tenants. They passed a boggy field, and Kitty offered, "I had some boggy fields. Mac planted water-loving trees like alder, birch, and willow along the highest edge of the field to take up the water. They are only two years old, so the trees are not fully performing their office, but it has helped already. We run sheep on those fields quite profitably."

Mr. Blanchard smiled. "I shall mention your sound suggestion to Mr. Lark, my land steward, whom I see just over there." He indicated a stout farmer with two other young men in the middle of a field to their left. They reined up, and by the time Mr. Blanchard had handed her down, Mr. Lark had approached the *curricle* trailed by the youths.

Introductions were made. The youths were Mr. Lark's sons.

Kitty's suggestion was passed on. A fascinating discussion concerning sheep breeding followed. They discussed the final complex details of a land-use agreement with some off-site shepherds. Kitty learnt much about farming as the day wore on. First, by listening intently to the conversations. Second, by asking questions in the *curricle* between visits.

She learnt even more about Mr. Blanchard, however. His tenants, while respectful, were not cringing lackeys. They all held him in esteem and sought his opinion, laughed at his jokes, and he at theirs. Some of the tenantss cottages were substantial stone and brick buildings and seemed comfortable and well kept.

One bold fellow tipped his hat to her, saying, "We were wonderin' what was takin' him so long to make the visits; well, now 'tis no wonder at all."

"Oh, I'm so pleased to hear you say so. I thought Mr. Blanchard just brought me along as ballast," Kitty replied with a coquettish twirl of her parasol.

When they were again in the *curricle* headed for Eynsham Hall, Mr. Blanchard smiled. "I started today thinking you would have the tenants eating out of your hand in two or three visits, but I perceive you have managed it in one."

"Oh, you give me too much credit!" Kitty cried gaily. "But I shall gladly accept."

Her eyes were sparkling, and her cheeks pink with delight at his compliment, Kitty was in her best looks. Mr. Blanchard contemplated her with admiration. He resumed his role as guide and told her all the local legends of various landmarks they passed on the way back to Eynsham.

For her part, Kitty was thinking admiring thoughts about a man who was obviously a good landlord and active steward of his own property. So many people were dependent upon him for their happiness, and he wore his responsibility well.

Kitty was eager to learn from Mr. Blanchard, an astute scientific farmer. He was conducting several interesting breeding experiments with heavy draft horses. She spent a very pleasant return ride plumbing the depths of his knowledge. He made her laugh with well-told tales of his tenant farmers and other locals.

Her entire day's adventure was promptly related to Marianne before everyone gathered for supper. "I had a very instructional tour of the estate."

"So, you enjoyed touring his holdings?" Marianne inquired, then teased, "How crassly ambitious of you."

"Yes, indeed," Kitty responded enthusiastically. "Eynsham Hall, with all its dependencies, is certainly superior to Mr. Peale's offer of two hundred pounds per year and the expectation of forty acres!" They both laughed at the memory.

"Are you so confident he will offer for you?" Marianne asked.

"Not at all. Not *yet*, anyway," Kitty replied. "But I am certain he is thinking of it. Why else would he invite all of us here?"

"Point taken. Mr. Blanchard is also materially aiding Wallace's career," Marianne reported. "He showed my dear Wallace's design sketches to Mr. Norton and the Parish Council, and they are debating on hiring him to design a new Chapter House."

"The parish certainly needs one," Kitty interjected.

"Yes, but that is not all," Marianne continued. "He has also shown your ink drawing of the terrace at Dixon Cottage to other friends. It looks as though dear Wallace is in contention for several larger commissions. I am convinced the harsh winter last year materially contributed to my difficulties with, you know, with the last time. I confess I would be much happier staying here in this gentler climate since the baby is due in March."

"I am sure you are right about the weather," Kitty agreed. "Oh, how delightful! This is such beautiful country, and with a much better climate than Keswick. Do you think your mother would come down here for your confinement? It is such a long way."

Marianne laughed. "I would be hard-pressed to keep her from it!"

"Oh, I believe this is a delightful development." Kitty clasped her hands in excitement. "This has sparked a hope in me; we may both settle here and remain close friends forever."

"I confess, the thought occurred to me," Marianne replied. The rest of their conversation had to be deferred, as it was time for supper.

THE EYNSHAM BALL

Friday evening, Taylor pinned up Kitty's hair, cut a very delicate fringe around the back, and styled her hair into large, loose curls, each highlighted with a tiny filigree pin. Kitty was very pleased with the effect and, confident in her appearance, fairly skipped down the stairs.

Mr. Blanchard and one of his guests were in the receiving hall at the base of the stairs. Mr. Blanchard smiled appreciatively. His guest, a very dandified young gentleman of sixteen or seventeen years, goggled at her. When she achieved the bottom of the stair, Mr. Blanchard introduced them.

"Lord Dankworth, may I present Miss Otis, of Dixon Cottage, Cumberland." Mr. Blanchard began smoothly, "Miss Otis, Lord Dankworth of Nuneham House, Nuneham Courtenay."

"How do you do," Kitty replied with a curtsey.

"Delighted to make your acquaintance, Miss Otis." Lord Dankworth made his bow with many ostentatious flourishes in keeping with his elaborate tailoring. Both gentlemen held out their arms to her, silently offering escort service. Kitty pretended not to have seen Lord Dankworth's gesture, took up Mr. Blanchard's arm, and they proceeded to the Green Hall.

A curious name for the room, as there was very little green in the *décor*. But, at a solid fifty feet by thirty feet, it was the most suitable room in the house for dancing. The Green Hall was just west of the library and opened out onto the back terrace. The large French windows were closed to protect the older guests from the soft summer breeze. The carpets had been removed from ancient parquetry floors, and the musicians were arrayed in a balcony overlooking the main body. The refreshments table was bright with summer flowers, beautiful cut glass cups, tempting piles of rout cakes, tiny sweetmeats, and several attractive punch bowls.

"May I offer you some punch, or perhaps champagne?" Mr. Blanchard offered.

"Oh, no. Not yet. After a few dances, perhaps," Kitty replied with a bright smile.

"Well, don't mind if *I* do," Lord Dankworth said and made a bee-line to the punch bowl.

The musicians started, and Kitty and Mr. Blanchard led off the first dance. As she recalled from her first season in London, Mr. Blanchard was a talented dancer, and the time passed quite enjoyably.

During the interval between dances, Mr. Blanchard went to fetch refreshments, and Kitty settled on a cool stone bench on the terrace. Almost immediately, she was accosted by Lord Dankworth, already well in his cups.

"Oh! Mish Ott ... Odd ... Odish, how de do." Lord Dankworth attempted a very wobbling bow.

"Far better than you, I expect," Kitty returned tartly.

"Sho bu ... boo ... beautiful." He hiccupped, and Kitty was treated to an overwhelming odour of strong spirits. "C'mon, give ush a kish." As he lunged for her, she turned her head, so his slobbering kiss landed on her upper cheek and ear.

Kitty leaned back on the bench and did her best to push him off. He was as relaxed as a rag doll; a very, *very* heavy rag doll. She was unsuccessful in pushing him away, but he succeeded in dragging her away from her seat.

As he reeled back, preparing for another assault, Kitty was seized by inspiration. She hopped up onto the bench and quickly down on the other side. Lord Dankworth blinked owlishly, obviously convinced Kitty had vanished altogether. Kitty's triumph was short-lived, however, as Lord Dankworth spun in a slow staggering circle and spied her in short order. As he came staggering towards her, Kitty backed towards the French doors.

"Stop before you embarrass yourself farther!" Kitty hissed before backing up into someone.

"Oh, so sorry." Kitty turned her head and realised it was Mr. Blanchard returning with refreshments. She perceived on his face an expression she had never seen there before, a stern purpose and aura of command. Kitty smiled gratefully up at her rescuer. "Just avoiding a drunken puppy."

"So I see. My apologies for my guest's behaviour," Mr. Blanchard gave the plate of sweetmeats and the glasses of punch to Kitty. In two quick strides, he reached Lord Dankworth, grabbed him by the collar of his coat, and shook him like an errant puppy.

"Uh-oh. Ah, noooo ..." Lord Dankworth moaned. Kitty immediately recognised the symptoms. She balanced the cups on the plate, used her other hand to gather up her skirts, and hopped up onto the stone bench again with great agility. And only just in time. Lord Dankworth vomited voluminously right where Kitty had been standing.

"Ugh, rum!" Mr. Blanchard commented.

"What?" Kitty asked, quivering with barely contained mirth. "All you have on offer is punch and wine."

"Must have brought his own supply," Mr. Blanchard returned sourly. "I recognise the smell from my tour as Snotty Keeper."

"*Snotty Keeper?*" Kitty asked, now openly laughing.

"Lieutenant in charge of newly commissioned ensigns on their first cruise," Mr. Blanchard enlightened her.

"Shall I send for someone?" Kitty inquired.

"Yes, please," Mr. Blanchard replied. "I shall continue walking him on the grass yard over there."

"I shall order volumes of weak tea and sops, my sovereign remedy for drunkenness," Kitty promised as she once again hopped off the bench on the dry side and hurried inside.

Mr. Blanchard's valet appeared in short order, and a footman followed with a large pot of tea and sops shortly thereafter. As a testament to the efficiency of the staff, Lord Dankworth's accident was being cleaned by the time Kitty completed her errand. She gathered up the plate and cups and returned to meet Mr. Blanchard on the other side of the terrace after he passed Dankworth off to a servant.

Kitty handed Mr. Blanchard a punch cup and set the plate down beside her on another stone bench. "Now, where were we?"

"I was about to demand the next two dances in honour of my timely rescue," Mr. Blanchard said.

"But will you not offend some of your other lady guests?" Kitty asked.

"Not at all. No one is counting." He shrugged and corrected himself with a grin. "Well, no one except my mother, and she approves."

"Ah. Well, with that authorisation, who could say no?" Kitty accepted.

"Let us be about it promptly, then; that reel is about to end," Mr. Blanchard said, smiling broadly.

Kitty boldly over-set convention to dance the next two with Mr. Blanchard and danced the night away happily with the rest of the guests. She paused only to converse with Marianne between sets, as Marianne, quite naturally, was avoiding dancing.

"I detect love in the air," Marianne said to her when Kitty sat down after dancing with Mr. Blanchard.

"Oh?" Kitty replied, fanning herself.

"*Three* dances with Mr. Blanchard. You are the talk of the ball," Marianne explained.

Kitty coloured slightly. "He said no one was counting except his mother, who would approve."

"Yes, I have heard gentlemen say very similar things, but they are invariably wrong. *Everyone* is counting," Marianne corrected.

"Oh, dear, I hope I have not offended anyone," Kitty remarked.

"Well, yes, some are offended," Marianne replied. "But those who are offended would be offended by anything you do. They find your very existence offensive, as they wanted to capture Mr. Blanchard's notice for themselves or for their daughters. You will never be able to please that crowd, so it is useless to worry. As to the rest of us, we all love you, and you are incapable of offending us, your greatest champions."

"I am vastly reassured," Kitty responded and promptly retailed her adventure with Lord Dankworth.

After laughing heartily at his youthful folly, Marianne remarked, "I shall assay no punishment for him. From the sound of things, his head-ache in the morning will be punishment enough!"

"No doubt!" Kitty replied before she was whisked away for another dance.

After having bid her *adieux* to the Blanchards, she rattled on happily about the party to Taylor whilst preparing for bed. Taylor was very pleased with this latest development, which she interpreted as a sign that Kitty's heart was on the mend. Kitty left orders to be awakened early, as she had an appointment to walk with Mrs. Blanchard and Georgiana the next morning in the garden.

As she, Mrs. Blanchard, and Georgiana were organising for a civilised hour of admiring flowers, very different preparations were being made on the other side of Eynsham Hall. After breakfast,

Mr. Blanchard called for his valet. "Abercrombie, we shall be making a schooling voyage this morning."

"Oh, aye, Sir?" Ambercrombie replied.

"Bring Old Bess, loaded with powder and wad, but no shot," Mr. Blanchard ordered. "I want the old blunderbuss to produce an impressive cloud of smoke but do no harm otherwise, understood?"

Ambercrombie nodded his understanding.

"When Lord Dankworth has his *phaeton* harnessed, I want to be informed immediately, and my *curricle* harnessed as well. Bolt and Challenger seem in fine fettle and should handily beat that flashy Yorkshire Trotter he uses. I believe this is a lesson best served in Ladywell Woods before we make the main road."

"Aye, sir," replied Ambercrombie.

Early that afternoon, Lord Dankworth finally dragged his aching head out of bed and ordered his phaeton. Mr. Blanchard's orders were carried out, and he and Ambercrombie set off only seconds after Lord Dankworth. They perceived the young Lord enter Ladywell Wood before them, and Mr. Blanchard shook out the reins. Bolt and Challenger responded beautifully, obviously excited to be pulling together, and the *curricle* overtook Lord Dankworth's *phaeton* in less than a minute.

"Have you got a bead on him?" Mr. Blanchard asked.

Ambercrombie settled the huge old duelling pistol on his forearm, "*Phaeton's* in the crosshairs, sir."

Reining in his team so as to pull even with the phaeton, Mr. Blanchard called out gaily, "Fire starboard guns!"

"Aye, aye, sir," Ambercrombie acknowledged and fired.

A huge cloud of burnt powder burst forth, and the whey-faced Lord Dankworth squealed like a frightened schoolgirl. He panicked, promptly overturned his *phaeton*, and was unceremoniously dumped in the thick leaf mould under the trees. Mr. Blanchard expertly reined in his horses and even backed them a bit to come level with the phaeton.

"See to Dankworth's poor horse, Abercrombie," Mr. Blanchard ordered as he tied off the reins of his own team. Mr. Blanchard stalked over to the green-faced young gentleman still sitting on the forest floor, clutching his head in his hands. He grabbed Dankworth's arm.

"Stand up," he ordered curtly and roughly hauled the boy to his feet.

"How dare you ..." the youth began before being intimidated into silence by Mr. Blanchard's well-practised glare.

"Evidently, you were attempting to impress Miss Otis last night. You should know 'drunk as a lord' is a figure of speech, not a prescription! What part of your performance do you think won her over? When you drooled in her ear, when you pushed her out of her seat, or when you puked on her shoes?"

Young Dankworth flinched as Mr. Blanchard ticked off his misbehaviour sarcastically. The youth hung his head, unable to meet Mr. Blanchard's steely glare.

"Furthermore, the 'prime article,' as you so vulgarly refer to her, is a lady of impeccable breeding, who should not be used like some common slattern!" His voice only now rising above conversational levels, Mr. Blanchard continued. "By what authority did you think yourself entitled to assault my guest? But finally, you young jackass, Miss Otis is the object of *my* affections. I suggest you limit your infatuations to under-bred schoolgirls. No real lady will have anything to do with you until you learn to act the gentleman! Have I made myself clear, Jack Dankworth!?"

Now completely deflated and miserable, flinching away from the sound of Mr. Blanchard's voice, the boy nodded.

Whilst Mr. Blanchard had been speaking, Ambercrombie had freed Dankworth's terrified horse and tied him off to a likely sapling. Mr. Blanchard and Abercrombie ascended into the *curricle*, and after some expert manoeuvring, returned to Eynsham Hall, laughing.

The tale of their "schooling voyage" quickly penetrated the household and became the topic of conversation at lunch. Many jests at the young lord's expense were made.

"But we should not judge him too harshly; he was in his cups," Alexander Tinsley assayed.

"And whose fault is that, I ask you?" his father replied vigorously. "I have seen far too many men use drunkenness as an excuse for all sorts of doltish behaviour. Stupidity is stupidity, whether self-inflicted by drink or not, and is always an appropriate target for ridicule."

Picking up the theme from his parents, Phillip Tinsley contributed. "Drink is dangerous as well. A fellow in the next form at Oxford managed to drown himself in a drunken stupor; broke his parents' hearts. Although I expect his horse is relieved to be rid of him."

Kitty had often seen the Tinsleys make use of such exemplars to impress wisdom upon their sons. She made a mental note to use the same tactic with her own children. This internal comment startled her. She realised she still hoped for children and therefore did not *actually* plan on pining away from disappointed hopes. Mr. Blanchard had initiated this sea-change in her heart. She was suddenly grateful to Blanchard and truly flattered by his attentions. Still cautious, she allowed herself to hope. Hope animated her, bringing back the lively effervescence she possessed before her Irish adventure.

NEWS FROM AUSTRALIA

O n the following day, a bundle of mail forwarded by
Mrs. Abernathy arrived. It included a long letter with the
sender's address marked Sydney Colony, Australia. Kitty ignored all
of her other correspondence and retreated to her room to devour it.

January 9, 1815
Sydney Colony, Australia

My Dearest Friend,

*I am now arrived at Sydney, Australia. No doubt you are et up
with curiosity, so I shall try to keep my narrative in order. The voyage
was mostly tedium, and toward the end, bad food. I have now eaten
enough exotic fish to stock a respectable aquarium and will limit
myself to beef, pork, and mutton for quite some time.*

*Most of the mares were carrying when they boarded. Three
slipped during the voyage, and their little foals were consigned to the
briny deep. One mare got cast in her box and had to be put down. The
sailors ate her up. I could not bring myself to eat horse flesh. Five of the
mares delivered early, and I landed with 119 mares, 111 pregnant and
ready to deliver, five stallions, and five young foals.*

*Fortunately, we only encountered one typhoon. A dreadful storm.
Quite the equal of any on the North Sea. The captain explained we
only caught the trailing edge of it, for had we encountered the main
storm, we should all have perished. The storm and its aftermath,
rain as warm as bath water, persisted for three days. I had not fully
appreciated the irony of the name "Pacific Ocean" until that moment!*

*All of the horses were thin and in poor condition, even Hercules,
by the time we landed. Fortunately, grassland is cheap. I was able
to rent several good fields for virtually nothing. Since we landed in
summer here, I could supplement their feed with carrots. Hercules
returned to his usual self, and the mares regained condition rapidly.
Freed of their on-board confinement, they dropped foals by the dozens.*

*My greatest difficulty has been convincing all and sundry I will
not sell my foundation herd; that everyone must wait until the new*

crop is at least yearlings. Then, at the suggestion of one of the officers, I set up a breed book. I listed the particulars of dam and sire and sold "places." In other words, took deposits on the foals.

My gravest error, it appears, is that I brought no heavy draft horses—a lack which I hope to remedy through correspondence with my favourite cold-blood breeder. I hope O'Donnell will accept what small sum I can send him with the promise of more. I desire to import two heavy stallions and at least forty mares. The interest my horses have already excited has encouraged me to believe I am poised to make my fortune, and I have high hopes for the future.

Quarters are hard to come by here, and I am sleeping in the rough for now. The locals all claim the winter is as mild as an Irish spring, and run-in sheds will do for the stock. However, I am not eager to spend more time in the human equivalent of a run-in shed and have commissioned a house.

The houses built here are quite curious. The weather is hot here, rather like Jamaica, with never any snow, and the houses are designed to defeat the heat. They are raised above the ground on stone support piers to encourage a breeze under the floorboards. They have very high ceilings and virtually no solid walls, just wooden screens that can be opened and closed to encourage a breeze through the house. The outer walls are surrounded by very deep, shaded porches to keep the sun off the walls. The kitchen is usually a separate shed, so the cooking fires will not heat up the house.

To build a house hereabouts, one must first buy a stand of trees, as there is no lumber mill yet built. So, I bought a stand of eucalypt, which have been felled and sawn into boards and timbers and are now curing. The wood should be dry in another month. I have begun erecting stone piers for the main house and the kitchen hut.

The native peoples are as dark as those of Africa. Properly referred to as "Aborigines," they are invariably spoken of as "Abbos." They are the very picture of wild, uncivilised people. They troop through town, men, women, and children together, stark naked. Quite a shocker when I first witnessed them. They plough no fields, nor do they plant any crops. They sustain themselves through hunting, fishing, and harvesting what wild produce they can find.

I enclose a spray of leaves from the mighty native eucalypt trees. The scent of a whole forest is overwhelming—a cross between medicine and cat piss. The natives claim the leaves drive off insects and are a remedy for infection. Based on the smell alone, I am inclined to believe them. I have the leaves stripped from local trees and sprinkled on the ground around the horse fields, and it seems to help keep the biting flies away.

I confess you were right, my dear friend, to choose England over this wild adventure. The few officers' wives who are here are a small, frightened band, trapped on the knife's edge between a criminal society and the fierce wilderness. There is only a make-shift church, and books are rare.

The vast majority of the females here are prisoners who rarely serve their sentences. Most of them are married before they achieve the end of the dock. The men here are so desperate they offer to marry a woman knowing nothing about her except that she is a convicted criminal!

I fear I have been spoilt and now expect intelligence and character in a woman, so I foresee no marriage for me for some time. Your adieux at the end of your last note, 'Do not renounce women for my sake,' was charity itself, and I return the sentiment. Be assured you made the right choice, and I wish you happy and well.

Yr. Most Obdt. Irish Giant,
Joseph McLaughlin

Kitty was relieved and joyful at discovering him safe. His charitable wish she should form a second attachment set her heart free. His letter prompted tears of joy, of loss, and, ultimately, of healing. At some point, she fell asleep and, after a short nap, completed reading the rest of her correspondence. Kitty hurried to the library, where the family were gathered before dinner. Kitty was so clearly in her best spirits, Mrs. Blanchard remarked.

"Oh, I have heard from Mr. McLaughlin," she replied. "It was a very satisfactory letter and has eased my heart immeasurably." She told of Mr. McLaughlin's account of Australia and passed around the eucalypt leaves. A lively conversation ensued. After dinner, a great atlas was brought forth, and they studied the geography of the Sydney Colony.

Finally, Kitty excused herself. "Well, I must not dawdle, for I have a long reply to write."

"But you are not engaged, so I thought ..." Georgina blurted out, surprised, before her mother cast a warning glance her way, and she stuttered to a halt.

"Yes, I know." Kitty smiled. "But first of all, I promised Mr. McLaughlin I would reply. Second, I fail to understand how this correspondence could represent any possible impropriety. My letter is hardly a *billet-doux*. The man is seventeen thousand miles from here! My aim is to encourage Mr. McLaughlin with his difficult emigration out of Christian charity."

"An excellent scheme," Mr. Blanchard interjected. "By his own admission, the poor man is in want of conversation, and your correspondence represents his only substitute."

"Thank you so much for understanding, Mr. Blanchard!" Kitty curtsied herself out.

June 17, 1815
Eynsham Hall, Oxfordshire

My Cara Daor,

I hope I have the Irish spelling of "Dearest Friend" correct! I am vastly relieved you and most of your cargo arrived safe and sound. I understand your survival rate is astonishing. Most exporters lose over half the stock on such a long voyage. Your trial on choppy waters was a stroke of genius. I, too, shall try to keep things in order.

I draped your lovely Irish cross about my neck before I left Dublin and have not removed it since and never intend to. The voyage back was quite rough, with heavy rain. There were several occasions when I was soaked through, and by the time I reached Dixon Cottage, I had contracted a chest complaint.

My dear Uncle Tinsley brought the eminent Dr. Jones to treat me, and he prescribed hydropathy. I was made to drink vile tisanes, laudanum, tea, and broth frequently through the day and night, and bathed in very hot herb-tinctured baths (a treatment which horrified my dear Aunt Tinsley). I was on the mend within three days. I am now in excellent health and spirits.

Dixon Cottage farm is returning an excellent profit. I have just acquired Micky and Molly, two vast shire horses of superior conformation and temperament. I promise to ship their get, should the foal prove to be sea-worthy, and will cheerfully accept whatever return you can give me.

I have had much greater luck romantically than you have (far greater opportunities). Perhaps you recall Mr. Blanchard? I believe

you met him on your last visit to London. He served under Captain
Edwards aboard the St. George.

  He has been widowed these last three years and has invited me
to his home, which I account as a sign of developing attachment. I was
reluctant to entertain Mr. Blanchard's advances and loathe to develop
an attachment, but your letter has set me free. I shall always regret
you and hold a special place in my heart for you, but I am no longer
shackled by grief. For that, I thank you most earnestly.

  As to Mr. Blanchard, he lost his first wife and their baby in
childbirth. He, too, has been shackled by grief. I, of course, seek a man
who will not begrudge me the space set aside in my heart for you. In
this, I am optimistic, as Mr. Blanchard encouraged me to write to you
upon hearing about your correspondence to me.

  My papa rarely emerges from his fog but is otherwise hale
and hearty. He is visiting here at Eynsham Hall in Oxfordshire
(Mr. Blanchard's home), together with my Aunt and Uncle Tinsley,
and the Wallaces (Marianne married James Wallace).

  Poor dear Mrs. Wallace lost her first baby, Angus, and is still
recovering from that heartbreak. Mr. Warden continues to be an
officious, interfering curmudgeon to the extent that the Wallaces
seek a home far away from Keswick. Mr. Wallace is now accepting
architectural commissions with a view of establishing his own
practise hereabouts.

  I invested in a Lloyd's syndicate on my Uncle Tinsley's advice.
It seems so much like gambling, but he assures me this is a good
bet. I wish there were a syndicate for your horses, for I should risk a
hundred or two quite serenely in such an adventure knowing your way
with horses.

  Let us never lose touch with one another, Cara Daor. *May God*
bless you and keep you.

Yr. Friend Forever, Kitty Otis

Kitty had arranged with Mr. Wright, the butler, to post the letter the
next morning. She joined Mrs. Blanchard and Georgina for a spell of
work before luncheon. The Tinsleys were visiting some of Phillip's
Oxford friends, the Wallaces were scouting for a likely house, and
Mr. Blanchard was away in Oxford, retrieving Mrs. Blanchard's
portrait from the framers.

"I hope you will not think me impertinent," Kitty addressed
Mrs. Blanchard. "Could you tell me why Mr. Blanchard has remained

widowed for so long? Surely, every match-making mama of the *ton* has thrown a daughter his way."

"Not impertinent at all, my dear. Perfectly natural," Mrs. Blanchard replied. "And you are absolutely correct about the match-making mamas. After the first year of desperate grief was spent and Sherry reappeared in Society, many a young lady set her cap for him. However, none of them had any sympathy for his feelings for Alice. One young lady I had high hopes for broke it off with Sherry because, in her words, she could not bear to share him with a ghost. After the double blow of losing his father and then Alice, he went numb, I think. He discharged all of his duties and kept civil company, but it was as if—as if he was sleepwalking. Now with you here, he's awakened. You are good for him, I think."

After a moment, whilst Kitty digested that information, she continued with "Sherry?"

Georgina explained, "His childhood nickname since his first name is my mother's maiden name, Sheridan."

"How long has it been since you lost Alice?" Kitty enquired.

"Three years exactly, come July twenty-fifth," Georgina said.

Mrs. Blanchard elaborated, "He built a lovely little folly on the tiny island in our lake as her memorial. He visits it every time he returns here and on the anniversary of their marriage and of her death."

"She must have been an extraordinary woman," Kitty said.

"Yes, she was. Not as pretty as you; bonier and somewhat freckled. Alice was not as athletic as you, either. She was a very talented musician, however. But I believe you are much alike in some ways. Alice was very clever and widely read, just as you are. Alice was also a merry soul; always optimistic and cheerful, with an infectious laugh and a generous spirit."

"And your granddaughter?"

"Was christened Agnes. That is why Sherry named his orphanage 'Asylum of St. Agnes," Mrs. Blanchard explained.

"I did not know Mr. Blanchard supported an orphanage."

"Oh, yes." Mrs. Blanchard smiled as Georgina nodded in agreement. "St. Agnes is his largest charity, situated just outside North Leigh. It houses up to one hundred girls and boys, and is set up as a series of home-like cottages rather than as a modern hospital. Sherry thought a large modern building would intimidate the little ones. The staff also take very great care to ensure the orphans go to good homes where they are adopted for love and not as slave labour. We are all unreasonably proud of Sherry's Asylum, as you can plainly see."

"I, too, have taken in an orphan. Well, a neglected child. Little Davey might have been better off as an orphan, actually." Kitty returned and told Davey's story. That led naturally enough to the story of Blanchard's hilarious misadventure shooting out of her house at high speed. His dearest loving relations showed no sympathy at all for poor Blanchard's dignity. They laughed until tears flowed.

Once they had recovered breath, Mrs. Blanchard resumed the conversation. "See, we are working on a christening gown, as a foundling has arrived. We are to christen her at St. Mary's tomorrow. Would you like to come?"

"I should be honoured." Kitty accepted. Shortly thereafter, Mr. Blanchard arrived with the framed portrait of Mrs. Blanchard, which was installed in the long gallery upstairs.

The christening was scheduled after two weddings in the morning. On the event, the tiny baby slept peacefully throughout the ceremony, only waking to protest the cold water before promptly resuming her slumber in Mr. Blanchard's arms. Kitty was forcibly struck by how well he looked in his *rôle* as a father and how cruelly death had deprived him of his own child.

Watching him, Kitty recognised in herself a romantic prejudice against second attachments she had not realised she possessed. It was obvious with Mr. Blanchard's example before her that a heart that had loved once could well learn to love again. She was fairly taken aback, not only for him, but also for herself. With barely controlled sentimental tears in her eyes, she admired the happy little group.

Mr. Blanchard told her the child was christened "Elizabeth" as it has so many nicknames; the child could select her own moniker when the time came. When they returned the baby to St. Agnes, Kitty observed the snug cottages, each managed by a couple with some servants shared among the cottages. The children were obviously healthy and well cared for, were taught to read and figure as well as useful trades. Kitty's heart swelled with admiration for Mr. Blanchard's charity. She admired him for fashioning this happy outcome from his own tragic loss and said as much to Marianne as they were preparing for supper.

"Oh, Kitty, I am so very pleased for you." Marianne rejoiced when they spoke next. "You have not admired a single gentleman since Mr. McLaughlin!"

"No, I suppose I have not," Kitty replied. "I also eradicated a prejudice which I never even knew I possessed. Today, when Mr. Blanchard was holding that baby, it struck me that I had dismissed second attachments as somehow second best." Kitty smiled consciously. "My opinions sprang from reading too many romances, I expect. At least, I am confident I admire him for something more substantial than his estate or a handsome countenance."

"I recall many young ladies who went mad for officers," Marianne opined. "They made minute observations about their appearance and did not care two pins for their character. I do not believe you or I ever fell into that error. At least, not after the age of fourteen. You esteem him for all the right reasons."

Kitty smiled in return. "I fear we are rather odd ducks."

"Perhaps," Marianne replied with insight. "But I would wager it is a result of parents who supplied us with improving educations rather than sending us off to seminaries exclusively designed to improve our chances on the marriage mart."

"I believe you have hit upon a home truth," Kitty replied. "I shall keep that in mind if ever I am in the position of educating a daughter."

As she was changing for dinner, Kitty spent an hour in deep thought. She realised she was becoming attached to Mr. Blanchard. Her feelings had none of the giddiness of her first attachment but were gentler. She wanted to attach Sherry and was hoping for his address. Kitty was dumbfounded to discover her allegiance had not excluded Joseph so much as it had expanded to include Sherry.

She finally understood she had been deaf and blind to her own heart! Kitty was simultaneously embarrassed and relieved. She was freed from the shackles of grief by Joseph's kind wishes, and realised Sherry needed similar help to move on. Now that securing Sherry's affection was an object, she thought long and hard on how to accomplish that feat. Finally, she was seized by inspiration. On her way to table, Kitty sought out the butler, Mr. Wright.

"Mr. Wright, I understand Mr. Blanchard makes a pilgrimage to Alice's memorial every year a few days hence?"

Mr. Wright nodded.

Kitty explained, "I would like to make it a special occasion for him on this anniversary. I would be happy to pay you a few guineas for your trouble. Could you contrive to clean the folly and stock it with flowers and garlands of greenery? Especially if anyone knows what her favourite flowers were? Perhaps include some memento of her life or accomplishments?"

Mr. Wright eyed her with unrestrained wonder. Kitty blushed. "I have had much help in overcoming my grief for my own lost love." She reached up and touched her cross, a gesture that was not lost on Mr. Wright. "I simply wish to give return to Mr. Blanchard."

Wright bowed and replied in a somewhat husky voice. "A gran' notion, Miss. I think I know exactly the thing. It'll be in place ready fer the day."

Kitty beamed and slipped two guineas into his hand. "I have every faith in your judgement, and even more in your remarkable organisation skills, Mr. Wright. I trust you entirely to supervise my little surprise!"

Georgina commented after luncheon one afternoon, "I notice you never waltz. I can understand at a public assembly like Almack's, but at a house party amongst those you know? Are your notions so very strict, then?"

"Not at all," Kitty assured them. "I have never learnt how."

"Well, that can be swiftly remedied!" Georgina cried. In a trice, Mrs. Blanchard joined them in the Green Hall. She played waltzes at a very sedate tempo whilst Georgina played the man and taught Kitty to waltz. Mrs. Blanchard gradually increased the tempo as Kitty became surer of the steps. Within an hour, Kitty was waltzing at full tempo, with only a few bobbles on the more complex twirls, and the lesson was pronounced complete.

That evening, Mr. Blanchard invited the entire party to extend their stay through the month of July. Mr. Tinsley needed to attend to his practice up north, but Phillip and Alexander would be starting at Oxford in the fall, Phillip, for his final term, Alexander for his first. To travel the whole length of the kingdom just to turn around again and return a few days later seemed silly. Soon, it was all settled. The Wallaces were to remain at Eynsham Hall until they arranged to let their own home. Kitty and Mr. Otis would extend their stay through July, and the boys would stay until the dormitories at the college opened for the term.

June 27, 1815
Eynsham Hall, Oxfordshire

Dear Mrs. Abernathy,

I hope this letter finds you all well and happy. Please convey my greetings to all in our household. Mr. Blanchard has invited me and Papa to spend the month of July at Eynsham Hall, and we have accepted.

One of Mr. Blanchard's dogs, a little russet-haired Spaniel, has permanently attached herself to Mr. Otis. She is always in his lap, following on his heels, or on his bed. I do not recall her name, but Mr. Otis calls her "Silky," and now, she answers to nothing else. She does not play fetch or perform tricks but seems bred exclusively to give and receive affection. She is doing Mr. Otis a world of good.

Mr. Hart asked me to convey to you all he is hale and hearty and enjoying being a valet which is rather an easier task than man-of-all-work. Eynsham Hall is an impressive house, and I dearly love it here, but still look forward to harvest and the hunt season at Dixon Cottage.

I have let Mr. Tinsley know to allow you to draw what funds are necessary for the hiring of farm labourers, as we did last season, in case you need to start hiring before I should arrive. I endorse Mac's ideas and encourage you to follow his precepts for the management of the home farm.

I wish you all happy and look forward to seeing you all this fall.

Sincerely, Miss Otis

P.S. Mrs. Taylor's note to you all is enclosed.

Mrs. Abernathy read the letter out to the entire staff and commented, "I wager the next time we see her, she'll be Mrs. Blanchard."

"Aye. What's to become of us?" Pike asked gloomily.

"Wishin' that bonnie young lass to dwindle into an old maid, just so as ye can keep yer position?" Mrs. Abernathy responded tartly, "Now *that's* Christian charity for ye!"

Mac jumped in, "I think this was her first house, and she loves it like her own bairn. I wager they'll keep it."

Mary and Mrs. Abernathy brightened up. "I think ye main be right, my love," Mary commented.

"Well, there's no sayin' what she'll decide." Mac ended the discussion. "But I know her; if she does sell this place, she'll write references that would put the psalmists to shame."

BLENHEIM PALACE

As the visit wore on, Kitty became acquainted with local society. She was frequently present when neighbours presented themselves for morning visits. Just as frequently, Kitty accompanied Mrs. Blanchard and Georgina on their morning calls and was introduced around in the Chapter House. Soon, rumours of impending nuptials flew.

As she became better known, she became more comfortable and began to feel more at home. Although, as Marianne had observed, several women of the Blanchard's acquaintance were offended that Kitty was Mr. Blanchard's choice. But Kitty never met with the cold civility which so repulsed her at Gleannri.

Kitty got some excellent news. Captain Jackson was as good as his word. Her payment from the Lloyd's syndicate was nearly seven hundred pounds. She promptly agreed to invest two hundred pounds in the next Captain Jackson syndicate at Lloyds. then wisely accepted Mr. Tinsley's advice to invest the rest in conservative consoles. Kitty saw the Tinsleys off at the end of June in good cheer.

"I would never have credited the sea-change in Kitty if I had not seen it with my own eyes," Mrs. Tinsley announced as their coach left Eynsham.

"Believed what, dear?" Mr. Tinsley responded.

"Why, her attachment to Mr. Blanchard," Mrs. Tinsley replied. "I believe you should start thinking on marriage articles for Kitty."

"Too late, my love," Mr. Tinsley replied, "For I have already rough-drafted them."

Mrs. Tinsley rapped him playfully on the shoulder with her fan, smiled, and said, "I should have known you would catch me out on this, Perry!"

"I am well content that God has granted her this hour of happiness after all of her early woes," Mr. Tinsley observed.

Meanwhile, James Wallace had arranged to lease a very agreeable property only a mile distant from the gates of Eynsham. At the

Wallace's newly leased home, Kitty was proving to be interfering, managing, and a very great help. Marianne was prone to indecision and procrastination, and Kitty was not. Marianne also had significant experience dealing with officious interference from her father. Since Kitty was far more rational and much less stubborn than Mr. Warden, the ladies got along very well, and the house was ready and the staff hired by their move-in date.

Marianne began to think on her baby. A very careful survey of local midwives netted Marianne a fairly young woman, Mrs. Sykes. She came with strong recommendations and was clean, orderly, and a Wesleyan Methodist who did not drink.

Marianne and Kitty plunged into preparations for the baby. Marianne had given away most of her original layette, on the grounds that it made her weep. Mr. Wallace came home one day with a little carved rocking crib, embellished all over with charming animal figures. Mr. Wallace hoped it would ward off bad luck. So, finally prepared as much as possible for their new arrival, Marianne settled in to wait.

"Oh, Georgina, Miss Otis!" Mrs. Blanchard exclaimed when they met for breakfast. "I have very happy news. We have all been invited by the Duke and Duchess of Marlborough to Blenheim Palace for a ball on Saturday the twenty-second!"

After the excitement had simmered down a bit, Kitty asked, "Oh, whatever shall I wear? I fear my country fashions are not suitable for so grand an event."

"Oh, fear not, there is enough time to secure the services of Mme. Gaudet," Mrs. Blanchard reassured her.

"But Taylor ..." Kitty began.

"Taylor is a *genius* milliner," Mrs. Blanchard interrupted firmly. "Never employ anyone else to trim up your hats, my dear. Her confections are enormously flattering to you. But Taylor is only a good seamstress, not a great *couturière*. For this occasion, it must be Mme. Gaudet. I shall send a footman to secure an appointment for us immediately." She pulled the bell-cord to summon Mr. Wright. "We should be able to see her next Monday, which should be ample time for Georgina's dress and your own. Mme. Gaudet employs a veritable army of seamstresses."

"That sounds lovely, and, since Captain Jackson's syndicate has just paid off, I can manage such a purchase," Kitty replied. "I shall apply to my uncle to release funds immediately."

"This ball is quite fortuitous, for I have ulterior motives," Mrs. Blanchard explained. "My Georgina here is pretty as a picture, and quite accomplished. How long before some Prince Charming captures her heart and takes her away from me?"

"Mama!" Georgina protested, blushing.

Mrs. Blanchard turned toward her daughter. "Georgina, your affections have not yet been engaged, but it is only a matter of time. Also, it is my dearest wish for you. But then what? Sherry rattling about this house all alone and myself with no companionship at Dower House?" Mrs. Blanchard turned to Kitty, with an arch little smile. "No, I wish to secure you as my daughter almost as much as Sherry wishes to secure you as his wife."

Kitty was much affected, and tears sprang in her eyes. She could not help but compare this open and unreserved declaration of affection to the cold prejudiced civility offered by Mrs. McLaughlin. Kitty's heart leapt in her chest, yearning for a motherly relationship.

"I too, wish to call you my sister," Georgina contributed, impulsively clasping Kitty's hand. "You are not just good for Sherry, but for all of us."

At this declaration, Kitty was unable to restrain tears. This appeared to flummox Mr. Wright, who had just entered the room.

"Happy tears, Mr. Wright," Mrs. Blanchard reassured him, "happy tears."

Kitty nodded vigorously, fanning her face with her hands to staunch the flow. Georgina rescued her by offering a kerchief. She sniffled and dabbed her eyes, struggling to compose herself.

Mrs. Blanchard arranged for a footman to open the London townhouse and secure their appointment. Kitty sent a note to Uncle Tinsley. They departed in good time the next morning and arrived in London only two days later on a Saturday. They attended services at Winchester Cathedral, much to Kitty's delight, and arrived promptly for their appointment Monday.

Mme. Gaudet greeted Kitty, "Ah, mademoiselle, so lovely to see you again."

"Mme. Gaudet's *saque* for my presentation was a triumph," Kitty explained to Mrs. Blanchard and Georgina. She turned back to Mme.

Gaudet. "That train-gathering cord was a stroke of genius, madam. I had no difficulties exiting the room, unlike several other ladies."

Mme. Gaudet smiled at the compliment. "And what is ze occasion zat brings you 'ere today?"

Mrs. Blanchard supplied, "The Duke's ball at Blenheim Castle. We are all of us conspiring to bring my son up to scratch and depend upon your genius towards that end for Miss Otis. With Georgina, we wish her to attract notice, you understand."

"*Parfaitement*!" Mme. Gaudet clapped her hands together sharply, and a shop clerk appeared. "Secure for us ze cream satin so mademoiselle may inspect. Also, bring out ze new net embroidered flounce." Mme. Gaudet began to take measurements whilst muttering under her breath, lost in a fugue of concentration. "For you, mademoiselle, it shall be simplicity and restraint." Mme. Gaudet held up a length of the silk. "We shall shape wiss delicate seaming, just so. Very simple lines, *très élégant, très subtile*, a Diana."

Kitty admired her form in the mirror with the goods draped about her. "It is inspired, madame. I eagerly await the moment I can try the gown on."

"But of course," Mme. Gaudet replied with a Gallic shrug. "We shall fit ze *toile* in two days."

"Now, for you, Mademoiselle Georgina, you shall be Venus. Soft, more lace ..."

The orders were quickly placed. Naturally, Kitty called on Mrs. Williamson with Mrs. and Miss Blanchard in attendance. Mrs. Williamson and Mrs. Blanchard promptly became fast friends. The week passed in a whirlwind. Even though not the Season, the public gardens were at their peak, and the ladies had enough acquaintance in town to pass the time quite amiably. Uncle Tinsley's bank instructions arrived in a timely manner, and Kitty's purchase was assured. At last, the day came for trying on the finished gowns. Kitty gawked at herself in the mirror with unrestrained vanity. By some subtle art of seaming, the gown enhanced every one of Kitty's best features.

"Well, if that does not bring Sherry up to scratch, nothing will!" Mrs. Blanchard teased her. Georgina stepped out in her new gown. The effect, while totally different than Kitty's gown, was just as amazing on Georgina.

"*Ainsi*!" Mme. Gaudet exclaimed, "*Diana et Vénus, la perfection!*" Mme. Gaudet accepted her clients' plaudits with no symptom of modesty, and the ladies left with their prizes in high good humour.

The night before the Duke's ball, Kitty was keyed up thinking about the grand event. She fantasised that Sherry would be so impressed by her beauty that he would propose on the spot. Those ideas prevented sleep. Finally, after two restless hours, she slipped into her dressing gown and slippers to go in search of a glass of sherry and a dull book.

She encountered Sherry as she rounded the corner into the long gallery. He was in his nightshirt, bare-headed and barefoot, marching up and down the gallery, with his hands clasped behind his back. He was clearly sound asleep. As she watched in astonishment, he dodged imagined obstacles, then wheeled around and headed back down the gallery. She considered waking him up but was too embarrassed to do so. So, she looked on silently.

A few moments later, it dawned on Kitty that he was—in his sleep—walking the deck of the St. George. It occurred to her that as much as he enjoyed his role as a gentleman farmer, he was haunted by the war.

As she watched him, she realised he was re-living a battle. Kitty admired him as a man who had clearly done his duty with courage at great personal cost. As he reached the "bow" of the ship, she deepened and roughened her voice as much as possible and barked out, "Dismissed, Lieutenant!" Sherry saluted, turned on his heel, and marched back towards his room.

Kitty retrieved the sherry, but not a book. She spent her time writing in her diary rather than reading. Eventually, she slipped into sleep. The next morning, after a late start, she related the whole to Marianne.

"Poor man! Condemned to re-live the war. I wonder if he is troubled by the brutality of battle or simply missing the sea?"

"Either way, he suffers. I am both grateful for his sacrifice to protect us all and horrified that he was called upon to make it. It just makes me loathe Bonaparte that much more."

Although it would be more diplomatic to let the whole incident pass without remark, Kitty could not overcome her curiosity. She succumbed to the temptation of asking about it when she was walking with Mrs. Blanchard.

"Yes. Sherry was prone to sleepwalking as a child. Many mornings were an adventure, as we searched the whole house for him. One time, we found him soundly asleep on Anna's tiny chaise that she had for her dolls," Mrs. Blanchard replied. "He had grown out of the habit, but he resumed after leaving the Navy. The worst one is when he re-lives the battle when his cabin boy, Jackie, was gruesomely killed in front of him. His valet, Ambercrombie, told me about it. That was a stroke of genius, dismissing him. You should pass that on to Ambercrombie."

"Thank you. I shall." Kitty pressed on, "Does he re-live the war often?"

"At first, nearly nightly. Now, the nightmares are much reduced, especially since you came along. Evidently, you fill his mind with much more pleasant thoughts."

"Delighted to hear it."

Mrs. Blanchard smiled. "I sent off an idealistic boy to the Navy and got back a man, better in many ways, but wounded in others."

Later that day, Taylor did up her hair in the fashion Mr. Blanchard admired. Kitty equipped herself with new satin gloves and her fretwork fan. She felt like a princess as she swept down the stairs. Mr. Blanchard evidently agreed, for she was greeted by a grin of appreciation before he handed her in to the *barouche-sociable*.

Blenheim Palace exceeded its reputation as enormous, elegant, and brilliantly decorated. The grand hall was almost entirely marble. It was three stories tall, the top story was exclusively wall-to-wall clerestory windows, the second story was a gallery supported by elaborate marble arches. Each arch contained a full size marble figure. Monumental Corinthian collumns supported the vault of the ceiling, leading the eye to the large scale oval ceiling mural. The white marble reflected the light of thousands of wax candles, and it was very nearly bright as day. The hall opened out to several other wood-floored salons with brilliant silk damask lined walls, comfortable furniture, and magnificent art.

The ball room's windows were shut up tight, in deference to the wishes of the older guests. Kitty escaped to the cool terrace several times during the evening. Mr. Blanchard had reserved the first and last dance, and they had already danced a reel happily together.

As Kitty re-entered the hallway giving out on to the ballroom, she spied a young lady speaking with Mr. Blanchard. The lady appeared to be very young and sported brassy curls elaborately arranged. Her gown was a virtually transparent gauze, covering nearly equally revealing undergarments, extravagantly trimmed with numerous flounces at the neckline and hem, and featured a number of trailing ribbons knotted at the waist. The dress had the unfortunate effect of making the young lady, already petite and somewhat plump, look rather like a squat pouter pigeon.

With some misgivings as to the propriety of her actions, but with undeniable curiosity, Kitty hovered in the shadows and listened to the exchange.

"Oh, Mr. Blanchard, you look very well tonight." The young lady said in breathless accents whilst fluttering her fan. "Very Beau Brummel, y'know."

"Thank you," Mr. Blanchard replied. "It seemed appropriate to the occasion."

"Oh." The young lady simpered, batting her eyelashes, "Here I thought you were trying to impress me."

"Not my object at all," Mr. Blanchard replied.

Oblivious to his hint, or so determined to flirt that no reply on his part would discourage her, the blonde continued. "Who was that drab brunette you danced the first reel with? You needn't do that again now I'm here."

"I do not recall dancing with a drab brunette," Mr. Blanchard returned.

"The first reel, the dark-haired girl," the girl said.

"Oh! You mean Miss Otis. The extraordinary beauty it was my privilege to escort," Mr. Blanchard said, feigning sudden enlightenment. "Her conversation is always so charming."

"Oh, Mr. Blanchard, I'm so thrilled to find"—the young woman lowered her voice theatrically—"that *conversation* is all you want of her." She tittered into her fan.

Kitty rolled her eyes in the privacy of the hallway. With her eyes dancing and colour heightened by Mr. Blanchard's compliment, she stepped around the corner.

"I did not know a theatrical performance was offered this evening, Mr. Blanchard," Kitty said.

"I am unaware of any such scheme, Miss Otis," Mr. Blanchard replied.

"Oh? How embarrassing." Kitty smiled prettily and turned to her rival. "I mistook you for an actress, Miss?"

The young lady stiffened, outrage declared in every part of her person.

"Excuse me, Miss Otis, may I present Miss Hawkins." Blanchard performed the introduction.

Kitty dropped a perfectly correct and graceful curtsey, whilst Miss Hawkins, still furious, only managed a short, awkward bob. Kitty opened her fan with an elegant gesture and fanned herself. Miss Hawkins's complexion turned an alarming blotchy red.

"You must tell me who ran up that dress for you," Miss Hawkins practically hissed. "It's so, so very plain."

Kitty smiled, turning the intended insult into a delightful compliment. "So kind of you to say so. Mme. Gaudet's first principle is, 'ze woman should wear ze gown, no?' And I always feel more secure in a heavier silk; I find it more flattering."

Kitty lowered her voice to a conspiratorial whisper and leaned close to Miss Hawkins, speaking to her from behind her fan. "As long as you avoid the brightest of the chandeliers, you will not risk any embarrassment." Resuming her normal tone, Kitty gestured to the balcony. "The musicians have returned. No doubt you are already promised for this dance; I shall not detain you any longer, Miss Hawkins, except to wish you a lovely evening."

They once again exchanged curtseys, and Miss Hawkins marched off, the very picture of offended dignity. Mr. Blanchard was not entirely successful at stifling his laughter but managed to turn his whoops into a cough pretty convincingly.

"Thank you for running off the most singularly vapid young woman in all of Britain." Mr. Blanchard fiddled with his cuffs, his face bright with mirth.

"You are most welcome, Mr. Blanchard," Kitty said before her hand was claimed by a young naval officer. The rest of the evening passed in giddy gaiety. Her final waltz with Mr. Blanchard was highly romantic, and Kitty felt she was dancing on air.

On the way home, Kitty was emboldened to confess. "Last night, I was keyed up and having difficulty falling asleep, so I ventured out of my room in search of a glass of sherry. I stumbled upon you sleepwalking in the long gallery. You appeared to be re-living a battle on the St. George. I barked out, 'Dismissed, Lieutenant!'

To my amazement, it worked. You saluted and went back to your bed chamber."

"Oh, how embarrassing!"

"Not at all, my dear Blanchard. I would think you *very* hard-hearted if you had no response to the brutality of the war you were called on to wage. I admire your personal sacrifice. Your example simply makes me loathe Bonaparte even more."

Blanchard grinned, delighted. "I repeat; Not just political opinions, but well-reasoned ones as well. You never cease to be a refreshment for my mind and spirit."

"I'm overjoyed to hear it since that is your effect on me." When they reached Eynsham, Kitty parted from him with her heart bright with hope.

On the evening before the anniversary of Alice's death, Kitty checked in with Mr. Wright. "Well, Mr. Wright, how goes our arrangement?"

Mr. Wright reported, "Very well, Miss. The late Mrs. Blanchard's favourites were snapdragons. So, the snaps are just about at their peak now, and the beds will be sadly stripped when you amble through the gardens. But I reckon you won't mind. She netted swaths for the babe's chamber, so we used them fringes. I have the gardeners' yonder working to clip all them shrubberies. It'll be a lush tribute to a luvly woman."

"Oh! It sounds wonderful. I knew I could count on you! Thank you again, Mr. Wright." Kitty tripped up the stairs cheerfully, granting Mr. Wright a little wave.

MEMORIAL

The next morning, Kitty met Mr. Blanchard after breakfast for one of their frequent rides together. She was arrayed in a lovely summer-weight riding habit of cotton sateen sprigged with tender pastels. She had on the most flattering bonnet that Taylor had trimmed up for her. Kitty was secure in her best looks.

They headed a little south and to the east of the house and circumnavigated the little lake there. The route offered the advantage of peaceful quiet and cool morning shade in the swath of forest that fringed the lake. When they approached very nearly the closest shore to the house, there was a small pole-boat tied up on the shore.

He invited her to dismount. They tied off the horses and descended to the diminutive craft. Mr. Blanchard poled them across the lake, heading for the tiny island, and as they grew close, he grew more pensive. They pulled up to the miniature dock, and Mr. Blanchard made fast the boat. As he turned from the dock to the tiny, elegant folly, he stopped dead in his tracks, and his jaw dropped open.

Mr. Wright and the rest of the staff had outdone themselves. The path was strewn with a lovely array of fresh flower petals. The low railing was festooned with garlands of fresh ivy and dill. The marble columns of the miniature Greek temple sported flower braids twining up their height. Huge bouquets of snapdragons mixed with other summer flowers were set on either side of the entrance. The floor was patterned with even more flower petals. A tiny arrangement of richly scented tuberoses was centred on the little marble table within the folly.

After a moment of goggling, Mr. Blanchard turned to Kitty. "Mother told you."

Kitty smiled and nodded affirmation.

"But how did you manage—"

"Mr. Wright was my co-conspirator, and a splendid conspirator he proved to be! Now go, admire the staff's handiwork and commune with Alice. I am perfectly comfortable in the shade and shall await you here." Kitty made little shooing motions with her hands and sat back down in the boat.

Mr. Blanchard made his way to the tiny marble Greek temple, and brushed his hands across the netted lace, drank in the scent of the flowers, and stared anew in amazement. After a moment, he took out his kerchief, wiped his eyes, blew his nose, and composed himself before returning for her.

He grasped her hand and threaded it through his arm. They made their way to Alice's memorial. Once seated there, Mr. Blanchard settled his elbows on his knees, his hands clasped together before him, and looking out at the lake, finally spoke.

"You do realise I will never 'get over her' and move on? My heart does not seem to work that way," he finally assayed.

"Neither does mine," Kitty confessed.

"You are the most generous ... amazingly generous woman I have ever known."

"If you can be content to let me reserve a tiny piece of my heart for Joseph, who am I to deny you the same favour for Alice?" He nodded, mute, obviously overcome with sentiment.

Kitty smiled. "My dear Blanchard, St. Luke promises those who attain the resurrection neither marry nor are given in marriage. I think, I *hope*, that means when our time here is done, you and I will be reunited with Alice and Joseph. From what I can tell, I will love Alice as much as you ever have, and I am certain you will get on brilliantly with my Joseph."

"Well, that is all right, then," he said huskily. "You know—you must know—how much I admire you."

"Well, I *hoped* my feelings were reciprocated," she whispered, overcome with feeling.

"Shall I apply to your father then, and put our relations out of the misery of suspense?" Blanchard smiled in return.

"I would be very much obliged," Kitty responded in trembling accents.

He swept her up in his arms, and they kissed, at first tentatively, but soon, passionately. Kitty was so overcome with giddiness as to be breathless. Her heart had never beat so fast! She experienced a wave of light-headedness. Both enraptured and alarmed by these symptoms, she stepped back. Sherry correctly diagnosed her distress and released her with a self-satisfied smile.

"A shame to waste this." He gestured to the lovely flowers. He held out his hand to her. "May I, Miss Otis?"

"Certainly, Mr. Blanchard," she said as she took his hand. They waltzed to the sigh of a summer breeze on a carpet of flowers. Kitty became convinced the joy she felt, the giddy delight of resting in his arms with her head pillowed on his chest and both hearts beating as one, was a foretaste of Heaven.

They returned to the house for luncheon, and Mr. Blanchard emerged from his very brief interview with Mr. Otis wreathed in smiles.

The announcement was quickly made. Many happy felicitations and handshakes were exchanged, and a gladsome lunch was enjoyed. Kitty hurried over to Marianne's immediately after lunch, with Mrs. Blanchard and Georgina in train. After the first ecstasies, the ladies set about planning the wedding and a shopping trip in London for Kitty's trousseau.

"I shall apply for a special license straight away, as this is not your home parish," Mrs. Blanchard began. "Besides, that will allow you to marry in summer, much easier to travel for our guests."

After much discussion, they set August 21st as the date.

"I shall pattern my wedding after yours, Marianne." Kitty tapped her pencil against her chin. "But I think I shall have Taylor do up my hair in loose curls, as I had it done for the Blenheim Ball."

Mrs. Blanchard agreed. "Yes, Sherry commented he liked your hair."

"Excellent!" Kitty exulted.

Georgina suggested, "White lace would look splendid against your dark hair."

"Perhaps." Kitty fretted. "I think it may be all wrong for my best gown."

"I think the gown you wore for the Blenheim Ball is inappropriate for an August morning. It will be quite warm then. I should think a silk gauze or a soft muslin overlaid with lace would be more the thing. Shall we consult Mme. Gaudet?" Mrs. Blanchard asked.

"Wonderful!" Kitty acquiesced. And soon, the ladies had settled all of the details of dress. They spent a very enjoyable afternoon planning the details of the wedding and breakfast to follow. The next few days were consumed in a frenzy of invitation writing. Mrs. Blanchard, Georgina, Mrs. Wallace, and Miss Otis informed all their acquaintance and family of the nuptials.

Kitty included all her acquaintance from Carlisle as well as Threlkeld and Keswick. She sent a note to her retired nurse, Mrs. McKittrick, and of course, her own staff. She reassured them she was keeping Dixon Cottage, which made Mac quite smug. Lord Dankworth rose to the occasion and franked all of the notes.

July 21, 1815
Eynsham Hall, Oxfordshire

Dearest Aunt and Uncle Tinsley,

I write to you to announce I am to be Mrs. Blanchard as of August the 21ˢᵗ and to request Articles. I also plan to draw out three hundred pounds you invested for me from Lloyd's London office, so I may indulge in trousseau shopping in London. I feel perfectly authorised to squander this vast sum, as I have managed a brilliant match and need not be as saving as I have been.

More importantly, though, I wish to invite you to the wedding. I realise you have just travelled the whole length of England and would have to make a nearly immediate return, but I selfishly request it of you, anyway.

If you cannot bear being cooped up in a coach again so soon, I shall try to understand. In any event, I shall not be angry, for I am far too pleased with myself to be capable of that emotion!

Yr. Loving & Hopeful Niece, Kitty

Kitty attended to all her social duties on a cloud of happiness and wrote out her fair share of the announcements. Then she undertook a very important note.

July 20, 1815
Eynsham Hall, Oxfordshire

Dearest Aunt Vivian,

I am thrilled to announce felicitations are in order. This is most certainly true love, since my dear Blanchard offered for me even <u>after</u> my gaffe at the cards table. I know the phrase is trite, and everyone says it, but I am the happiest woman in England today!

> *The only tiny cloud on my horizon is your difficulty travelling.*
> *We are to be wed on August 21St. Mr. Blanchard has a leaf-spring*
> *barouche-sociable with a silky ride, more swaying than bouncing, and*
> *will happily send it up to collect you. A two-day excursion is required,*
> *and you could stay here and recover for as long as you would like*
> *before returning home.*
>
> *If it is too painful for you, of course, you must decline. But know*
> *my happiness will overflow if you can be with me on my wedding day*
> *in place of my mother.*

> *Yr. Loving Niece, Kitty*

Sherry's brother-in-law and sister, Sir and Lady Leyton, responded to the summons quite promptly, as they lived only thirty miles distant. Anna, at age twenty-nine, was only two years older than Sherry. She was blonder than either of her siblings, and already the mother of two robust and active young children. She was pleasingly plump after her two pregnancies, and had a sharper, more sarcastic sense of humour than her sister, but was equally adept at cards. Anna, like her sister, was an accomplished musician. Although the demands of two young children had sharply limited her practice hours, she and Georgina delighted the family with many performances during their visit.

Later that week, Kitty received a note from Mr. Tinsley informing her a withdrawal from Lloyd's had been arranged, and the ladies set off for the Blanchards' London townhouse. After reviewing all the finest goods at the best warehouses, they made their way to Grafton's, and, after considerable hustle and bustle and inordinately long waits for service, Kitty spent nearly three hundred pounds duplicating those goods there. They made a long, leisurely lunch, since Marianne was fatigued due to her delicate condition.

"I see ze gown, it was *accomplissement*, and now, mademoiselle returns for ze wedding gown, no?" Mme. Gaudet greeted them that afternoon. Mme. Gaudet made recommendations, and the order was placed.

Mr. Otis elected to stay at Eynsham, offering the excuse he might lose Silky if he was to attempt to take her to Dixon Cottage with him. Kitty decided to ship the rest of his effects from Dixon Cottage to Eynsham when they next went there for hunt season. Marianne stood as her matron of honour, and Georgina as her maid. Mr. Blanchard chose his brother-in-law as the best man and to honour his new family, Phillip Tinsley, as the groom's man. Mr. and Mrs. Tinsley arrived only fifteen days after Miss Otis's missive reached them with Articles in hand. Aunt Vivian accepted the use of Mr. Blanchard's *barouche-sociable* and stayed for a very satisfactory two-month long visit. Kitty and Sherry were married in the morning, and M. Colgate outdid himself for the breakfast.

For the next four and a half months, Marianne followed every precept of her doctor and Mrs. Sykes. Every evening, *not* on doctor's order, she crooned lullabies to her rapidly expanding abdomen. Once again, she reached confinement. Once again, she laboured for less than six hours. But this time, her anxious family was rewarded with the lusty cry of an outraged new-born.

"Six and a half pounds! I had the maid bring up the sugar scale from the kitchen to weigh him," Kitty crowed triumphantly from the top of the stairs, her own pregnancy just beginning to show. "You put her to the trouble of delivering *such* a monster! Go and see all his perfect little parts. Ginger-haired too, just like his father!" Kitty wept tears of joy and relief. When she had composed herself, she spread the glad tidings to the rest of both houses, and they made merry well into the night.

CODICIL

Mr. and Mrs. Blanchard named their first child Joseph, and their next, Alice. Mr. and Mrs. Wallace produced a lovely family of four children, and the Blanchards were blessed with five children. Mrs. Wallace or Mrs. Blanchard, or both, were either pregnant or nursing for the next fourteen years, since neither of them could bear to part with their offspring to a wet nurse. Their children grew up together, were tutored and went to school together, and played together. This continued even after the Wallaces built their own home on the north side of Ladywell Woods.

Sir Richard sold some family heirlooms, purchased a commission when Napoleon escaped Elba, and was lost at Waterloo. Lady Margaret sold the family estate to an ambitious 'beer baron', to the everlasting benefit of the tenants, and paid all her son's arrears in tithes from the proceeds. She also disposed of the little hunting box and took Kitty's advice to settle in London. They maintained their acquaintance to the end of Lady Margaret's days. With no immediate family heirs, the bulk of her estate was willed to the Asylum of St. Agnes.

Mr. Warden died of apoplexy only a year after the Blanchards' wedding. Mrs. Warden survived him by thirty-five years; long enough to see all of her grandchildren grown and married. Mr. Otis lived another fifteen years, long enough to see all of his grandchildren born. He passed on peacefully in his sleep, followed only days later by his faithful little dog, Silky. Betsy Taylor married Mr. Cox, one of Mr. Blanchard's footmen, and remained Mrs. Blanchard's abigail until her retirement.

The Blanchards eventually sold Dixon Cottage to Robert MacDonald and his wife, Mary. She was a prodigious mother who produced eight siblings for Davey. Davey Burton's childhood friend, George, succumbed to fever as a young man. Davey eventually purchased Coldbrook Farm and lived next door to his adoptive parents for the rest of their lives. When the time came, Mr. Hart retired to the MacDonald's honeymoon cottage.

Kitty Blanchard shared the nursing of her Aunt Vivian during her final illness with her cousin, Mrs. Edwards. Lady Vivian Shackford passed peacefully in 1828. Kitty lost her beloved Aunt Eliza Tinsley in 1853. She shared the nursing of her dearest Uncle Pericles Tinsley with his daughters-in-law until he joined his wife in rest only six months later.

Mr. McLaughlin made a handsome fortune importing horses and other domestic livestock to Australia. He financed those ventures through Lloyd's syndicates promoted by Mr. Tinsley, and later, by Mr. Tinsley's sons. In 1817, he married Mrs. John Fenton, *née* Lydia Moore, the relict of an officer killed in the line of duty, and adopted her son. The McLaughlins produced six more children, one of whom was named Katherine. Mr. McLaughlin used a significant part of his fortune to help found Adelaide in 1832, where criminals were excluded, and moved his family there.

Correspondence between Mr. McLaughlin and Mrs. Blanchard, *née* Otis never slackened in fifty years, until, in 1865, Mrs. Blanchard received a package with an enclosure note from Adelaide instead of the usual letter.

February the Tenth, 1865
Adelaide, Australia

Dear Mrs. Blanchard,

It is my sad duty to report that my father, Joseph McLaughlin, suffered a series of heart attacks which confined him to his bed for the last four months of his life. He passed away peacefully in his sleep, January 12, 1865. I have enclosed his obituary, his most recent photograph, and copies of the correspondence from you that he carefully saved in a tin box. I felt that both sets of letters should be brought together and preserved, for I believe that the history contained therein to be quite interesting.

> *Yr. Obdt. &ct.,*
> *Mrs. Robert Whitehead,*
> *née Kitty McLaughlin*

Kitty sighed heavily. Sherry looked up from his book and asked, "What is it, my dear?"

"Joseph McLaughlin has died," she replied, with tears in her eyes.

He reached over and took her hand. "Do you ever regret choosing England over Australia?"

Kitty smiled. "No. Joseph was everything my 18-year-old heart desired. But I am far too domestic for Australia. I am much happier doing some good in my small way locally than I would have been taming a raw wilderness." Kitty stood, leaned over Sherry and kissed him on the forehead. "But more important than all that—he wasn't you."

Sherry smiled and pulled her into his lap. They both laughed as her hoops flew up. "At a stroke, you have made me the happiest man in all of England." He kissed her soundly.

DEDICATION

Well, Maureen, here's your book. I say 'your' because it wouldn't exist without you. I cannot express the gratitude I have for you—my enthusiastic cheerleader, critique partner, editor, life-story-contributor, and eternally patient re-reader.

This book wouldn't be what it is without the talents of editor extraordinaire, Emily Poole of Midnight Owl Editors, and the astute feedback from dedicated beta readers Mark Kilfoil, Jesse Savage, and several others, together with the dozens of fellow writers who patiently taught me my craft. I want to thank Kit for proofreading the book. Finally, the book looks as good as it does inside and out because of the design talent and skill of typesetter Eugene (xchats on Fiverr) and cover designer Nirosha, (printok on Fiverr).

I give you all my heartfelt gratitude,

Lincoln

AFTERWORD

"Those who cannot remember the past are condemned to repeat it."

George Santayana

First, thank you for reading *Dauntless Hearts*. There is nothing so precious as one's time, and I am honoured that you spent some of it on my novel. I sincerely hope you felt your time was well-spent.

I wrote this book to enlighten my descendants. I am a retired teacher and routinely encountered students (including my own kids) who were convinced that prejudice against the Irish didn't happen, or didn't happen in America, or that it wasn't as crippling as prejudice against people of color. My students were horrified when I showed them the want ads in a newspaper from 1970—six years *after* the Kennedy administration and the Equal Rights Amendment— and they discovered gender-divided want ads with *columns* of ads ending in "no Negroes, Chinese or Irish need apply."

My father was a second generation Irish immigrant, and my mother's English ancestors first stepped foot in American in 1630. When my mother announced her engagement, my grandmother said, "Good grief, Betty, you're a good-looking girl; you can hold out for better!" Mother's parents agreed to pay for her wedding on the condition that she get married at her college, 1,700 miles away from their stately Winnetka home, since it would be less embarrassing that way. So, this book is also written in their memory; two pioneers who dared to love where bigotry had been sown and were a power couple for over fifty years.

I discovered as a teacher that telling instructive stories is the best way to inform young minds. The stories stick long after memories of factual lectures have faded. So, while the names, circumstances, and several plot points are pure fiction, most of this book is firmly grounded in my personal and familial experience. It took ten years of writing classes, researching, revising and rewriting, but I finally crafted a novel that I would want to read.

Your feedback is invaluable to me and will help other readers decide whether or not to read the book. If you enjoyed *Dauntless Hearts* (or even if you didn't) please visit http://www.amazon.com/review/create-review?&asin=B0C36D41JB to leave a brief review.

ABOUT LINCOLN TUVELAIS

I am a retired Texan currently residing in Kuala Lumpur. I was inspired to pick up my pen out of sheer frustration. As a voracious reader, I discovered it was impossible to find books to satisfy my need for a factually accurate, engrossing historical tale. I succumbed to the madness that compels otherwise normal people to write novels.

After working on my book for a decade, I prepared to publish. To my dismay, I discovered that my legal name is a marketing fiasco. My first and last name is already taken *five* times. Yep, five other authors are publishing or blogging under my name. {Sigh} It's a marketing disaster to be Ms. Common, the Sixth!

Lincoln is my legit on-the-birth-certificate middle name. After jiggering around first and last and middle names in as many combinations as possible, I was still hip-deep in other writers with identical names.

In exasperation, I logged on to Google translate, translated "into the future" from English to Finnish and then subtracted letters until it was vaguely pronounceable.

Job done. *Nobody's* got Lincoln Tuvelais! Except that nobody knows how to pronounce it. 🖼

So here you go: "Two-Vuh-Laze"; it rhymes with Rabelais.

Made in United States
North Haven, CT
29 May 2023

37104899R00155